Five Little Peppers
ABROAD

Five Little Peppers
ABROAD

MARGARET SIDNEY

ÆGYPAN PRESS

Special thanks to Michelle Shephard, Charles Franks, and the On-line Distributed Proofreading Team.

Five Little Peppers Abroad
A publication of
ÆGYPAN PRESS

www.aegypan.com

Preface

When the friends of the Pepper family found that the author was firm in her decision to continue their history no further, they brought their appeals for the details of some of those good times that made the "little brown house" an object-lesson.

In these appeals, the parents were as vigorous as the young people for a volume of the stories that Polly told, to keep the children happy in those hard days when her story-telling had to be a large factor in their home-life; and also for a book of their plays and exploits, impossible to be embodied in the continued series of their history, so that all who loved the "Five Little Peppers" might the better study the influences that shaped their lives.

Those requests were complied with; the author realizing that the detailed account held values, by which stronger light might be thrown on the family life in the "little brown house."

And now the pressure is brought to bear for a book showing the Little Peppers over the ocean, recorded in "Five Little Peppers Midway." And the author is very glad to comply again; for foreign travel throws a wholly different sidelight upon the Pepper family. So here is the book.

It is in no sense to be taken as a story written for a guide-book, — although the author lives in it again her repeated enjoyment of the sights and scenes which are accurately depicted. A "Baedeker," if carefully studied, is really all that is needed as a constant companion to the traveler; while for supplementary helps and suggestions, there are many valuable books along the same line. This volume is given up to the Peppers; and they must live their own lives and tell their own story while abroad just as they choose.

As the author has stated many times, her part is "simply to set down what the Peppers did and said, without trying to make them say or do anything in particular." And so over the ocean they are just as much the makers of their own history as when they first opened the door of the "little brown house" to

MARGARET SIDNEY

I

OVER THE OCEAN

"*D*ear me," said Polly, "I don't see wherever she can be, Jasper. I've searched just everywhere for her." And she gave a little sigh, and pushed up the brown rings of hair under her sailor cap.

"Don't worry, Polly," said Jasper, with a reassuring smile. "She's with Matilda, of course. Come, Polly, let's you and I have a try at the shuffle-board by ourselves, down on the lower deck."

"No, we can't," said Polly, with a dreadful longing at her heart for the charms of a game; "that is, until we've found Phronsie." And she ran down the deck. "Perhaps she is in one of the library corners, though I thought I looked over them all."

"How do you know she isn't with Matilda, Polly?" cried Jasper, racing after, to see Polly's little blue jacket whisking ahead of him up the companion-way.

"Because" — Polly stopped at the top and looked over her shoulder at him — "Matilda's in her berth. She's awfully seasick. I was to stay with Phronsie, and now I've lost her!" And the brown head drooped, and Polly clasped her hands tightly together.

"Oh, no, she can't be lost, Polly," said Jasper, cheerfully, as he bounded up the stairs and gained her side; "why, she couldn't be!"

"Well, anyway, we can't find her, Jasper," said Polly, running on. "And it's all my fault, for I forgot, and left her in the library, and went with Fanny Vanderburgh down to her state-room. O dear me!" as she sped on.

"Well, she's in the library now, most likely," said Jasper, cheerfully, hurrying after, "curled up asleep in a corner." And they both ran in, expecting to see Phronsie's yellow head snuggled into one of the pillows.

But there was no one there except a little old gentleman on one of the sofas back of a table, who held his paper upside down, his big spectacles on the end of his nose, almost tumbling off as he nodded drowsily with the motion of the steamer.

"O dear me!" exclaimed Polly; "now we shall wake him up," as they tiptoed around, peering in every cozy corner and behind all the tables for a glimpse of Phronsie's little brown gown.

"No danger," said Jasper, with a glance over at the old gentleman; "he's just as fast asleep as can be. Here, Polly, I think she's probably tucked up in here." And he hurried over to the farther side, where the sofa made a generous angle.

Just then in stalked a tall boy, who rushed up to the little old gentleman. "Here, Granddad, wake up." And he shook his arm smartly. "You're losing your glasses, and then there'll be a beastly row to pay."

"O dear me!" cried Polly aghast, as she and Jasper whirled around.

"Hey — what — what!" exclaimed the old gentleman, clutching his paper as he started forward. "Oh, — why, I haven't been asleep, Tom."

"Ha! Ha! tell that to the marines," cried Tom, loudly, dancing in derision, "You've been sleeping like a log. You'd much better go down and get into your state-room. But give me a sovereign first." He held out his hand as he spoke. "Hurry up, Granddad!" he added impatiently.

The old gentleman put his hand to his head, and then rubbed his eyes.

"Bustle up," cried the boy, with a laugh, "or else I'll run my fist in your pocket and help myself."

"Indeed, you won't," declared the old gentleman, now thoroughly awake.

"Ha! Ha!" laughed the boy. "You see if I won't, Granddad." Yet he dropped his imperious tone, and waited, though impatiently, while the big pocketbook was drawn out.

"What do you want with money on board the boat?" demanded the old gentleman.

"Give me a sovereign, Granddad," cried Tom, controlling his impatience as best he might, with many a cross look at the wrinkled old face under the white hair.

His Grandfather slowly drew out the coin, and Tom twitched it eagerly from the long, thin fingers.

"I don't see how you can need money on board the boat," repeated the old gentleman.

"Never you mind what I want it for, Grand-daddy," said Tom, laughing loudly and shaking the sovereign at him as he ran off; "that's my business, and not yours."

Polly had not taken her eyes off their faces. Now she turned toward Jasper. "Oh, how very dreadful!" she gasped — then would have given everything if she had kept still, for the old gentleman whirled around and saw them for the first time.

"Hey — who are you — and what are you listening there for — hey?" he demanded sharply. He had little black eyes, and they now snapped in a truly dreadful way at them.

"We came to find her little sister," said Jasper, politely, for Polly was quite beyond speaking.

"Sister? I don't know anything about your sister," said the old gentleman, irascibly. "And this room isn't a place for children, I can tell you," he added, as if he owned the library and the whole ship.

Jasper made no reply.

"Phronsie isn't here." Polly clasped her hands again tighter than ever. "And, oh, Jasper!" and she looked at the angry old face before them with pitying eyes.

"What I say to my grandson, Tom, and what he says to me, is our own business!" exclaimed the old gentleman in a passion, thumping the table with his clenched hand. "And no one else has a right to hear it."

"I am so very sorry we heard it," said Polly, the color which had quite gone from her cheek now rushing back. "And we are going right away, sir."

"You would much better," said the old man, nodding angrily. "And you, boy, too; I suppose you think yourself better than my Tom. But you are not — not a bit of it!" And suddenly he tried to start to his feet, but lurched heavily against the table instead.

Polly and Jasper rushed over to him. "Lean on me, sir," said Jasper, putting both arms around him, while Polly ran to his other side, he was shaking so dreadfully.

The old gentleman essayed to wave them off. "Let me alone," he said feebly; "I'm going after my grandson, Tom." His voice sank to a whisper, and his head dropped to his breast. "He's got money — he's always getting it, and I'm going to see what he's doing with it."

"Polly," said Jasper, "you help me put him back on the sofa; there, that's it," as the old man sank feebly down against the cushions; "and then I'll run and find his grandson."

It was just the time when everybody seemed to be in the state-rooms, or out on deck in steamer chairs, so Polly sat there at the old man's head, feeling as if every minute were an hour, and he kept gurgling, "Tom's a bad boy — he gets money all the time, and I'm going to see what he's doing with it," with feeble waves of his legs, that put Polly in a fright lest he should roll off the sofa at every lurch of the steamer.

"Tom is coming," at last she said, putting her hand on the hot forehead. "Please stay still, sir; you will be sick."

"But I don't want Tom to come," cried the old gentleman, irritably. "Who said I wanted him to come? Hey?" He turned up his head and looked at her, and Polly's hand shook worse than ever when the little snapping eyes were full on her face, and she had all she could do to keep from running out of the room and up on deck where she could breathe freely.

"I am so sorry," she managed to gasp, feeling if she didn't say something, she should surely run. "Does your head feel better?" And she smoothed his hot forehead gently just as Phronsie always did Grandpapa's when it ached. And when she thought of Phronsie, then it was all she could do to keep the tears back. Where could she be? And would Jasper never come back?

And just then in ran Tom with a great clatter, complaining noisily every step of the way. "I told you you'd much better get off to your stateroom, Granddad!" he exclaimed. "Here, I'll help you down there." And he laid a hasty hand on the feeble old arm.

"I think he is sick," said Polly, gently. Jasper came hurrying in. "Phronsie is all right," he had time to whisper to Polly.

"Oh, Jasper!" the color rushed into her cheek that had turned quite white. "I am so glad."

"Nonsense!" exclaimed Tom, abruptly. "It's only one of his crotchets. You don't know; he gets up plenty of 'em on occasion."

"What did you want a sovereign for?" asked the old gentleman, querulously, taking his sharp little eyes off Polly to fasten them on his grandson's face. "Say, I *will* know."

"And I say no matter," retorted Tom, roughly. "And you ought to come down to your state-room where you belong. Come, Granddad!" And he tried again to lay hold of his arm. But the little old gentleman sank back, and looked up at Polly again. "I think I'll stay here," he said.

"I say," began the boy, in an embarrassed way, "this is dreadfully rough on you," and then he looked away from Polly to Jasper. "And if you knew him as well as I do," nodding his head at his Grandfather, "you wouldn't get in such a funk."

Polly was busy smoothing the hot forehead under the white hair, and appeared not to notice a word he said.

"Your Grandfather really appears ill," said Jasper. "And the doctor might give him something to help him."

Tom burst into a short laugh and kicked his heel against the table. "Hoh! hoh! I say, you don't know him; oh, what muffs you are! He's well enough, only he's determined not to go to his state-room where he belongs, but to kick up a row here."

"Very well," said Jasper, coolly, "since you are determined to do nothing for his relief, I shall take it upon myself to summon the doctor." He stepped to a table a bit further off, and touched the electric button back of it.

"Here, don't do that," remonstrated Tom, springing forward. But it was too late, and the steward who attended to calls on the library stepped in.

"It isn't the hour for giving out books," he began.

Tom was stamping his foot impatiently, and scowling at Jasper, alternately casting longing glances out the nearest port-hole.

"It isn't books we want," said Jasper, quickly, "but this old gentleman" — whose head was now heavily sunken on his breast, and whose cheek was quite white — "appears to be very ill, and to need the doctor."

"Is that so?" The steward leaned over and peered into the old face. "Well, he doesn't look just right, and that's a fact. Is he your father?"

"Oh, no," said Jasper, quickly, "I don't know who he is. But, do hurry, for he's sick, and needs the doctor at once."

"I'll get Dr. Jones." Off ran the steward toward the surgeon's cabin.

"See what you've done," cried Tom, in a towering passion. "Kicked up a pretty mess — when I tell you I've seen my Grandfather just as bad a hundred times."

Jasper made no reply, and Polly continued to stroke gently the poor head.

"Well — well — well!" exclaimed Mr. King, coming in, "to be sure, it's very stupid in me not to think of looking in the library for both of you before. O dear me — bless me!" And he came to a dead stop of astonishment.

"Father," cried Jasper, "this poor man seems very ill."

"Oh, yes," breathed Polly, pitifully, "he really is, Grandpapa." And she put out her hand to seize one of Mr. King's. "And Jasper has sent for the doctor."

"And none too soon, I should say," remarked Mr. King, grimly, with a keen glance into the old man's face. "Raise his feet a little higher, Jasper; put a pillow under them; there, that's it. Well, the doctor should be hurried up." He glanced quickly around. "Here, you boy," seeing Tom, "run as you never have run before, and tell the doctor to come quickly."

"There isn't any need," began Tom.

"Do you *go!*" commanded Mr. King, pointing to the door. And Tom went.

"Father, that boy is his grandson," said Jasper, pointing to the sick man.

Mr. King stared into Jasper's face, unable to make a reply.

"He is," declared Polly. "Oh, Grandpapa, he really is!" Then she buried her flushed face up against Mr. King's arm.

"There is no need to waste words," said Mr. King, finding his tongue. "There, there, Polly, child," fondling her brown head, "don't feel badly. I'm sure you've done all you could."

"'Twas Jasper; he did it all — I couldn't do anything," said Polly.

"Oh, Polly, you did everything," protested Jasper.

"Yes, yes, I know, you both did," said Mr. King. "Well, here's the doctor, thank the Lord!"

And then when nobody wanted them, the library seemed to be full of people, and the news spreading out to the decks, many of the passengers got out of their steamer chairs, and tried to swarm into the two doorways.

Tom, who never knew how he summoned Dr. Jones, being chiefly occupied in astonishment at finding that he obeyed a command from a perfect stranger, did not come back to the library, but kept himself with the same amazed expression on his face, idly kicking his heels in a quiet corner of the deck near by. He never thought of such a thing as being worried over his Grandfather, for he couldn't remember when the old gentleman hadn't been subject to nervous attacks; but somehow since "a row," as he expressed it, "had been kicked up," it was just as well to stay in the vicinity and see the end of it. But he wasn't going inside — no, not he!

After awhile, Tom was just beginning to yawn, and to feel that no one could expect him to waste time like that, and probably his Grandfather was going to sleep it out on the sofa, and the stupid doctor would find that there was nothing the matter, only the old man was nervous. "And I'm going back to the fellows," decided Tom, shaking his long legs.

"Oh, here you are!" cried Jasper, running up to him. "Come quickly," seizing his arm.

"Hey, here, what are you about?" roared Tom at him, shaking off the hand.

"You must excuse me for wasting no ceremony," said Jasper, sternly. It struck Tom that he looked very much like the old gentleman who had told him to *go!* "Your Grandfather is very ill; something is the matter with his heart, and the doctor has sent me for you. He says he may not live an hour." It was necessary to tell the whole of the dreadful truth, for Tom was still staring at him in defiance.

II

TWO ENGLISH FRIENDS

"*I* don't want you," muttered the old gentleman, feebly, turning his head away from Tom, and then he set his lips tightly together. But he held to Polly's hand.

"You would better go out," Dr. Jones nodded to Tom. "It excites him."

The second time Tom was told to go. He stood quite still. "He's my Grandfather!" he blurted out.

"Can't help it," said Dr. Jones, curtly; "he's my patient. So I tell you again it is imperative that you leave this room." Then he turned back to his work of making the sick man comfortable without taking any-more notice of the boy.

Tom gave a good long look at as much of his Grandfather's face as he could see, then slunk out, in a dazed condition, trying to make himself as small as possible. Jasper found him a half hour afterward, hanging over the rail away from curious eyes, his head buried on his arms.

"I thought you'd like to know that your Grandfather is better," said Jasper, touching the bent shoulder.

"Get away, will you?" growled Tom, kicking out his leg, unmindful where it struck.

"And the doctor has gotten him into his state-room, and he is as comfortable as he could be made." Jasper didn't add that Dr. Jones had asked him to come back, and that the old man was still insisting that Polly should hold his hand.

"In that case," declared Tom, suddenly twitching up his head, "I will go down there." His face was so drawn that Jasper started, and then looked away over the sea, and did not appear to notice the clenched hand down by the boy's side.

"I — I — didn't know he was sick." Tom brought it out in gusts, and his face worked worse than ever in his efforts not to show his distress.

The only thing he could do was to double up his hand tighter than ever, as he tried to keep it back of him.

"I understand," nodded Jasper, still looking off over the blue water.

"And now I'll go down," said Tom, drawing a long breath and starting off. Oh! and Dr. Jones had said the last thing to Jasper as he rushed off with the good news to Tom, "On no account let that boy see his Grandfather. I won't answer for the consequences if you do."

"See here," Jasper tore his gaze off from the shimmering water. "The doctor doesn't — doesn't think you ought to see your Grandfather now."

"Hey!" cried Tom, his drawn lips flying open, and his big blue eyes distending in anger. "He's my Grandfather. I rather think I shall do as I've a mind to," and he plunged off.

"Tom!" Jasper took long steps after him. "Beg your pardon, this is no time for thinking of anything but your Grandfather's life. Dr. Jones said you were not to see him at present." The truth must be told, for in another moment the boy would have been off on the wings of the wind.

"And do you think that I will mind in the least what that beastly doctor says?" cried Tom, getting redder and redder in the face, his rage was so great. "Hoh! no, sir."

"Then your Grandfather's life will be paid as a sacrifice," said Jasper calmly. And he stood quite still; and surveyed the boy before him.

Neither spoke. It seemed to Jasper an age that they stood there in silence. At last Tom wavered, put out his hand unsteadily, leaned against a steamer chair, and turned his face away.

"Let us do a bit of a turn on the deck," said Jasper, suddenly, overcoming by a mighty effort his repugnance to the idea.

Tom shook his head, and swallowed hard.

"Oh, yes," said Jasper, summoning all the cheerfulness he could muster to his aid. "Come, it's the very thing to do, if you really want to help your Grandfather."

Tom raised his head and looked at him. "I never supposed the old man was sick," he said brokenly, and down went his head again, this time upon his hands, which were grasping the top of the chair.

"I don't believe you did," answered Jasper. "But come, Tom, let's walk around the deck; we can talk just as well meanwhile."

Two or three young men, with cigarettes in their mouths, came sauntering up. "Tom Selwyn, you're a pretty fellow —"

Tom raised his head and looked at them defiantly.

"To give us the slip like this," cried one, with a sneer, in which the others joined, with a curious look at Jasper.

"Well, come on now," said one. "Yes — yes — come along," said another; "we've waited long enough for you to get back."

"I'm not coming," declared Tom, shortly.

"Not coming back? Well —" One of the young men said something under his breath, and the first speaker turned on his heel, tossing his cigarette over the railing.

"No," said Tom, "I'm not coming. Did you hear me?"

"I believe I had that pleasure," said the last named, "as I am not deaf. Come on, fellows; our little boy has got to wait on his Grandpappy. Good-bye, kid!" He snapped his fingers; the other two laughed derisively, and sauntered off down the deck as they came.

Tom shook with passion. "I'd like to walk," he said, drawing a long breath, and setting off unsteadily.

"All right," said Jasper, falling into step beside him.

Meantime the old gentleman, in his large handsome state-room, showed no sign of returning to the consciousness that had come back for a brief moment. And he held to Polly's hand so tightly, as she sat at the head of the berth, that there was no chance of withdrawing her fingers had she so desired. And Father Fisher with whom Dr. Jones had of course made acquaintance, before the steamer fairly sailed, sat there keeping watch too, in a professional way, the ship's doctor having called him in consultation over the case. And Phronsie, who had been in deep penitence because she had wandered off from the library with another little girl, to gaze over the railing upon the steerage children below, thereby missing Polly, was in such woe over it all that she was allowed to cuddle up against Polly's side and hold her other hand. And there she sat as still as a mouse, hardly daring to breathe. And Mr. King, feeling as if, after all, the case was pretty much under his supervision, came softly in at intervals to see that all was well, and that the dreadful boy was kept out.

And the passengers all drifted back to their steamer chairs, glad of some new topic to discuss, for the gossip they had brought on board was threadbare now, as they were two days at sea. And the steamer sailed over the blue water that softly lapped the stout vessel's side, careless of the battle that had been waged for a life, even then holding by slender threads. And Fanny Vanderburgh, whose grandfather was a contemporary in the old business days in New York with Mr. King, and who sat with her mother at the next table to the King party, spent most of her time running to Mrs. Pepper's state-room, or interviewing anyone who would be able to give her the slightest encouragement as to when she could claim Polly Pepper.

"O dear me!" Fanny cried, on one such occasion, when she happened to run across Jasper. "I've been down to No. 45 four times this morning, and there's nobody there but that stupid Matilda, and she doesn't know or won't tell when Polly will get through reading to that tiresome old man. And they won't let me go to his state-room. Mrs. Fisher and your father are there, too, or I'd get them to make Polly come out on deck. We all want her for a game of shuffle-board."

Jasper sighed. So did he long for a game of shuffle-board. Then he brought himself up, and said as brightly as he could: "Mr. Selwyn begs Polly to stay, and won't have anyone else read to him, Miss Vanderburgh, so I don't see as it can be helped. He's been very sick, you know."

Fanny Vanderburgh beat the toe of her boot on the deck floor. "It's a perfect shame. And that horrible old man, he's so seedy and common – just think of it – and spoiling all our fun!"

Jasper looked off over the sea, and said nothing.

"As for that dreadful boy, his grandson, I think he's a boor. Goodness me – I hope nobody will introduce him. I'm sure I never'll recognize him afterward."

Jasper turned uneasily. "Please, Mr. King, do make Polly listen to reason," begged Fanny. "There isn't another girl on board I care to go with – at least not in the way I would with her. The Griswolds are well enough to play games with, and all that; but you know what I mean. Do make her come out with us this morning, and listen to reason," she repeated, winding up helplessly.

"But I think she is just right," said Jasper, stoutly.

"Right!" cried Fanny, explosively; "oh, how can you say so, Mr. Jasper! Why, she is losing just every bit of the fun."

"I know it," said Jasper, with a twinge at the thought. "Well, there is nothing more to be said or done, Miss Vanderburgh, since Polly has decided the matter. Only I want you to remember that I think she is just right about it."

Fanny Vanderburgh pouted her pretty lips in vexation. "At least, don't try to get that dreadful boy into our own set to play games," she cried venomously, "for I won't speak to him. He's a perfect boor. 'Twas only yesterday he brushed by me like a clumsy elephant, and knocked my book out of my hand, and never even picked it up. Think of that, Mr. King!"

"I know – that was dreadful," assented Jasper, in dismay at the obstacle to the plan he had formed in his own mind, to do that very thing he was now being warned against. "But you see, Miss Vanderburgh, he's all upset by his Grandfather's sickness."

"And I should think he would be," cried Fanny Vanderburgh, with spirit. "Mrs. Griswold says she's heard him domineering over the old man, and then his Grandfather would snarl and scold like everything. She has the next state-room, you know. I don't see how those Selwyns can afford such a nice cabin," continued Fanny, her aristocratic nose in the air, "they look so poor. Anyway that boy is a perfect beast, Mr. King."

"He's very different now," said Jasper, quickly. "He had no idea his Grandfather was so poorly. Now I'll tell you, Miss Vanderburgh," Jasper turned sharply around on his heel so that he faced her. It was necessary with a girl like her to state plainly what he had to say, and to keep to it. "I am going to ask Tom Selwyn to play games with all us young people. If it distresses you, or anyone else, so that you cannot join, of course I will withdraw, and I know Polly will, and we will get up another circle that will play with him."

It was almost impossible to keep from laughing at Fanny's face, but Jasper was very grave as he waited for an answer. "O dear me, Mr. Jasper," she cried, "haven't I told you I don't really care for anyone on board but Polly Pepper, and Mamma doesn't want me to mix up much with those Griswolds?" She lowered her voice and glanced over her shoulder. "It would make it so awkward if they should be much in New York, and we should meet. So of course I've got to do as Polly and you do. Don't you see? — it's awfully hard on me, though," and she clasped her hands in vexation.

"Very well, then," said Jasper; "now that's decided. And seeing it is, why the next thing to do, is to bring Tom down, and we'll get up a game of shuffle-board at once. He's not needed by his Grandfather now." He didn't think it necessary to add, "for the old gentleman won't see him, and Tom is forbidden the room by the doctor."

Fanny's aristocratic nose went up in alarm, and her whole face was overspread with dismay. It was one thing to anticipate evil, and quite another to find it precipitated upon one. "I — I don't — believe I can play this morning, Mr. Jasper," she began hurriedly, for the first time in her young life finding herself actually embarrassed. She was even twisting her fingers.

"Very well," said Jasper, coolly, "then I understand that you will not play with us at any time, for, as we begin today, we shall keep on. I will set about getting up another party at once." He touched his yacht cap lightly, and turned off.

"I'll go right down on the lower deck with you now." Fanny ran after him, her little boot heels clicking excitedly on the hard floor. "The steward has marked it all for us. I got him to, while I ran to find Polly so as to engage the place," she added breathlessly.

"That's fine," said Jasper, a smile breaking over the gloom on his face; "now we'll have a prime game, Miss Vanderburgh."

Fanny swallowed hard the lump in her throat, and tried to look pleasant. "Do you go and collect the Griswolds," cried Jasper, radiantly, "and I'll be back with Tom," and he plunged off. It was all done in a minute. And the thing that had been worrying him — how to get Tom into good shape, and to keep him there — seemed fixed in the best way possible. But Tom wouldn't go. Nothing that Jasper could do or say would move him out of the gloom into which he was cast, and at last Jasper ran down for a hurried game with the party awaiting him, to whom he explained matters in the best way he could.

At last, old Mr. Selwyn was able to emerge from his state-room. Mr. King and he were the best of friends by this time, the former always, when Polly read aloud, being one of the listeners. At all such hours, indeed, and whenever Polly went to sit by the invalid, Phronsie would curl up at Polly's side, and fondle the doll that Grandpapa gave her last, which had the honor to take the European trip with the family. Phronsie would smooth the little dress down carefully, and then with her hand in Polly's, she would sit motionless till the reading was over. Mamsie, whose fingers could not be idle, although the big mending basket was left at home, would be over on the sofa, sewing busily; and little Dr. Fisher would run in and out, and beaming at them all through his spectacles, would cry cheerily, "Well, I declare, you have the most comfortable place on the whole boat, Mr. Selwyn." Or Dr. Jones, whom Polly thought, next to Papa Fisher, was the very nicest doctor in all the world, would appear suddenly around the curtain, and smile approval through his white teeth. At last on the fifth day out, the old man was helped up to sun himself in his steamer chair on deck. And then he had a perfect côterie around him, oh-ing and ah-ing over his illness, and expressing sympathy in every shape, for since Mr. King and his party took him up, it was quite the thing for all the other passengers to follow suit.

When a few hours of this sort of thing had been going on, the old man called abruptly to Polly Pepper, who had left him, seeing he had such good company about him, and had now skipped up with Jasper to toss him a merry word, or to see if his steamer rug was all tucked in snugly around him.

"See here, Polly Pepper, do you play chess?"

"What, sir?" Polly thought she had not heard correctly.

"Do you play chess, I say?" demanded old Mr. Selwyn, bringing his sharp little eyes to bear on her.

"No, sir, that is — only a little," stammered Polly.

"Well, that will do for a start," the old gentleman nodded in satisfaction. "And I'll give you some points later on about the game. Well, and you play backgammon, of course." He didn't wait for her to answer, but finished, "These people here drive me almost crazy, asking me how I feel, and what was the matter with me, and all that rubbish. Now, I'm going into the library, and you shall go too, and we'll have a game of backgammon."

He flung back his steamer rug with a determined hand.

Jasper began, "Oh, Polly!" in dismay, but she broke in, "Yes, indeed, I do play backgammon, Mr. Selwyn, and it will be fine to have a game." And together they helped him up and into a cozy corner of the library.

"There, now," said Polly, with a final little pat on the sofa pillows tucked up at his back. "I believe you are as comfortable as you can be, Mr. Selwyn."

"Indeed I am," he declared.

"And now, Jasper, do get the backgammon board," cried Polly. "There it is over there," spying it on a further table.

Old Mr. Selwyn cast a hungry glance on it as it was brought forward, and his sharp little eyes sparkled, as Polly threw it open. He even chuckled in delight as he set the men.

Tom Selwyn came up to the door, and standing in its shadow, looked in. Jasper flung himself down on the sofa by the old gentleman's side to watch the game. Suddenly he glanced up, caught sight of Tom, although the latter's head was quickly withdrawn, and jumping up, he dashed after him.

"Here — see here, Tom!" he called to the big figure before him, making good time down the stairs. "I can't go chasing you all over the boat in this fashion. Stop, will you?"

"What do you want?" demanded Tom, crossly, feeling it impossible to elude such a pursuer, and backing up against a convenient angle.

"I want you to come up into the library and watch the game. Do, it'll be the best time," — he didn't say "to make it all up."

"Can't," said Tom, "he won't see me."

"Oh, yes, he will; I almost know he will," declared Jasper, eagerly feeling this minute as if the most unheard-of things were possible.

"And beside, your sister — I mean the Pepper girl — Miss Pepper —" Tom corrected himself clumsily. "She can't bear me — I won't come."

"Oh, yes, she can now," said Jasper, just as eagerly, "especially since I've told her all you've told me."

"Well, I hate girls anyway," declared Tom, in his most savage fashion; "always have hated 'em, and always shall. I won't come!"

III

PHRONSIE GOES VISITING

"Grandpapa," said Phronsie, softly, as she clung to his hand, after they had made the descent to the lower deck, "I think the littlest one can eat some of the fruit, don't you?" she asked anxiously.

"Never you fear," assented old Mr. King, "that child that I saw yesterday can compass anything in the shape of food. Why, it had its mouth full of teeth, Phronsie; it was impossible not to see them when it roared."

"I am so glad its teeth are there," said Phronsie, with a sigh of satisfaction, as she regarded her basket of fruit, "because if it hadn't any, we couldn't give it these nice pears, Grandpapa."

"Well, here we are," said Mr. King, holding her hand tightly. "Bless me — are those your toes, young man?" this to a big chubby-faced boy, whose fat legs lay across the space as he sprawled on the deck; "just draw them in a bit, will you? — there. Well, now, Phronsie, this way. Here's the party, I believe," and he led her over to the other side, where a knot of steerage passengers were huddled together. In the midst sat a woman, chubby faced, and big and square, holding a baby. She had a big red shawl wrapped around her, in the folds of which snuggled the baby, who was contentedly chewing one end of it, while his mother had her eyes on the rest of her offspring, of which there seemed a good many. When the baby saw Phronsie, he stopped chewing the old shawl and grinned, showing all the teeth of which Mr. King had spoken. The other children, tow headed and also chubby, looked at the basket hanging on Phronsie's arm, and also grinned.

"There is the baby!" exclaimed Phronsie, in delight, pulling Grandpapa's hand gently. "Oh, Grandpapa, there he is."

"That's very evident," said the old gentleman. "Bless me!" addressing the woman, "how many children have you, pray tell?"

"Nine," she said. Then she twitched the jacket of one of them, and the pinafore of another, to have them mind their manners, while the baby kicked and crowed and gurgled, seeming to be all teeth.

"I have brought you some fruit," said Phronsie, holding out her basket, whereat all the tow headed group except the baby crowded each other dreadfully to see all there was in it. "I'm sorry the flowers are gone, so I couldn't bring any today. May the baby have this?" holding out a pear by the stem.

The baby settled that question by lunging forward and seizing the pear with two fat hands, when he immediately sank into the depths of the old shawl again, all his teeth quite busy at work. Phronsie set down her basket on the deck, and the rest of the brood emptied it to their own satisfaction. Their mother's stolid face lighted up with a broad smile that showed all her teeth, and very white and even they were.

"Grandpapa," said Phronsie, turning to him and clasping her hands, "if I only might hold that baby just one little bit of a minute," she begged, keenly excited.

"Oh, Phronsie, he's too big," expostulated Mr. King, in dismay.

"I can hold him just as easy, Grandpapa dear," said Phronsie, her lips drooping mournfully. "See." And she sat down on a big coil of rope near by and smoothed out her brown gown. "Please, Grandpapa dear."

"He'll cry," said Mr. King, quickly. "Oh, no, Phronsie, it wouldn't do to take him away from his mother. You see it would be dreadful to set that child to roaring — very dreadful indeed." Yet he hung over her in distress at the drooping little face.

"He won't cry." The mother's stolid face lighted up a moment. "And if the little lady wants to hold him, he'll sit there."

"May I, Grandpapa?" cried Phronsie, her red lips curling into a happy smile. "Oh, please say I may, Grandpapa dear," clasping her hands.

"The family seems unusually clean," observed Mr. King to himself. "And the doctor says there's no sickness on board, and it's a very different lot of steerage folks going this way from coming out, all of which I've settled before coming down here," he reflected. "Well, Phronsie — yes — I see no reason why you may not hold the baby if you want to." And before the words were hardly out of his mouth, the chubby-faced woman had set the fat baby in the middle of the brown gown smoothed out to receive him. He clung to his pear with both hands and ate away with great satisfaction, regardless of his new resting-place.

"Just come here!" Mrs. Griswold, in immaculately fitting garments, evidently made up freshly for steamer use, beckoned with a hasty hand to her husband. "It's worth getting up to see." He flung down his novel and tumbled out of his steamer chair. "Look down there!"

"*Whew!*" whistled Mr. Griswold; "that *is* a sight!"

"And that is the great Horatio King!" exclaimed Mrs. Griswold under her breath; "down there in that dirty steerage — and look at that child — Reginald, did you ever see such a sight in your life?"

"On my honor, I never have," declared Mr. Griswold, solemnly, and wanting to whistle again.

"Sh! — don't speak so loud," warned Mrs. Griswold, who was doing most of the talking herself. And plucking his sleeve, she emphasized every word with fearful distinctness close to his ear. "She's got a dirty steerage baby in her lap, and Mr. King is laughing. Well, I never! O dear me, here come the young people!"

Polly and Jasper came on a brisk trot up the deck length. "Fifteen times around make a mile, don't they, Jasper?" she cried.

"I believe they do," said Jasper, "but it isn't like home miles, is it, Polly?" — laughing gaily — "or dear old Badgertown?"

"I should think not," replied Polly, with a little pang at her heart whenever Badgertown was mentioned. "We used to run around the little brown house, and see how many times we could do it without stopping."

"And how many did you, Polly?" asked Jasper, — "the largest number, I mean."

"Oh, I don't know," said Polly, with a little laugh; "Joel beat us always, I remember that."

"Yes, Joe would get over the ground, you may be sure," said Jasper, "if anybody could."

Polly's laugh suddenly died away and her face fell. "Jasper, you don't know," she said, "how I do want to see those boys."

"I know," said Jasper, sympathizingly, "but you'll get a letter, you know, most as soon as we reach port, for they were going to mail it before we left."

"And I have one every day in my mailbag," said Polly, "but I want to *see* them so, Jasper, I don't know what to do." She went up to the rail at a remove from the Griswolds and leaned over it.

"Polly," said Jasper, taking her hand, "you know your mother will feel dreadfully if she knows you are worrying about it."

"I know it," said Polly, bravely, raising her head; "and I won't — why Jasper Elyot King!" for then she saw Grandpapa and Phronsie and the steerage baby.

Jasper gave a halloo, and waved his hand, and Polly danced up and down and called, and waved her hands too. And Phronsie gave a little crow of delight. "See, Grandpapa, there they are; I want Polly — and Jasper, too." And old Mr. King whirled around. "O dear me! Come down, both of you," which command it did not take them long to obey.

"Well, I never did in all my life," ejaculated Mrs. Griswold, "see anything like that. Now if some people" — she didn't say "we" — "should do anything like that, 'twould be dreadfully erratic and queer. But those Kings can do anything," she added, with venom.

"It's pretty much so," assented Mr. Griswold, giving a lazy shake. "Well, I'm going back to my chair if you've got through with me, Louisa." And he sauntered off.

"Don't go, Reginald," begged his wife; "I haven't got a soul to talk to."

"Oh, well, you can talk to yourself," said her husband, "any woman can." But he paused a moment.

"Haven't those Pepper children got a good berth?" exclaimed Mrs. Griswold, unable to keep her eyes off from the small group below. "And their Mother Pepper, or Fisher, or whatever her name is — I declare it's just like a novel, the way I heard the story from Mrs. Vanderburgh about it all."

"And I wish you'd let me get back to my book, Louisa," exclaimed Mr. Griswold, tartly, at the mention of the word "novel," beginning to look longingly at his deserted steamer chair, "for it's precious little time I get to read on shore. Seems as if I might have a little peace at sea."

"Do go back and read, then," said his wife, impatiently; "that's just like a man, — he can't talk of anything but business, or he must have his nose in a book."

"We men want to talk sense," growled her husband, turning off. But Mrs. Griswold was engrossed in her survey of Mr. King and the doings of his party, and either didn't hear or didn't care what was remarked outside of that interest.

Tom Selwyn just then ran up against someone as clumsily as ever. It proved to be the ship's doctor, who surveyed him coldly and passed on. Tom gave a start and swallowed hard, then plunged after him. "Oh, I say."

"What is it?" asked Dr. Jones, pausing.

"Can I — I'd like — to see my Grandfather, don't you know?"

Dr. Jones scanned him coolly from top to toe. Tom took it without wincing, but inwardly he felt as if he must shake to pieces.

"If you can so conduct yourself that your Grandfather will not be excited," at last said the doctor, — what an age it seemed to Tom, — "I see no reason why you shouldn't see your Grandfather, and go back to your state-room. But let me tell you, young man, it was a pretty close shave for him the other day. Had he slipped away, you'd have had that on your conscience that would have lasted you for many a day." With this, and a parting keen glance, he turned on his heel and strode off.

Tom gave a great gasp, clenched his big hands tightly together, took a long look at the wide expanse of water, then disappeared within.

In about half an hour, the steerage baby having gone to sleep in Phronsie's arms, the brothers and sisters, finding, after the closest inspection, nothing more to eat in the basket, gathered around the center of attraction in a small bunch.

"I hope they won't wake up the baby," said Phronsie, in gentle alarm.

"Never you fear," said old Mr. King, quite comfortable now in the camp-chair one of the sailors had brought in response to a request from Jasper; "that child knows very well by this time, I should imagine, what noise is."

But after a little, the edge of their curiosity having been worn off, the small group began to get restive, and to clamor and pull at their mother for want of something better to do.

"O dear me!" said Phronsie, in distress.

"Dear, dear!" echoed Polly, vainly trying to induce the child next to the baby to get into her lap; "something must be done. Oh, don't you want to hear about a funny cat, children? I'm going to tell them about Grandma Bascom's, Jasper," she said, seeing the piteous look in Phronsie's eyes.

"Yes, we do," said one of the boys, as spokesman, and he solemnly bobbed his tow head, whereat all the children then bobbed theirs.

"Sit down, then," said Polly, socially making way for them, "all of you in a circle, and I'll tell you of that very funny cat." So the whole bunch of tow-headed children sat down in a ring, and solemnly folded their hands in their laps. Jasper threw himself down where he could edge himself in. Old Mr. King leaned back and surveyed them with great satisfaction. So Polly launched out in her gayest mood, and the big blue eyes in the round faces before her widened, and the mouths flew open, showing the white teeth; and the stolid mother leaned forward, and her eyes and mouth looked just like those of her children, only they were bigger; and at last Polly drew a long breath and wound up with a flourish, "And that's all"

"Tell another," said one of the round-eyed, open-mouthed children, without moving a muscle. All the rest sat perfectly still.

"O dear me," said Polly, with a little laugh, "that was such a good long one, you can't want another."

"I think you've gotten yourself into business, Polly," said Jasper, with a laugh. "Hadn't we better go?"

Polly gave a quick glance at Phronsie. "Phronsie dear," she said, "let us go up to our deck now, dear. Shall we?"

"Oh, no, Polly, please don't go yet," begged Phronsie, in alarm, and patting the baby softly with a gentle little hand. Polly looked off at Grandpapa. He was placidly surveying the water, his eyes occasionally roving over the novel and interesting sights around. On the other side of the deck a returning immigrant was bringing out a jew's-harp, and two or three of his fellow-passengers were preparing to pitch quoits. Old Mr. King was actually smiling at it all. Polly hadn't seen him so contented since they sailed.

"I guess I'll tell another one, Jasper," she said. "Oh, about a dog, you wanted, did you?" nodding at the biggest boy.

"Yes," said the boy, bobbing his tow head, "I did;" and he unfolded and folded his hands back again, then waited patiently.

So Polly flew off on a gay little story about a dog that bade fair to rival Grandma Bascom's cat for cleverness. He belonged to Mr. Atkins who kept store in Badgertown, and the Pepper children used to see a good deal of him, when they took home the sacks and coats that Mamsie sewed for the storekeeper. And in the midst of the story, when the stolid steerage children were actually laughing over the antics of that remarkable dog, Jasper glanced up toward the promenade deck, took a long look, and started to his feet. "Why, Polly Pepper, see!" He pointed upward. There, on the curve, were old Mr. Selwyn and Tom walking arm in arm.

IV

STEAMER LIFE

*A*nd after that, it was "My grandson, Thomas," on all occasions, the old gentleman introducing the boy to the right and to the left, as he paraded the deck, his old arm within the younger one. And the little, sharp black eyes snapped proudly and the white head was held up, as he laughed and chattered away sociably to the passengers and the ship's crew, at every good opportunity.

"Yes, my grandson, Thomas, is going back to school. We've been running about in your country a bit, and the boy's mother went home first with the other children —" Polly heard him say as the two paused in front of her steamer chair.

"Indeed!" ejaculated Mrs. Vanderburgh, as he addressed her, and raising her eyebrows with a supercilious glance for his plain, unprepossessing appearance. "Yes, Madam, and glad shall I be to set my foot on Old England again Hey, Tom, my boy, don't you say so?"

Tom looked off over the sea, but did not speak.

Neither did Mrs. Vanderburgh answer, but turned her face away in disdain that was very plainly marked.

"Home is the best place, Madam," declared old Mr. Selwyn emphatically. "Well, Old England is our home, and nothing will induce me to leave it again, I can assure you."

Again Mrs. Vanderburgh did not reply, but looked him up and down in cold silence. Old Mr. Selwyn, not appearing to notice, chattered on. At last she deliberately turned her back on him.

"Isn't he common and horrid?" whispered Fanny Vanderburgh, in the steamer chair next to Polly, thrusting her face in between her and her book. And she gave a little giggle.

"Hush!" said Polly, warningly, "he will hear you."

"Nonsense — it's impossible; he is rattling on so; and do look at Mamma's face!"

He didn't hear, but Tom did; and he flashed a glance — dark and wrathful — over at the two girls, and started forward, abruptly pulling his Grandfather along.

"O dear me!" exclaimed Polly, in distress, dropping her book in her lap; "now he *has* heard."

"Oh, that dreadful boy," said Fanny, carelessly, stretching out in her steamer chair comfortably; "well, who cares? he's worse than his Grandfather."

"Yes, he has heard," repeated Polly, sorrowfully looking after the two, Tom still propelling the old gentleman along the deck at a lively rate; "now, what shall we do?"

"It isn't of the least consequence if he has heard," reiterated Fanny, "and Mamma has been frightfully bored, I know. Do tell us, Mamma," she called.

Mrs. Vanderburgh turned away from the rail, where she had paused in her constitutional when addressed by the old gentleman, and came up to the girls.

"Do sit down, Mamma, in your steamer chair," begged Fanny; "I'll tuck you up in your rug." And she jumped lightly out of her own chair. "There, that's nice," as Mrs. Vanderburgh sank gracefully down, and Fanny patted and pulled the rug into shape. "Now tell us, wasn't he the most horrible old bore?"

As she cuddled back into her own nest, Mrs. Vanderburgh laughed in a very highbred manner. "He was very amusing," she said.

"Amusing! I should say so!" cried Fanny. "I suppose he would have told you all his family history if he had stayed. O dear me, he is such a common, odious old person."

Polly twisted uneasily under her rug.

Mrs. Vanderburgh glanced into the steamer chair on the other side. It had several books on top of the rug. "I don't believe he can take that seat," she said; "still, Fanny, I think it would be well for you to change into it, for that old man may take it into his head, when he makes the turn of the deck, to drop into it and give us the whole of his family history."

"Horrors!" ejaculated Fanny, hopping out of her chair again. "I'll make sure that he doesn't. And yet I did so want to sit next to Polly Pepper," she mourned, ensconcing herself under the neighboring rug, and putting the books on the floor by her side.

"Don't do that; give them to me," said her mother; "I'll put them in your chair unless Miss Polly will take that place, only I don't like to disturb you, dear," she said with a sweet smile at Polly.

"Why, that would make matters' worse, Mamma," said Fanny. "Don't you see, then, that old bore would put himself into Polly's chair, for he likes her, anyway. Do leave it as it is."

So Mrs. Vanderburgh smiled again. "I don't know but that you are right," she said, and leaned back her head restfully. "Dear me, yes, he *is* amusing."

"They are terribly common people," said Fanny, her aristocratic nose well in the air, "aren't they, Mamma? And did you ever see such a clumsy thing as that dreadful boy, and such big hands and feet?" She held up her own hands as she spoke, and played with her rings, and let the jingling bracelets run up and down her wrists.

"Fanny, how often must I tell you to wear gloves on shipboard?" said her mother, in a tone of reproof. "Nothing spoils the hands so much as a trip at sea. They won't get over it all summer; they're coarsened already," and she cast an alarmed glance at the long, slender fingers.

"I'm so tired of gloves, Mamma." Fanny gave a restful yawn. "Polly Pepper doesn't wear them," she cried triumphantly, peering past her mother to point to Polly's hands.

Mrs. Vanderburgh hesitated. It wouldn't do to say anything that would reflect against the Peppers — manners, or customs, or bringing up generally. So she leaned over and touched Polly's fingers with her own gloved ones.

"You don't wear gloves, do you, my dear?" she said, in gentle surprise, quite as if the idea had just struck her for the first time.

"No, Mrs. Vanderburgh, I don't," said Polly, "at least not on shipboard, unless it is cold."

"There, now, Mamma," laughed Fanny, in a pleased way; "you'll stop teasing me about wearing them, I'm sure."

Mrs. Vanderburgh turned and surveyed her daughter; but she didn't smile, and Fanny thought it as well to begin again on the old topic.

"They're awfully common people, aren't they, Mamma, — those Selwyns?"

"They are, indeed," replied Mrs. Vanderburgh, "quite commonplace, and exceedingly tiresome; be sure and not speak to them, Fanny."

"Trust me for that," said Fanny, with a wise little nod. "The old man stopped me and asked me something this morning, as I was coming out of the dining room, after breakfast, but I pretended I didn't hear, and I skipped upstairs and almost fell on my nose."

"You were fortunate to escape," said her mother, with a little laugh. "Well, let us drop the subject and talk of something else much more important. Polly, my dear." She turned again and surveyed the young girl at her side. "You are coming home this autumn, aren't you?"

"Oh, no," said Polly, "Grandpapa expects to stay over in Europe a year."

"Is that so?" said Mrs. Vanderburgh, and her face fell; "I regret it exceedingly, for I should be glad if you would visit Fanny this winter in New York."

"Thank you; but I couldn't anyway," said Polly. Then the color flew up to her cheek. "I mean I am in school, you know, Mrs. Vanderburgh, but I thank you, and it is so good of you to want me," she added, hurriedly, feeling that she hadn't said the right thing at all.

"I do want you very much, my dear child," said Mrs. Vanderburgh, "and I am very sorry you are to remain abroad over the winter, for your Grandfather would be persuaded, I feel quite sure, to have you leave school for a while, and come to us for a visit."

"Oh, no, he wouldn't," cried Polly, quickly. "I beg pardon, Mrs. Vanderburgh, but I never leave school for anything unless I am sick, and I am almost never sick."

"Well, then, you could come for the Christmas holidays," said Mrs. Vanderburgh, with ladylike obstinacy like one accustomed to carrying her point.

"The Christmas holidays!" exclaimed Polly, starting forward in her chair. "Oh, I wouldn't leave home for anything, then, Mrs. Vanderburgh. Why, we have the most beautiful times, and we are all together — the boys come home from school — and it's just too lovely for anything!" She clasped her hands and sighed — oh, if she could but see Ben and Joel and David but once!

Mrs. Vanderburgh was a very tall woman, and she gazed down into the radiant face, without speaking; Polly was looking off over the sea, and the color came and went on her cheek.

"We would soon get her out of all such notions, if we once had her with us, wouldn't we, Mamma?" said Fanny, in a low tone close to her mother's ear.

Mrs. Vanderburgh gave her a warning pinch, but Polly's brown eyes were fastened on the distant horizon, and she hadn't heard a word.

"Well, we'll arrange it sometime," said Fanny's mother, breaking the silence; "so you must remember, Polly dear, that you are engaged to us for a good long visit when you do come home."

"I will tell Grandpapa that you asked me," said Polly, bringing her eyes back with a sigh to look into Mrs. Vanderburgh's face.

"Oh, he will fall into the plan quite readily, I think," said Mrs. Vanderburgh, lightly. "You know we are all very old friends — that is, the families are — Mr. Vanderburgh's father and Mr. King were very intimate. Perhaps you don't know, Polly," — and Fanny's mamma drew herself up to her extreme height; it was impossible for her to loll back in her chair when talking of her family, — "that we are related to the Earl of Cavendish who owns the old estate in England, and we go back to William the Conqueror; that is, Fanny does on her father's side."

Fanny thereupon came up out of her chair depths to sit quite straight and gaze with importance at Polly's face. But Polly was still thinking of the boys, and she said nothing.

"And my family is just as important," said Mrs. Vanderburgh, and she smiled in great satisfaction. "Really, we could make things very pleasant for you, my child; our set is so exclusive, you could not possibly meet anyone but the very best people. Oh, here is your mother." She smiled enchantingly up at Mrs. Fisher, and held out her hand. "Do come and sit here with us, my dear Mrs. Fisher," she begged, "then we shall be a delightful group, we two mothers and our daughters."

"Thank you, Mrs. Vanderburgh." Mrs. Fisher smiled, but she didn't offer to take the steamer chair. "I have come after Polly."

"Mamsie, what is it? I'll come," said Polly, tumbling out of her steamer chair in a twinkling.

"O dear me!" exclaimed Mrs. Vanderburgh, in regret, "don't take Polly away, I do implore you, my dear Mrs. Fisher — I am *so* fond of her."

"I must," said Mother Fisher, smiling again, her hand now in Polly's, and before anymore remonstrances were made, they were off.

"Oh, Mamsie!" breathed Polly, hanging to the dear hand, "I am so glad you came, and took me away."

"Polly," said Mother Fisher, suddenly, "Grandpapa asked me to find you; he thinks you could cheer old Mr. Selwyn up a bit, perhaps, with backgammon. I'm afraid Tom has been behaving badly again."

"Oh, Mamsie!" exclaimed Polly, in dismay. And then the story came out.

"Grandpapa," said Phronsie, pulling at his hand gently, as they walked slowly up and down the deck, "does your head ache?" And she peered anxiously up into his face.

"No, child — that is, not much," said old Mr. King, trying to smooth his brows out. He was thinking — for it kept obtruding at all times and seasons — of that dreadful scrap of paper that Cousin Eunice had imposed upon him at the last minute before they sailed, announcing that she had had her way, and would at last compel acceptance of such a gift as she chose to make to Phronsie Pepper.

"If it aches at all," said Phronsie, decidedly, "I wish you would let me rub it for you, Grandpapa. I do, truly."

"Well, it doesn't," said Grandpapa; "that is it won't, now that I have you with me. I was thinking of something unpleasant, Phronsie, and then, to tell you the truth, that old Mr. Selwyn tires me to death. I can't talk to him, and his grandson is a cad."

"What is a cad?" asked Phronsie, wonderingly.

"Oh, well, a boy who isn't nice," said Mr. King, carelessly.

"Grandpapa, why isn't that boy nice to that poor old man?" asked Phronsie, a grieved look coming into her blue eyes.

"Goodness me, child, you ask me too much," said Mr. King, quickly; "oh, a variety of reasons. Well, we must take things as we find them, and do what we can to help matters along; but it seems a hopeless case, — things were in better shape; and now they seem all tangled up again, thanks to that boy."

"Grandpapa," said Phronsie, earnestly, "I don't believe that boy means to be bad to that poor old man, I don't really and truly, Grandpapa," she added, shaking her head.

"Well, he takes a queer way to show it, if he means to be good," said old Mr. King, grimly.

"Oh, is that you, Master Tom?" as they turned a corner to find themselves face to face with Tom Selwyn.

"Mr. King," Tom began very rapidly so that the words ran all over each other, "I'm no end sorry — don't think hard things of me — it's not my fault this time; Grandfather heard it as well as I — at least, I caught a little and he asked me what it was, and I had to tell him, and it upset him."

Old Mr. King stood gazing into the big boy's face in utter bewilderment. "As I don't know in the least what you are trying to tell me, my boy," at last he said, "I shall have to ask you to repeat it, and go slowly."

So Tom tried again to tell his story, and by the time that it was all out, Mr. King was fuming in righteous indignation.

"Well, well, it's not worth thinking of," at last he said at sight of the flashing eyes before him and the angry light on the young face. "You take my arm, or I'll take yours, Master Tom, — there, that's better, — and we'll do a bit of a turn on the deck. Your grandfather'll come out of it, for he's busy over the backgammon board. But it was an ugly thing to do just the same."

Just then Mrs. Vanderburgh and Fanny passed them, all sweet smiles for him and for Phronsie, but with no eyes for the boy.

V

A FISH STORY AND OTHER THINGS

"Oh, Polly! Polly!" Phronsie came running along the deck, and up to the little group playing shuffle-board; "there's such a very big whale." And she clasped her hands in great excitement. "There truly is. Do come and see him."

"Is there, Pet?" cried Polly, throwing down her shovel, "then we must all go and see him. Come, Jasper, and all of you," and she seized Phronsie's hand.

"He is very dreadful big," said Phronsie, as they sped on, Jasper and the other players close behind. "And he puffed, Polly, and the water went up, oh, so high!"

"That's because he came up to breathe," said Polly, as they raced along. "Dear me, I hope he won't be gone when we get there."

"Can't he breathe under the water?" asked Phronsie, finding it rather hard work to perform that exercise herself in such a race. "What does he stay down there for, then, say, Polly?"

"Oh, because he likes it," answered Polly, carelessly. "Take care, Phronsie, you're running into all those steamer chairs."

"I'm sorry he can't breathe," said Phronsie, anxiously trying to steer clear of the bunch of steamer chairs whose occupants had suddenly left them, too, to see the whale. "Poor whale — I'm sorry for him, Polly."

"Oh, he's happy," said Polly, "he likes it just as it is. He comes up for a little while to blow and —"

"I thought you said he came up to breathe, Polly," said Phronsie, tugging at Polly's hand, and guilty of interrupting.

"Well, and so he does, and to blow, too, — it's just the same thing," said Polly, quickly.

"Is it just exactly the same?" asked Phronsie.

"Yes, indeed; that is, in the whale's case," answered Polly, as they ran up to Grandpapa and the rest of their party, and the knots of other passengers, all staring hard at a certain point on the sparkling waste of water.

"I thought you were never coming," said old Mr. King, moving away from the rail to tuck Polly and Phronsie in where they could get a good view. "Oh, there he is — there he is — Jasper, look!" cried Polly.

"There he is!" crowed Phronsie, now much excited. "Oh, isn't he big, Grandpapa?"

"I should say he was," declared Mr. King. "I think I never saw a finer whale in my life, Phronsie."

"He comes up to blow," said Phronsie, softly to herself, her face pressed close to the rail, and her yellow hair floating off in the breeze; "and Polly says it doesn't hurt him, and he likes it."

"What is it, Phronsie child?" asked old Mr. King, hearing her voice.

"Grandpapa, has he got any little whales?" asked Phronsie, suddenly raising her face.

"Oh, yes, I imagine so," said old Mr. King; "that is, he ought to have, I'm sure. Porpoises go in schools, — why shouldn't whales, pray tell?"

"What's a porpoise?" asked Phronsie, with wide eyes.

"Oh, he's a dolphin or a grampus."

"Oh," said Phronsie, much mystified, "and does he go to school?"

"Well, they go ever so many of them together, and they call it a school. Goodness me — that *is* a blow!" as the whale spouted valiantly, and looked as if he were making directly for the steamer.

"Oh, Grandpapa, he's coming right here!" screamed Phronsie, clapping her hands in delight, and hopping up and down, — Polly and Jasper were almost as much excited, — while the passengers ran hither and thither to get a good view, and leveled their big glasses, and oh-ed and ah-ed. And some of them ran to get their cameras. And Mr. Whale seemed to like it, for he spouted and flirted his long tail and dashed into the water and out again to blow, till they were all quite worn out looking at him. At last, with a final plunge, he bade them all good-bye and disappeared.

Phronsie, after her first scream of delight, had pressed her face close to the rail and held her breath. She did not say a word, but gazed in speechless enjoyment at the antics of the big fish. And Grandpapa had to speak two or three times when the show was all over before she heard him.

"Did you like it, Phronsie?" he asked, gathering her hand up closely in his, as he leaned over to see her face.

Phronsie turned away with a sigh. "Oh, Grandpapa, he was so beautiful!" She drew a long breath, then turned back longingly. "Won't he ever come back?" she asked.

"Maybe not this one," said old Mr. King; "but we'll see plenty more, I imagine, Phronsie. At least, if not on this voyage, — why, some other time."

"Oh, wasn't it splendid!" exclaimed Polly, tossing back the little rings of brown hair from her brow. "Well, he's gone; now we must run back, Jasper, and finish our game." And they were off, the other players following.

"I'd like to see this very whale again," said Phronsie, with a small sigh; "Grandpapa, I would, really; he was a nice whale."

"Yes, he was a fine one," said old Mr. King. "I don't know as I ever put eyes on a better specimen, and I've seen a great many in my life."

"Tell me about them, do, Grandpapa," begged Phronsie, drawing nearer to him.

"Well, I'll get into my steamer chair, and you shall sit in my lap, and then I'll tell you about some of them," said Mr. King, much gratified. As they moved off, Phronsie clinging to his hand, she looked back and saw two children gazing wistfully after them. "Grandpapa," she whispered, pulling his hand gently to attract attention, "may that little boy and girl come, too, and hear about your whales?"

"Yes, to be sure," cried Mr. King. So Phronsie called them, and in a few minutes there was quite a big group around Grandpapa's steamer chair; for when the other children saw what was going on, they stopped, too, and before he knew, there he was perfectly surrounded.

"I should very much like to hear what it is all about." Mrs. Vanderburgh's soft voice broke into a pause, when old Mr. King stopped to rest a bit. "You must be very fascinating, dear Mr. King; you have no idea how pretty your group is." She pulled Fanny forward gently into the outer fringe of the circle. "Pray, what is the subject?"

"Nothing in the world but a fish story, Madam," said the old gentleman.

"Oh, *may* we stay and hear it?" cried Mrs. Vanderburgh, enthusiastically, clasping her gloved hands. "Fanny adores such things, don't you, dear?" turning to her.

"Yes, indeed, Mamma," answered Fanny, trying to look very much pleased.

"Take my word for it, you will find little to interest either of you," said Mr. King.

"Oh, I should be charmed," cried Mrs. Vanderburgh. "Fanny dear, draw up that steamer chair to the other side." But a stout, comfortable-looking woman coming down the deck stopped directly in front of that same chair, and before Fanny could move it, sat down, saying, "This is my chair, young lady."

"That vulgar old woman has got it," said Fanny, coming back quite crestfallen.

"Ugh!" Mrs. Vanderburgh shrugged her shoulders as she looked at the occupant of the chair, who surveyed her calmly, then fell to reading her book. "Well, you must just bear it, dear; it's one of the annoyances to be endured on shipboard."

"I suppose the lady wanted her own chair," observed Mr. King, dryly.

"Lady? Oh, my dear Mr. King!" Mrs. Vanderburgh gave a soft little laugh. "It's very good of you to put it that way, I'm sure. Well, now do let us hear that delightful story. Fanny dear, you can sit on part of my chair," she added, regardless of the black looks of a gentleman hovering near, who had a sharp glance on the green card hanging to the back of the chair she had appropriated and that bore his name.

So Fanny perched on the end of the steamer chair, and Mr. King, not seeing any way out of it, went on in his recital of the whale story, winding up with an account of some wonderful porpoises he had seen, and a variety of other things, until suddenly he turned his head and keenly regarded Fanny's mother.

"How intensely interesting!" she exclaimed, opening her eyes, and trying not to yawn. "Do go on, and finish about that whale," feeling that she must say something.

"Mamma!" exclaimed Fanny, trying to stop her.

"I ended up that whale some five minutes ago, Madam," said Mr. King. "I think you must have been asleep."

"Oh, no, indeed, I have been charmed every moment," protested Mrs. Vanderburgh sitting quite erect. "You surely have the gift of a *raconteur,* Mr. King," she said, gracefully recovering herself. "O dear me, here is that odious boy and that tiresome old man!" as Tom Selwyn came up slowly, his Grandfather on his arm.

Mr. King put Phronsie gently off from his lap, still keeping her hand in his. "Now, children, the story-telling is all done, the whales and porpoises are all finished up — so run away." He touched his sea-cap to Mrs. Vanderburgh and her daughter, then marched up to the old man and Tom.

"I am tired of sitting still," he said. "May my little granddaughter and I join you in a walk?"

Tom shot him a grateful look. Old Mr. Selwyn, who cared most of all for Polly, mumbled out something, but did not seem especially happy. But Mr. King did not appear to notice anything awry, but fell into step, still keeping Phronsie's hand, and they paced off.

"If you know which side your bread is buttered, Mamma," said Fanny Vanderburgh, shrewdly, looking after them as they disappeared, "you'll make up to those dreadful Selwyn people."

"Never!" declared her mother, firmly. "Fanny, are you wild? Why, you are a Vanderburgh and are related to the English nobility, and I am an Ashleigh. What would your father say to such a notion?"

"Well, Papa isn't here," said Fanny, "and if he were, he'd do something to keep in with Mr. King. I hate and detest those dreadful Selwyns as much as you do, Mamma, but I'm going to cultivate them. See if I don't!"

"And I forbid it," said her mother, forgetting herself and raising her voice. "They are low bred and common. And beside that, they are eccentric and queer. Don't you speak to them or notice them in the slightest."

"Madam," said the gentleman of the black looks, advancing and touching his cap politely, "I regret to disturb you, but I believe you have my chair."

Mrs. Vanderburgh begged pardon and vacated the chair, when the gentleman touched his cap again, and immediately drew the chair up to the one where the stout, comfortable-looking woman sat.

"It seems to me there are more ill-bred, low-lived people on board this boat than it has been my lot to meet on any voyage," said Mrs. Vanderburgh, drawing her sea coat around her slight figure and sailing off, her daughter in her wake.

VI

A LITTLE SURPRISE

"Sir," said little Mr. Selwyn, bringing his sharp black eyes to bear upon old Mr. King, "you've been very good to me, and I've not been always pleasant. But it's my way, sir; it's my way."

Mr. King nodded pleasantly, although deep in his heart he agreed with the choleric old gentleman. "But as for Polly, why, she's good — good as gold, sir." There was no mistaking Mr. Selwyn's sentiments there, and his old cheek glowed while giving what to him meant the most wonderful praise to be paid to a person.

Old Mr. King straightened up. "You've said the right thing now," he declared.

"And I wish I could see that girl when she's grown up," added the little old gentleman. "I want really to know what sort of a woman she'll make. I do, indeed, sir."

"It isn't necessary to speculate much on it," answered Mr. King, confidently, "when you look at her mother and remember the bringing up that Polly Pepper has had."

The little old gentleman squinted hard at the clouds scudding across the blue sky. "That's so," he said at last. "Well, I'm sorry we are to part," he added. "And, sir, I really wish you would come down to my place with your party and give me a fortnight during your stay in England. I really do, sir, upon me word." There was no mistaking his earnestness as he thrust out one thin, long-fingered hand. With the other, he set a card within Mr. King's fingers.

"Arthur Selwyn, The Earl of Cavendish," met Mr. King's eyes.

"I had a fancy to do this thing," said the little old gentleman, "to run across from America in simple fashion, and it pleased the boy, who hates a fuss. And we've gotten rid of all sorts of nuisances by it; interviews, and tiresome people. And I've enjoyed it mightily." He chuckled away till it seemed as if he were never going to stop. Old Mr. King burst out laughing, too; and the pair were so very jolly that the passengers, grouped together waiting for the Liverpool landing, turned to stare at them.

"Just see how intimate Mr. King is with that tiresome, common, old Mr. Selwyn!" exclaimed Mrs. Vanderburgh to her daughter. "I never was so surprised at anything in all my life, to see that he keeps it up now, for I thought that aristocratic Horatio King was the most fastidious being alive."

"The Kings have awfully nice times," grumbled Fanny, picking her gloves discontentedly. "And you keep me mewed up, and won't let me speak to anybody whose grandfather wasn't born in our set, and I hate and loathe it all."

"You'll be glad when you are a few years older, and I bring you out in society, that I always have been so particular," observed Mrs. Vanderburgh, complacently, lifting her head in its dainty bonnet, higher than ever.

"I want some nice times and a little fun now," whined Fanny, with an envious glance over at Polly and Jasper with the dreadful Selwyn boy between them, and Phronsie running up to join them, and everybody in their party just bubbling over with happiness.

"I wish Mr. King and his party would go to Paris now," said her mother, suddenly.

"Oh, don't I just wish it!" cried Fanny, in a burst. "Did you ask him, Mamma?"

"Yes, indeed; I talked for fully half an hour yesterday, but it was no use. And he doesn't seem to know how long he is going to stay in England; 'only a few days,' he said, vaguely, then they go to Holland."

"Oh, why couldn't we go to Holland!" exclaimed Fanny, impulsively, and her eyes brightened; "splendid Holland, that would be something like, Mamma!"

"You forget the Van Dykes are to be in Paris awaiting us."

"Oh, those stupid Van Dykes!" exploded Fanny. "Mamma, don't go there now. Do change, and let us go to Holland with the Kings. Do, Mamma," she implored.

"Why, Fanny Vanderburgh!" exclaimed her mother, sharply, "what is the matter with you? You know it was settled long ago, that we should meet Mrs. Van Dyke and Eleanor in Paris at just this very time. It would never do to offend them, particularly when Eleanor is going to marry into the Howard set."

"And I'll have the most stupid time imaginable," cried Fanny, passionately, "dragging around while you and the Van Dykes are buying that trousseau."

"Yes, that's one thing that I wanted the Kings to go to Paris for," said Mrs. Vanderburgh; "you could be with them. And really they are much more important than anyone to get in with. And I'd keep up the friendship with the Van Dykes. But that Mr. King is so obstinate, you can't do anything with him." A frown settled all across her pretty face, and she beat her foot impatiently on the deck.

"You spoil everything, Mamma, with your sets and your stupid people," declared Fanny, her passion by no means cooled. "When I come out in society I'm going to choose my own friends," she muttered to herself, and set her lips tightly together.

Mr. King was saying, "Thank you, so much, Mr. Selwyn, for I really think I'd prefer to call you so, as I knew you so first."

"So you shall," cried the little Earl, glancing around on the groups, "and it's better just here, at all events," and he chuckled again. "Then you really will come?" and he actually seized Mr. King's hand and wrung it heartily.

"No, I was about to say it is quite impossible."

The Earl of Cavendish stared blankly up out of his sharp little black eyes in utter amazement into the other's face. "My stay in London is short, only a few days," Mr. King was saying, "and then we go directly to Holland. I thank you all the same — believe me, I appreciate it. It is good of you to ask us," he cordially added.

The little Earl of Cavendish broke away from him, and took a few hasty steps down the deck to get this new idea fairly into his brain that his invitation had not been accepted. Then he hurried back. "My dear sir," he said, laying his hand on Mr. King's arm, "will you do me the favor to try to come at some future time — to consider your plans before you return to America, and see if you can't manage to give me this great pleasure of welcoming you to my home? Think of it, I beg, and drop me a line; if at home, I shall always be most glad to have you with me. I should esteem it a privilege." The Earl of Cavendish was astonished to find himself beseeching the American gentleman without a title. And then they awaked to the fact that the groups of passengers were merging into a solid mass, and a slow procession was beginning to form for the stairway, and the landing episode was well under way.

Mrs. Vanderburgh, determined not to bid good-bye on the steamer but to be with the Kings till the last moment, rushed up to them on the wharf, followed by Fanny.

"Oh, we are *so* sorry you are not going to Paris with us," cried Mrs. Vanderburgh, while Fanny flew at Polly Pepper and engrossed her hungrily. "Can't you reconsider it now?" she asked, with a pretty earnestness.

"No, it is impossible," answered Mr. King, for about the fiftieth time. "Our plans will not allow it. I hope you and your daughter will have the best of times," he remarked politely.

"Yes, we shall; we meet old friends there, and Paris is always delightful." Mrs. Vanderburgh bit her lip in her vexation. "I was going to see you and beg you even now to change your plans, while we were on the steamer waiting to land," she went on hurriedly, "but you were bored — I quite pitied you — by that tiresome, common, old Mr. Selwyn."

"Yes, I was talking with him," said Mr. King, "but excuse me, I was not bored. He is peculiar, but not at all common, and he has many good qualities as a man; and I like the boy immensely."

"How can you?" Mrs. Vanderburgh gave a little highbred laugh. "They are so insufferably common, Mr. King, those Selwyns are."

"Excuse me," said Mr. King, "that was the Earl of Cavendish; it will do no harm to mention it now, as they have gone."

"Who — who?" demanded Mrs. Vanderburgh in a bewildered way.

"I did not know it till this morning," Mr. King was explaining, "but our fellow-passenger, Mr. Selwyn, chose to cross over keeping his real identity unknown, and I must say I admire his taste in the matter; and anyway it was his affair and not mine." It was a long speech, and at its conclusion Mrs. Vanderburgh was still demanding, "Who — who?" in as much of a puzzle as ever.

"The Earl of Cavendish," repeated Mr. King; "Mr. Selwyn is the Earl of Cavendish. As I say, he did not wish it known, and —"

"Fanny — Fanny!" called her mother, sitting helplessly on the first thing that presented itself, a box of merchandise by no means clean. "Fan-ny! the — the Earl of Cavendish!" She could get no further.

Little Dr. Fisher, who administered restoratives and waited on Mrs. Vanderburgh and her daughter to their London train, came skipping back to the Liverpool hotel.

"I hope, wife, I shan't grow uncharitable," — he actually glared through his big spectacles, — "but Heaven defend us on our travels from any further specimens like that woman."

"We shall meet all sorts, probably, Adoniram," said his wife, calmly; "it really doesn't matter with our party of eight; we can take solid comfort together."

The little doctor came out of his ill temper, but he said ruefully, "That's all very well, wife, for you and the Hendersons; for you steered pretty clear, I noticed, of that woman. Well, she's gone." And he smiled cheerfully. "Now for dinner, for I suppose Mr. King has ordered it."

"Yes, he has," said his wife. "And you have a quarter of an hour. I've put your clothes out all ready."

"All right." The little doctor was already plunging here and there, tearing off his coat and necktie and boots; and exactly at the time set, he joined the party, with a bright and shining face, as if no Mrs. Vanderburgh, or anyone in the least resembling her, had ever crossed his path.

"Jasper," cried Polly, as they hurried along out of the Harwich train to the steamer that was to take them to the Hook of Holland, "can you really believe we are almost there?"

"No, I can't," said Jasper, "for I've wanted to see Holland for such a time."

"Wasn't it good of Grandpapa," cried Polly, "to take us here the first thing after London?"

"Father always does seem to plan things rightly," answered Jasper, with a good degree of pride. "And then 'it's prime,'" "as Joel used to say," he was going to add, but thought better of it, as any reference to the boys always set Polly to longing for them.

"Indeed, he does," exclaimed Polly, in her most earnest fashion; "he's ever and always the most splendid Grandpapa. Oh, I wish I could do things for him, Jasper," she mourned; "he's so good to us."

"You do things for him all the while, Polly," Jasper made haste to say, as they ran along to keep up with the Parson and Mrs. Henderson's comfortable figures just before them; "you are all the while doing something for him."

"Oh, no, I don't," said Polly, "there isn't anything I can do for him. Don't you suppose there ever will be, Jasper?" she asked imploringly.

"Yes, indeed," said Jasper; "there always are things that hop up to be done when people keep their eyes open. But don't you worry about your not doing anything for him, Polly. Promise me that." Jasper took her hand and stopped just a minute to look into her face.

"I'll try not to," promised Polly, "but, oh, Jasper, I do so very much wish there might be something that I could do. I do, indeed, Jasper."

"It was only yesterday," said Jasper, as they began to hurry on once more, "that father said 'you can't begin to think, Jasper, what a comfort Polly Pepper is to me.'"

"Did he, Jasper?" cried Polly, well pleased, the color flying over her cheek, "that was nice of him, because there isn't anything much I can really do for him. O dear! there is Grandpapa beckoning to us to hurry." So on they sped, having no breath for words. And presently they were on the boat, and little Dr. Fisher and Mr. Henderson went forward into the saloon, where the rooms reserved beforehand were to be given out, and the rest of the party waited and watched the stream of people of all ages and sizes and nationalities who desired to reach Holland the next morning.

To Polly it was a world of delight, and to Jasper, who watched her keenly, it was a revelation to see how nothing escaped her, no matter how noisy and dirty or turbulent the crowd, or how annoying the detention, — it was all a marvel of happiness from beginning to end. And Jasper looking back over the two times he had been before to Europe with his father, although he had never seen Holland, remembered only a sort of dreary drifting about with many pleasant episodes and experiences, it is true, still with the feeling on the whole of the most distinct gladness when their faces were turned homeward and the journeying was over.

"Mamsie," cried Polly, poking her head out from the upper berth of the stuffy little state-room assigned to Mrs. Fisher, Mrs. Henderson, Phronsie, and herself; "was anything ever so delicious as this boat? — and to think, Mamsie," — here Polly paused to add as impressively as if the idea had never been voiced before, — "that we are really to see Holland tomorrow."

"You'd better go to sleep now, then," said Mrs. Fisher, wisely, "if you want to be bright and ready really to see much of Holland in the morning, Polly."

"That's so," answered Polly, ducking back her head to its pillow, and wriggling her toes in satisfaction; "Phronsie is asleep already, isn't she, Mamsie?"

"Yes," said Mrs. Fisher, "she dropped off as soon as her head touched the pillow. Good night, Polly, you would better do the same."

"Good night, Mamsie," said Polly, with a sleepy little yawn, "and good night, dear Mrs. Henderson," she added, already almost in dreamland.

VII

OFF FOR HOLLAND

*I*t seemed to Polly as if she had only breathed twice, and had not turned over once, when there was Mamsie's voice calling her, and there was Mamsie's face looking into hers over the edge of the berth. "Wake up, Polly, child, you have only about ten minutes to dress in."

"O dear me! what — where?" exclaimed Polly, springing to a sitting position, thereby giving her brown head a smart thump on the ceiling of the berth, "where are we, Mamsie? why, it is the middle of the night, isn't it?" she cried, not stopping to pity her poor head.

"We are almost at the Hook of Holland," said Mrs. Fisher, busily buttoning Phronsie's shoes. Phronsie sat on the lower berth, her sleepy little legs dangling over the edge, and her sleepy little head going nid-nodding, despite all her efforts to keep herself awake.

"O dear me!" cried Polly, remorsefully, when she saw that. "I ought to have dressed Phronsie. Why didn't you wake me up earlier, Mamsie?"

"Because I wanted you to sleep all you could," said Mrs. Fisher, "and now if you'll only dress Polly Pepper as quickly as possible, that's all I ask."

"I will dress Polly Pepper in a twinkling, Mamsie," declared Polly, laughing merrily; "O dear me, where *is* my other stocking?" She stuck out one black foot ready for its boot. "Is it down there, Mamsie?" All the while she was shaking the bedclothes violently for any chance glimpse of it in the berth.

"Where did you put it last night when you took it off, Polly?" asked Mrs. Fisher, buttoning away for dear life on Phronsie's shoes. "There now, Pet, those are done; hop out now, and fly into your clothes."

"I thought I put 'em both in the corner here," cried poor Polly, twitching everything loose. Thereupon her big hat, hung carefully upon a high hook, slipped off and fell to the floor.

"Take care, Polly," warned her mother, "haste only makes matters worse."

"But I can't go with only one stocking on," said Polly, quite gone in despair now. "Oh, dear Mrs. Henderson, don't you see it on the floor?" For that good woman had dropped to her knees, and was busily prowling around among the accumulation of bags and clothing.

"That's what I'm hoping to do," she answered, "but I don't see it as yet, Polly."

"I'll help Polly to find it," cried Phronsie, now thoroughly awake and dropping her small skirts to get down on the floor by Mrs. Henderson's side. "Don't feel badly, Polly; I'll find your stocking for you."

"No, Phronsie," said her mother, "you must get into your own clothes. And then Mrs. Henderson is nearly all ready, and you can go out with her, and that will leave more room, so that Polly and I can search more carefully. And the stocking has got to come, for it couldn't walk off of itself," she added cheerily as she saw Polly's face. "Why — what?" as she happened to look upward. And then Polly looked, too, and there was her stocking dangling from the very high hook where the big hat had been.

"You tossed it up there, I suppose, when you shook up the bedclothes so quickly," said Mrs. Fisher. "Well, now," as Polly pounced on the stocking, "see how fast you can hop into your clothes, daughter." Then she began to put the things for the bags into their places, and Matilda, coming in, finished the work; and Polly flew around, buttoning and tying and patting herself into shape, and by the time that little Dr. Fisher's voice called at the door, "Well, wife, are you ready?" there they all were, trim and tidy as ever for a start.

"Where is it, Grandpapa?" asked Phronsie, peering around on either side, — Dr. Fisher and Jasper had gone off to attend to the examination of the luggage by the customs inspectors, — and then coming up gently to pull his arm. "I don't see it anywhere."

"What, child?" answered Grandpapa, looking down at her. "See here, wait a minute," to the others who were ahead, "Phronsie has lost something."

"Oh, no, Grandpapa, I haven't," began Phronsie, in gentle protestation, "all my things are in here." She patted her little bag that hung on her arm, a gift of old Mr. King's for her to carry her very own things in, that yielded her immense satisfaction every time she looked at it, which was very often.

"Didn't you say you wanted to find something, dear?" he asked, quite puzzled, while the others surrounded them wonderingly.

"No," said Phronsie, "only where is the hook, Grandpapa? I don't see it." She lifted her little face and gazed up at him confident that he knew everything.

"She has lost her button-hook!" exclaimed Polly, "the cunning little silver one Auntie Whitney gave her Christmas. I'll run back and get it; it must be in the state-room."

"Stay, Polly," commanded Mr. King. And, "Oh, no, I haven't," piped Phronsie, as Polly was flying off. "It's here in my bag," patting Grandpapa's gift hanging on her arm. "I couldn't lose that, Polly," she cried in horror at the thought, as Polly hurried back.

"Well, what is it, then, you've lost?" demanded Polly, breathlessly.

"I haven't lost anything," reiterated Phronsie, pushing back the yellow hair from her face. "Grandpapa, tell them, please, I haven't lost anything," she kept repeating, appealing to him.

"She says she hasn't lost anything, so we won't say that again," echoed old Mr. King. "Now, Phronsie, child, tell me what it is you mean; what hook you want."

"The hook," said Phronsie; "here, Grandpapa," and she looked all around in a troubled way, "they said it was here; I don't see it, Grandpapa."

"She means the Hook of Holland," burst out Polly, "don't you, Phronsie pet?" And she threw her arms around her while Mr. Henderson exclaimed, "Of course, why didn't we think of it, to be sure?"

"Yes, Polly." Phronsie gave a glad little cry, and wriggled in great satisfaction in her arms. "Grandpapa, where is it, — the Hook of Holland?"

"Oh, bless me, child!" exclaimed Mr. King, "that is the name of the place; at least, to be accurate, it is Hoek van Holland. Now, just as soon as we get fairly started on our way to Rotterdam, I'll tell you all about it, or Polly shall, since she was clever enough to find out what you meant."

"Oh, no, Grandpapa," cried Polly, "I'd so much rather you told her — please do, dear Grandfather?"

"And so I will," he promised, very much pleased, for Mr. King dearly loved to be the one to relate the history and anecdotes about the places along which they traveled. And so, when they were steaming off toward Rotterdam, as he sat in the center of the compartment he had reserved for their use, Phronsie next to him, and Polly and Jasper opposite, he told the whole story. The others tucked themselves in the remaining four seats, and did not lose a word. Matilda and Mr. King's valet, in a second-class compartment, took charge of the luggage.

"I like it very much," declared Phronsie, when the story was all finished, and smoothing down her little brown gown in satisfaction.

"I like it very much, Grandpapa's telling it," said Polly, "but the Hook of Holland isn't anything to what we shall see at Rotterdam, while, as for The Hague and Amsterdam — oh, Grandpapa!"

That "oh, Grandpapa" just won his heart, and Mr. King beamed at her as her glowing face was turned first to one window and then to the other, that she might not lose anything as the train rumbled on.

"Just wait till we get to Marken," broke in Jasper, gaily, "then if you want to see the Dutch beat the Dutch — well, you may!" he ended with a laugh.

"Oh, Jasper, do they really beat each other?" cried Phronsie, quite horrified, and slipping away from Grandpapa to regard him closely.

"Oh, no! I mean — they go ahead of everything that is most Dutch," Jasper hastened to say; "I haven't explained it very well."

"No, I should think not," laughed his father, in high good humor. "Well, Phronsie, I think you will like the folks on the Island of Marken, for they dress in funny quaint costumes, just as their ancestors did, years upon years ago."

"Are there any little children there?" asked Phronsie, slipping back into her place again, and nestling close to his side.

"Hundreds of them, I suppose," replied Mr. King, with his arm around her and drawing her up to him, "and they wear wooden shoes or sabots, or klompen as they call them, and —"

"Wooden shoes!" cried Phronsie; "oh, Grandpapa," clasping her hands, "how do they stay on?"

"Well, that's what I've always wondered myself when I've been in Holland. A good many have left off the sabots, I believe, and wear leather shoes made just like other people's."

"Oh, Grandpapa," cried Phronsie, leaning forward to peer into his face, "don't let them leave off the wooden shoes, please."

"I can't make them wear anything but what they want to," said old Mr. King, with a laugh; "but don't be troubled, child, you'll see all the wooden shoes you desire, in Rotterdam, and The Hague, too, for that matter."

"Shall I?" cried Phronsie, nestling back again quite pleased. "Grandpapa, I wish I could wear wooden shoes," she whispered presently in a burst of confidence, sticking out her toes to look at them.

"Bless me! you couldn't keep them on," said Mr. King.

"Don't the little Dutch children keep them on?" asked Phronsie. "Oh, Grandpapa, I think I could; I really think I could," she added earnestly.

"Yes, they do, because they are born and brought up to it, although, for the life of me, I don't see how they do it; but you couldn't, child, you'd fall the first minute and break your nose, most likely."

Phronsie gave a sigh. "Should I, Grandpapa?"

"Yes, quite likely; but I'll tell you what I will do. I will buy you a pair, and we will take them home. That will be fine, won't it, dear?"

"Yes," said Phronsie, wriggling in delight. Then she sat quite still.

"Grandpapa," she said, reaching up to whisper again, "I'm afraid it will make Araminta feel badly to see me with my beautiful wooden shoes on, when she can't have any. Do you suppose there are little teenty ones, Grandpapa dear, and I might get her a pair?"

"Yes, indeed," cried Grandpapa, nodding his white head in delight, "there are shoals of them, Phronsie, of all sizes."

"What are shoals?" queried Phronsie.

"Oh, numbers and numbers — so many we can't count them," answered Mr. King, recklessly.

Phronsie slid down into her place again, and sat quite still lost in thought. So many wooden shoes she couldn't count them was quite beyond her. But Grandpapa's voice roused her. "And I'll buy a bushel of them, Phronsie, and send them home, so that all your dolls at home can each have a pair. Would that suit you, Pet?"

Phronsie screamed with delight and clapped her hands. Polly and Jasper who had changed places, as Dr. Fisher and Mr. Henderson had made them take theirs by one window, now whirled around. "What is it?" cried Polly of Phronsie. "What is it?"

"I'm going to have wooden shoes," announced Phronsie, in a burst of confidence that included everybody in the compartment, "for my very own self, and Araminta is going to have a pair, and every single one of my children at home, too. Grandpapa said so."

"Whew!" whistled Jasper. "Oh, what fun," sighed Polly.

"And you shall have a pair, too, if you want them, Polly," Grandpapa telegraphed over to her in the corner.

"And Jasper can, too, can't he, Grandpapa? And, oh, thank you *so much*," cried Polly, all in one breath.

"I guess it's as well I shall be on hand to set the broken bones," said little Dr. Fisher, "with all you children capering around in those wooden abominations."

"Oh, Dr. Fisher, we are not going to fall!" exclaimed Jasper, in disdain, at the very thought. And "No, indeed," came merrily from Polly. And then they all fell to work admiring the numberless windmills past which their train was speeding toward Rotterdam.

"To think it is only six o'clock!" exclaimed Polly, looking at her little traveling watch that Grandpapa had given her. "Now, what a fine long day we are going to have, Jasper, for sightseeing in Rotterdam."

As the train came to a standstill, the guards threw open compartment doors, and all the people poured out calling for porters to see to their luggage, and everything was in confusion at once on the platforms.

"Indeed, you won't, Miss Polly," declared Mr. King, overhearing it, as they waited till all was ready for them to get into the hotel coach, — "we are all going to spend this day at the hotel — first, in getting a good breakfast, and then, dear me, I shall sleep pretty much all of the morning, and I'd advise the rest of you to jump into your beds and get good naps after the experience on that atrocious steamboat last night."

"Oh, Grandpapa, must we really go to bed?" cried Polly, in horror at the mere thought.

"Well, not exactly into your beds," laughed Mr. King, as Jasper, announcing that all was ready, piloted them into the coach, "but you've got to rest like sensible beings. Make up your mind to that. As for Phronsie," and he gallantly lifted her up to the step, "she's half asleep already. She's got to have a splendid nap, and no mistake."

"I'm not sleepy," declared Phronsie, stumbling into the high coach to sit down next to Mother Fisher. "No, Grandpapa dear, not a bit." And before anybody knew it, and as soon as the coach wheels spun round, she rolled over into Mamsie's lap. There she was as fast asleep as could be!

VIII

"WE WILL COME AGAIN AND STAY A WEEK"

*T*hey had been several days at The Hague, running about in a restful way in the morning, and driving all the long golden afternoons. "Don't you dare to go into a picture-gallery or a museum until I give the word," Grandpapa had laid down the law. "I'm not going to begin by being all tired out." So Polly and Jasper had gone sometimes with Mr. King and Phronsie, who had a habit of wandering off by themselves; or, as the case might be, Mr. Henderson would pilot them about till they learnt the ways of the old town. And Mrs. Fisher and Mrs. Henderson would confess now and then that they would much rather take a few stitches and overlook the traveling clothes than do anymore sight-seeing. And then again, they would all come together and go about in a big party. All but Dr. Fisher — he was for hospitals every time.

"That's what I've come for, wife," he would reply to all remonstrance, "and don't ask me to put my head into a cathedral or a museum." To Mr. King, "Land alive, man, I've got to find out how to take care of living bodies before I stare at bones and relics," and Mr. King would laugh and let him alone. "He's incorrigible, that husband of yours, Mrs. Fisher," he would add, "and we must just let him have his way." And Mamsie would smile, and every night the little doctor would tome from his tramps and medical study, tired but radiant.

At last one morning Grandpapa said, "Now for Scheveningen today!"

"Oh, goody!" cried Polly, clapping her hands; then blushed as red as a rose. They were at breakfast, and everybody in the vicinity turned and stared at their table.

"Don't mind it, Polly," said Jasper, her next neighbor, "I want to do the same thing. And it will do some of those starched and prim people good to hear a little enthusiasm." Polly knew whom he meant, — some young Englishmen. One of them immediately put up his monocle and regarded her as if she had been a new kind of creature displayed for his benefit. Jasper glared back at him.

"Yes, we'll go to Scheveningen this morning," repeated Mr. King, smiling approvingly at poor Polly, which caused her to lift her head; "the carriages are ordered, so as soon as we are through breakfast we will be off."

"Oh, father," exclaimed Jasper, in dismay, "must we go in carriages?"

"How else would you go, Jasper?" asked his father.

"Oh, by the tramway; oh, by all means," cried Jasper, perfectly delighted that he could get his father even to listen to any other plan.

"The dirty tram-cars," ejaculated Mr. King, in disgust. "How can you ask it, Jasper? No, indeed, we must go in carriages, or not at all."

"But, father," and Jasper's face fell, "don't you see the upper deck of the tram-car is so high and there are fine seats there, and we can see so much better than driving in a stupid carriage?"

Polly's face had drooped, too. Mr. King, in looking from one to the other, was dismayed and a good bit annoyed to find that his plan wasn't productive of much happiness after all. He had just opened his mouth to say authoritatively, "No use, Jasper, either you will go in the way I have provided, or stay at home," when Phronsie slipped out of her chair where she happened this morning to be sitting next to Mother Fisher, and running around to his chair, piped out, "Oh, Grandpapa, if you please, do let us sit up top."

"We'll do it now, Polly," whispered Jasper, in a transport, "when Phronsie looks like that. See her face!"

"Do you really want to go in a dirty old tram-car, Phronsie, instead of in a carriage?" Old Mr. King pushed back his chair and looked steadily at her.

"Oh, yes, yes, Grandpapa, please" — Phronsie beat her hands softly together — "to ride on top; may we, *dear* Grandpapa?" That "dear Grandpapa" settled it. Jasper never heard such a welcome command as that Mr. King was just issuing. "Go to the office and countermand the order for the carriages, my son; tell them to put the amount on my bill, the same as if I'd used them, unless they get a chance to let them to someone else. They needn't be the losers. Now then," as Jasper bounded off to execute the command, "get on your bonnets and hats, all of you, and we'll try this wonderful tram-car. I suppose you won't come with us, but will stay behind for the pleasures of some hospital here," he added to Dr. Fisher.

"On the contrary," said the little doctor, throwing down his napkin and getting out of his chair. "I am going, for there is a marine hospital for children there, that I wouldn't miss for the world."

"I warrant you would find one on a desert island," retorted old Mr. King. "Well, hurry now, all of you — and we will be off."

"Now, then, all scramble up here. Phronsie, you go with me," cried old Mr. King, as they stood in *plein*, and the tram-car halted before them. He was surprised to find that he liked this sort of thing, mixing with a crowd and hurrying for seats just like common ordinary individuals. And as he toiled up the winding stairs, Phronsie in front of him, he had an exhilaration already that made him feel almost as young as Polly and Jasper, scampering up the circular stairway at the other end. "Well, bless me, we are up, aren't we?" he exclaimed, sitting down and casting a glance around.

"Did you ever see anything so fascinating?" cried Polly Pepper, clasping her hands in delight, and not stopping to sit down, but looking all around.

"You had better sit down," advised Mother Fisher, "else when the car starts you may go over the railing."

"Oh, I can't fall, Mamsie," said Polly, carelessly, yet she sat down, while Jasper got out of his seat and ran up to old Mr. King.

"Now, father, don't you like it?" he cried. "And isn't it better than a stuffy old carriage?"

"Yes, I do, my boy," answered his father, frankly. "Now run off with you, you've planned it well." So Jasper, made happy for the day, rushed back to his seat. A hand not over clean was laid on it, and a tall individual, who was pouring out very bad provincial French at a fearful rate, was just about to worm himself into it. Polly, who sat next, had turned around to view the scenery from the other side, and hadn't seen his advance.

"Excuse me," said Jasper, in another torrent of the same language, only of a better quality, "this is my seat — I only left it to speak to my father."

But the Frenchman being there, thought that he could get still further into the seat. So he twisted and edged, but Jasper slipped neatly in, and looked calmly up at him. The Frenchman, unable to get his balance, sat down in Jasper's lap. But he bounded up again, blue with rage.

"What's all this?" demanded Mr. King, who never could speak French in a hurry, being very elegant at it, and exceedingly careful as to his accent. Phronsie turned pale and clung to his hand.

"Nothing," said Jasper, in English, "only this person chose to try to take my seat, and I chose to have it myself."

"You take yourself off," commanded Mr. King, in an irate voice to the French individual, "or I'll see that someone attends to your case."

Not understanding the language, all might have gone well, but the French person could interpret the expression of the face under the white hair, and he accordingly left a position in front of Jasper to sidle up toward Mr. King's seat in a threatening attitude. At that Jasper got out of his seat again and went to his father's side. Little Dr. Fisher also skipped up.

"See here you, Frenchy, stop your parley vousing, and march down those stairs double quick," cried the little doctor, standing on his tiptoes and bristling with indignation. His big spectacles had slipped to the end of his nose, his sharp little eyes blazing above them.

"Frenchy" stared at him in amazement, unable to find his tongue. And then he saw another gentleman in the person of the parson, who was just as big as the doctor was small. With one look he glanced around to see if there were anymore such specimens. At any rate, it was time to be going, so he took a bee-line for the nearest stairway and plunged down. But he gave the little doctor the compliment of his parting regard.

"Well," ejaculated Mr. King, when his party had regained their seats and the car started off, "if this is to be the style of our companions, I think my plan of carriages might be best after all. Eh, my boy?" with a sly look at Jasper.

"But anything like this might not happen again in a hundred times, father," said Jasper.

"I suppose I must say 'yes, I know it' to that," said his father. And as everybody had regained composure, he was beginning to feel very happy himself as the car rumbled off.

"This is fine," he kept saying to himself, "the boy knew what was best," and he smiled more than once over at Jasper, who was pointing out this and that to Polly. Jasper nodded back again.

"Don't let him bother you to see everything, Polly," called Grandpapa. "Take my advice — it's a nuisance to try to compass the whole place on the first visit." But Polly laughed back, and the advice went over her head, as he very well knew it would.

"Was anything ever more beautiful?" exclaimed Mother Fisher, drawing in long breaths of delight. The little doctor leaned back in his seat, and beamed at her over his big glasses. She began to look rested and young already. "This journey is the very thing," he declared to himself, and his hard-worked hand slipped itself over her toil-worn one as it lay on her lap. She turned to him with a smile.

"Adoniram, I never imagined anything like this," she said simply.

"No more did I," he answered. "That's the good of our coming, wife."

"Just see those beautiful green trees, so soft and trembling," she exclaimed, as enthusiastically as Polly herself. "And what a perfect arch!" And she bent forward to glance down the shaded avenue. "Oh, Adoniram!"

"What makes the trunks look so green?" Polly was crying as they rumbled along. "See, Jasper, there isn't a brown branch, even. Everything is green."

"That's what makes it so pretty," said Jasper. "I don't wonder these oaks in the *Scheveningsche Boschjes* — O dear me, I don't know how to pronounce it in the least — are so celebrated."

"Don't try," said Polly, "to pronounce it, Jasper. I just mark things in my Baedeker and let it go."

"Our Baedekers will be a sight when we get home, won't they, Polly?" remarked Jasper, in a pause, when eyes had been busy to their utmost capacity.

"I rather think they will," laughed Polly. "Mine is a sight now, Jasper, for I mark all round the edges — and just everywhere."

"But you are always copying off the things into your journal," said Jasper, "afterward. So do I mark my Baedeker; it's the only way to jot things down in any sort of order. One can't be whipping out a notebook every minute. Halloo, here we are at the château of the Grand Duke of Saxe-Weimar. Look, Polly! look!"

As they looked back in the distance to the receding ducal estate, Polly said: "It isn't one-half as beautiful as this delicious old wood is, Jasper. Just see that perfectly beautiful walk down there and that cunning little trail. Oh, I do so wish we could stay here."

"Some day, let us ask Dr. Fisher to come out with us, and we will tramp it. Oh, I forgot; he won't leave the hospitals."

"Mr. Henderson might like to," said Polly, in a glow, "let's ask him sometime, anyway, Jasper. And then, just think, we can go all in and out this lovely wood. How fine!"

"Father will come over to Scheveningen again and stay a few days, maybe," said Jasper, "if he takes a fancy to the idea. How would you like that, Polly?"

"I don't know," said Polly, "because I haven't seen it yet, Jasper."

"I know — I forgot — 'twas silly in me to ask such a question," said Jasper, with a laugh. "Well, anyway, I think it more than likely that he will."

"I just love The Hague," declared Polly, with a backward glance down the green avenue. "I hope we are going to stay there ever so long, Jasper."

"Then we shan't get on to all the other places," said Jasper. "We shall feel just as badly to leave every other one, I suppose, Polly."

"I suppose so," said Polly, with a sigh.

When they left the tram-car at the beginning of the village of Scheveningen they set off on a walk down to the *Curhaus* and the beach. Old Mr. King, as young as anyone, started out on the promenade on the undulating terrace at the top of the Dunes, followed by the rest of his party.

Down below ran a level road. "There is the Boulevard," said Grandpapa. "See, child," pointing to it; but Phronsie had no eyes for anything but the hundreds and hundreds of Bath chairs dotting the sands.

"Oh, Grandpapa, what are they?" she cried, pulling his hand and pointing to them.

"Those are chairs," answered Mr. King, "and by and by we will go down and get into some of them."

"They look just like the big sunbonnets that Grandma Bascom always wore when she went out to feed her hens, don't they, Jasper?"

"Precisely," he said, bursting into a laugh. "How you always do see funny things, Polly."

"And see what queer patches there are all up and down the sides of some of them," cried Polly. "Whatever can they be, Jasper?"

"Oh, those are the advertisements," said Jasper. "You'll find that everything is plastered up in that way abroad."

"Just as the omnibuses in London are all covered over with posters," said Polly; "weren't they funny, Jasper?"

"Yes, indeed, — 'Lipton Teas,' — I got so tired of that. And these, — cocoa or chocolate. You know Holland is full of manufactories of it."

"And isn't it good?" cried Polly, smacking her lips, as she had feasted on it since their arrival in Holland, Grandpapa considering it especially good and pure.

"I should say so," echoed Jasper, smacking his lips, too.

"Dr. Fisher —" The parson turned to address his neighbor, but there was no little doctor.

"Oh, he is off long ago," said his wife, "to his beloved hospital. What is it, Samuel?"

"I was only going to remark that I don't believe I ever saw so many people together before. Just look!" he pointed down to the Boulevard and off to the sands along the beach.

"It is a swarm, isn't it?" said his wife. "Well, we must go, for Mr. King is going down to the Boulevard."

Polly and Jasper, running in and out of the fascinating shops by the Concert terrace, had minds divided by the desire to stay on the sands, and to explore further the tempting interiors. "We must get something for the boys," she declared, jingling her little silver purse; "just let us go in this one now, then we'll run after Grandpapa; he's going down on the sands."

"He's going to sit with Phronsie in some of those big sunbonnets of yours, Polly," said Jasper. "There they are," pointing to them. "Well, we'll go in this shop. I want to get a pair of those wooden shoes for Joel." And they hurried in.

"Oh, how fine!" exclaimed Polly. "Well, I saw a carved bear I think Davie would like, and —" the rest was lost in the confusing array of tempting things spread out for their choice by deft shopkeepers.

When they emerged, Polly had a china windmill, and an inkstand of Delftware, and several other things, and Jasper carried all the big bundles. "O dear me," said Polly, "now we must run, or we shan't have much time to stay on the beach; and besides, Grandpapa will worry over us if we're not there."

"We can't run much, loaded down with this," said Jasper, looking at his armful and laughing, "or we'd likely drop half of them, and smash them to pieces. Wait a bit, Polly, I'm going to buy you some fruit." They stopped at the top of the stone stairway leading down to the sands, where some comely peasant women, fishermen's wives, held great baskets of fruit, and in one hand was a pair of scales. "Now, then, what will you have, Polly?"

"Oh, some grapes, please, Jasper," said Polly. "Aren't they most beautiful?"

"I should say they were; they are black Hamburgs," declared Jasper. "Now, then, my good woman, give us a couple of pounds." He put down the coin she asked for, and she weighed them out in her scales, and did them up in a piece of a Dutch newspaper.

"We are much worse off now, Jasper," laughed Polly, as they got over the stairs somehow with their burdens, "since we've all these grapes to carry. O dear me, there goes one!"

"Never mind," said Jasper, looking over his armful of presents, to investigate his paper of grapes; "if we don't lose but one, we're lucky."

"And there goes another," announced Polly, as they picked their way over and through the thick sand.

"Well, I declare," exclaimed old Mr. King, peering out of his Bath chair, "if you children aren't loaded down!" He was eating black Hamburg grapes. Phronsie sat opposite him almost lost in the depth of another Bath chair, similarly occupied. And at a little remove was the remainder of the party, and they all were in Bath chairs, and eating black Hamburg grapes.

"We've had such fun," sighed Polly, and she and Jasper cast their bundles on the soft sand; then she threw herself down next to them, and pushed up the little brown rings from her damp brow.

Jasper set his paper of grapes in her lap, then rushed off. "I'll get you a Bath chair," he said, beckoning to the attendant.

"Oh, Jasper, I'd so much rather sit on the sand," called Polly.

"So had I," he confessed, running back and throwing himself down beside her. "Now, then, do begin on your grapes, Polly."

"We'll begin together," she said, poking open the paper. "Oh, aren't they good, though!"

"I should rather say they were," declared Jasper; "dear me, what a bunch!"

"It's not as big as mine," said Polly, holding up hers to the light. "You made me take that one, Jasper."

"It's no better than mine," said Jasper, eating away.

"I'm going to hop into one of the chairs just a minute before we go," said Polly, nodding at the array along the beach, and eating her grapes busily, "to see how they feel."

"Oh, Polly, let me get you a chair now," begged Jasper, setting down the remainder of his bunch of grapes, and springing up.

"Oh, I don't want to, I really and truly don't, Jasper," Polly made haste to cry. "I like the sand ever and ever so much better. I only want to see for a minute what it's like to be in one of those funny old things. Then I should want to hop out with all my might, I just know I should."

"I'm of your mind," said Jasper, coming back to his seat on the sand again. "They must be very stuffy, Polly. Well, now you are here, would you like to come back to Scheveningen for a few days, Polly?"

"I think I should," said Polly, slowly, bringing her gaze around over the sea, to the Dunes, the beach, with the crowds of people of all nationalities, and the peasant folk, "if we could stay just as long, for all that, at the dear old Hague."

And just then old Mr. King was saying to Phronsie, "We will come out here again, child, and stay a week. Yes," he said to himself, "I will engage the rooms before we go back this afternoon."

"Grandpapa," asked Phronsie, laying her hand on his knee, "can I have this very same little house next time we come?"

"Well, I don't know," said Mr. King, peering up and down Phronsie's Bath chair adorned with the most lively descriptions of the merits of cocoa as a food; "they're all alike as two peas, except for the matter of the chocolate and cocoa trimmings. But perhaps I can fix it, Phronsie, so that you can have this identical one," mentally resolving to do that very thing. "Well, come, Phronsie, we must go now and get our luncheon."

"I am so glad if I can have the same little house," said Phronsie, with a sigh of contentment, as she slowly got out of her Bath chair. "It is a nice little house, Grandpapa, and I love it very much."

IX

A BOX FOR THE PEPPER BOYS

"Mamsie, have we been here a whole week in Amsterdam," cried Polly, leaning out of the window to look up and down the canal where the many-colored boats lay, "beside all those days at Scheveningen? I can't believe it!"

"It doesn't seem possible," Mother Fisher answered musingly, and her hands dropped to her lap, where they lay quietly folded.

"Mamsie," — Polly suddenly drew in her gaze from the charming old canal and its boats, and sprang to Mrs. Fisher's side, — "do you know, I think it was just the loveliest thing in all the world for Grandpapa to bring dear Mr. and Mrs. Henderson abroad with us? I do, Mamsie."

"Mr. King is always doing good, kind things," said Mrs. Fisher, coming out of her reverie, as Polly threw herself down on the floor and laid her head in her mother's lap, just as she used to do at home. "I haven't done this for so long," she said, "and it is so good!"

"That is the only drawback about travel," observed Mother Fisher, her hand passing soothingly over Polly's head, "that there never seems to be time for the little home ways that are so good. Now we must make the time and keep it, Polly."

"Indeed we will," cried Polly, seizing Mamsie's other hand to cuddle it under her chin, "and I'm going to begin right now. It makes me think of the little brown house, Mamsie, whenever you smooth my hair. What good times we used to have there!"

Mrs. Fisher's hand trembled a bit, but the black eyes were as serene as ever. "You used to work pretty hard, Polly," she said.

"Oh, but it was fun!" said Polly, merrily, "only I didn't like the old stove when it acted badly. But then came my new stove. Mamsie, wasn't Papa Fisher splendid? And then he saved my eyes. Just think, Mamsie, I never can love him half enough. I wish I could do something for him," she mourned, just as she did in the old days.

"You do, Polly; you are doing something every day of your life," said her mother, reassuringly. "Never think that you don't do anything. Why, it was only this very morning that your father told me that you were his little helper, and that he depended on you to cheer him up."

"Did he say that?" asked Polly, much gratified, poking up her head to look at her mother. "Oh, I want to be, but I don't know how to help him. Papa Fisher always seems to be doing something for other people, and not to need anybody to do things for him."

"Ah, Polly, when you have lived longer," said Mrs. Fisher, "you will know that those who are doing things always for other people, are the very ones who need cheering up, for they never complain. Your father, in going about as he does, day after day, to the hospitals and everywhere, where he can learn anything that will make him a better doctor, is working very hard indeed, and yet think how cheerful he is when he comes home! And he says you help to keep him so, Polly." She bent over and set a kiss on Polly's red cheek.

"Mamsie," cried Polly, with a glow where the kiss had dropped, "I'm going to try harder than ever to see wherever I can find a time to help Papa-Doctor. And I hope that one will come soon."

"And you'll find just such a time will come; it never fails to when you watch for it," said Mother Fisher, wisely. Just then the door opened, and Phronsie, fresh from the hands of Matilda, who had been changing her gown, came in with Araminta in her arms. When she saw Polly on the floor with her head in Mamsie's lap, she got down by her side and curled up there, too.

"Smooth my hair, do, Mamsie," she begged.

"Mamsie's got her two bothers," said Polly, with a little laugh.

"Mamsie doesn't mind her bothers," said Mrs. Fisher, her other hand going softly over Phronsie's yellow hair, at which Phronsie gave a small sigh of content, and wriggled her toes as they were stretched out straight before her on the carpet, "if only they grow up a little better every day than they were the day before."

"We'll try to, Mamsie," said Polly, "won't we, Pet?" leaning over and kissing her.

"I'll try to," promised Phronsie, with another wriggle of her small toes.

"That's right," said Mother Fisher, smiling approval.

"Mrs. Fisher!" called Grandpapa's voice at the door. Thereupon Polly and Phronsie sprang to their feet, and a lively race ensued to see which should be there the first to open it. The consequence was that both faces met him at once.

"Bless me!" cried old Mr. King, laughing gaily, as the door flew open, and they both rushed into his arms; "so you did like to have your old Grandfather come to see you," he exclaimed, mightily pleased.

"I should think we did!" cried Polly, as they escorted him in, and led him to the seat of honor, a big carved armchair, with a faded tapestry covering.

"I should very much like to get into your lap, Grandpapa dear," said Phronsie, surveying him gravely as he sat down and leaned his head against the chair back.

"So you shall," cried Mr. King, lifting her up to his knee, Araminta and all. She perched there in quiet content, while he set forth his business which he had come to talk over with Mother Fisher.

"Now, you know those three boys of yours are the most splendid boys that ever were in all this world, and they are working away at home, studying and all that, Joel and David are, and Ben is pegging away at business." Old Mr. King thought best to go to the heart of the matter at once without any dallying.

Mrs. Fisher's cheek grew a shade paler, but she said not a word as she fastened her black eyes on his face.

"Hem — well, we don't talk much about those boys," observed the old gentleman, "because it makes us all homesick after them, and it's best that they should be there, and that we should be here, so that was settled once for all by our coming."

Still Mrs. Fisher said not a word.

"Well, now, the fact of it is," continued old Mr. King, still keeping to the main point with wonderful directness, "I think the time has come for us to act, which is much better than talking, in my opinion; and I want to do something for those boys."

A pin could have been heard to drop. Polly leaned over his chair and hung on his words, while Mrs. Fisher never took her eyes from his face.

"In short," continued old Mr. King, well pleased with the attention of his audience, "I propose that we send a box of good things of various descriptions to Ben and Joel and David."

A small howl of delight from Polly broke the silence. When she heard that, Phronsie gave a little crow. "Oh, Grandpapa!" exclaimed Polly, "do you really mean it?" and she threw her arms around his neck. Phronsie immediately clambered up and did the same thing.

"That's just as your mother shall decide," said Mr. King, immensely pleased with the way his news was received. "She hasn't said a word yet whether she likes the idea or not."

"It's just because I couldn't speak at first," said Mrs. Fisher, wiping her eyes; and her voice trembled. "But it's the very thing; and oh! thank you, sir, for thinking of it. The boys won't be so homesick for us when they get the box. And it will be the best thing in the world for us to keep busy, so we can't worry about them."

"Mamsie *has* said 'yes'!" exclaimed Polly, flying off to dance around and around in the middle of the room. "Oh, I wish Jasper was here!" she cried regretfully, breaking short off.

"Go and call him, then, — he's down in the reading room, writing to the boys, — and bring him up here," said old Mr. King. "No, no, Phronsie, you want to stay and take care of me," as Phronsie showed signs of slipping down from his lap to go too.

"I'll stay and take care of you," said Phronsie, obediently; "just let me lay Araminta down, Grandpapa, on the sofa, and then I'll come back and rub your head."

So she got down and set Araminta up straight against the sofa back, and then came and clambered up again into his lap. By this time Polly and Jasper, racing along the hall, had reached Mother Fisher's room.

"That's regularly splendid, father." Jasper tossed his dark hair back from his forehead, and his eyes sparkled. "Oh, can't we go out right away and begin to buy the presents?"

"I shouldn't think that idea was a half-bad one," said old Mr. King. "What do you say, Mrs. Fisher? If we are going to send the box, why isn't it best to begin the work at once? There's never so good a time as now, in my opinion. I'm sure you agree with me."

On Mother Fisher saying "yes," all three of the young people took hold of hands, and danced around the room in glee. For old Mr. King set Phronsie down, with, "There, go, child, and spin with the others; then all hurry and get your hats on, and we'll be off."

And in less time than it takes to write it, old Mr. King and Mother Fisher and Jasper and Polly and Phronsie all hurried out of the hotel, and began a round of the shops to get the things together for the wonderful box to go home to the boys. And though Polly didn't know it, several other things, that boys wouldn't be supposed to care for in the least, were slyly added to the purchases, when she wasn't looking, to be sent home to the hotel in separate parcels to Mr. King. For Polly was going to have a birthday before very long; though she had quite forgotten it in the excitement over this box for Ben and Joel and David.

"It's just like buying things for Christmas, isn't it, Jasper?" said Polly, as they hung over the show-cases and peered into windows; "only everything is so funny here. Oh, no, Phronsie, that won't do; it's too big," as Phronsie protested that nothing was so nice as a huge Delft plate hanging on the wall. There was a big windmill and several little wind-mills in the distance along a Dutch canal, and two or three cows in the foreground, and a peasant girl with a basket in her hand. Phronsie stood and gazed at it all the time they were in this particular shop.

"I like that little girl," she said, "and those cows; and they are like Deacon Blodgett's cows at home in Badgertown. And Ben would like it, and Joel, and David." And all Polly could do, she would still say, "I like it, Polly, and I want Grandpapa to send it."

At last Polly turned in despair to Jasper. "Oh, what can we do?" she cried; "she is just as determined as she was when she would send the gingerbread boy to Grandpapa."

"Well, I think we would better not try to get her away from the idea," said Jasper, with a look at the rapt little face. Phronsie was now kneeling on a Flemish oak chair, and studying the Delft plate with absorbed attention.

"No," said Polly, with a sigh, "I suppose it isn't any use to try when she looks like that." Just then old Mr. King, who had been busy in a farther corner with the proprietor of the shop, picking out some small articles that struck his fancy, turned and called Phronsie. She didn't hear him, being too absorbed. And so he laid down the little silver paper-cutter he was looking at, and came over to see what was the matter.

"Well, child," he said, looking over her shoulder. "And so you like that, hey?"

Phronsie drew a long breath. "I do, Grandpapa, like it very much indeed," she said.

"Well, then, I don't see but what you must have it. And it shall hang in your own little room at home, Phronsie."

"But I don't want it for my very own, Grandpapa," said Phronsie; "it must go in the box for Ben and Joel and David."

"Dear me! You think they would like it, Phronsie?" he asked doubtfully, and just on the point of saying, like Polly, "it's too big, child," when he stopped himself and finished up — "and so it pleases you, Phronsie?"

"Yes, it does," said Phronsie, with an emphatic little nod; "I love that nice cow, and that little girl. Grandpapa, I think I should like to live in a windmill."

"Bless me! I think you wouldn't want to live there very long, child. Well, the plate shall go to the boys, and I only hope they will like it," he said to himself, dubiously.

"He is going to send it," Jasper and Polly said to each other, peering round an angle in the shop at the two. "Well, it's a mercy it's got a cow on it instead of a cat," said Jasper. "How Joel would howl if Phronsie sent him the picture of a cat!"

"She would if there were a cat to be found," said Polly; "don't you believe, Jasper, but what she would?"

X

DANGER

*W*ell, the box that went home across the seas to the Pepper boys was a marvel, stuffed in every nook and cranny where there was a possibility that the tiniest parcel could be tucked, until Phronsie, who kept bringing up more bundles, had to be told by Polly and Jasper, who did the packing, that no more could go in.

"They are very small," sighed Phronsie, curling up on the floor by the side of the big box, almost overflowing with billows of the soft white paper on top, and holding up two pudgy little bundles.

"So you've said for the last hour, Phronsie," exclaimed Polly, in despair, and sitting quite straight, her hands in her lap. "Jasper, what *shall* we do?" He was over by the window laying out the long nails that were to fasten the cover on; for no one must touch this precious box, but the loving hands that got it ready.

"Oh, we can't," began Jasper. Then he turned and saw Phronsie's face. "Perhaps one might be crowded in," he added, with a look at Polly. "Which one would you rather have Polly make a try at, Phronsie?"

"This one," she said, holding up the pudgiest bundle, "because this is the china cat, and I want Joel to have that."

Down went Polly's head on the edge of the box. Jasper dropped the long nails and hurried over to her.

"I can't help it." Polly's shoulders were shaking, and she added gustily, "O dear me — and Joel does so hate cats!"

"Phronsie, I think I can tuck in that parcel," Jasper made haste to say. "There, give it to me, child," and he took it out of her hand. "For Joel" was written across it in unsteady letters.

"Is Polly sick?" asked Phronsie, wonderingly, as she resigned her cat into his hands.

"No, only a bit tired, I think," answered Jasper. "Well, now, Phronsie, I think there is just room enough to tuck that parcel in this corner," said Jasper, crowding his fingers down in between the various bundles to make a space. "There, in it pops!" suiting the action to the word.

"I am so very glad," said Phronsie, smoothing her brown gown in great satisfaction; "for then Joel will know that I sent it all by myself."

"He'll know that nobody else sent it," said Polly to herself. "And I know it's a perfectly awful cat, for Phronsie always picks out the very ugliest she can find."

Well, the box was off, at last, the Pepper children and Jasper seeing it till the very last minute. And old Mr. King was nearly as excited as the young folks, and the Parson and Mrs. Henderson said it reminded them of Christmas times over again, and Mother Fisher and the little doctor were in a great state of happiness.

And that night when Polly was in bed, and Mother Fisher came into her room and Phronsie's, which opened into her own, to say "Good night," Polly turned on her pillow. "Mamsie," she said, "I do so very much wish that we could send a box to the Henderson boys. They must be so homesick for their mother and father."

Mrs. Fisher stopped and thought a bit, "A very good idea, Polly," she said, "and I'm glad you thought of it. I'll speak to your father and see if he approves, before we say anything to Mr. King."

"You see," said Polly, rolling over to get hold of one of Mother Fisher's hands, and speaking very fast, "of course the Henderson boys are having a good time at dear Deacon Blodgett's, but then their mother and father are away off. Oh, Mamsie!" She reached over and threw both arms around her mother and hugged her tightly.

"Yes, I know, Polly," said Mother Fisher, holding her big girl to her heart, "and we must look out for other people's boys; that's what you mean to say, isn't it?"

"Yes," said Polly, happy that Mamsie always understood, "and now that Ben's and Joel's and David's box is off, why, I wish we could, Mamsie, send the other one."

"I really think it can be done," said Mrs. Fisher, "but I must ask your father first. And now, daughter, go to sleep, like Phronsie." She glanced over at the other little bed, where Phronsie's yellow head was lost in dreams.

"You know we are going to Marken tomorrow."

"I know," said Polly, with a happy little wriggle under the bedclothes.

"And it never would do for you to be all tired out in the morning. That would be very unkind to dear Mr. King, who is trying so hard to make us all happy," continued Mrs. Fisher.

"I know," said Polly, again. "Well, good night, Mamsie." She set three or four kisses on Mother Fisher's cheek, then turned over, with her face to the wall.

"I'll shut the door until you get to sleep, Polly," said Mrs. Fisher, "then I will open it again," as she went out.

As Mother Fisher had said, they were going to the Island of Marken tomorrow; and Polly tumbled asleep with her head full of all the strange things they were to see there, and that Jasper and she had been reading about, — how the people wore the same kind of funny costume that their great-great-ever-so-many-times great-grandfathers and grandmothers had worn; and how the houses were of different colors, and built in different layers or mounds of land, with cunning little windows and scarcely any stairs; and how they were going in the haying season when everybody would be out raking up and gleaning — and — and — Polly was completely lost in her happy dreams.

Somebody seemed to be pulling her arm. What! Oh, she remembered they were going to Marken, and she must hurry and get her bath and fly into her clothes. "Yes, Mamsie!" she cried, flying up to sit straight in the bed. "I'll get right up and dress; oh, won't we have fun!"

"Polly," said Mother Fisher. She had on a dressing gown, and her black hair was hanging down her back. She looked pale and worried; Polly could see that, although she blinked at the sudden light. "It isn't morning, but the middle of the night. You must get up this minute. Pull on your shoes; don't stop for stockings, and slip into your wrapper. Don't ask questions," as Polly's lips moved.

Polly obeyed with an awful feeling at her heart. She glanced at Phronsie's little bed; she was not there! Mrs. Fisher threw the pink wrapper over her head; Polly thrust her arms into the sleeves, feeling as if she were sinking way down. "Now come." And Mamsie seized her hand and hurried her through her own room without another word. It was empty. Father Fisher and Phronsie were nowhere to be seen. And now for the first time Polly was conscious of a great noise out in the corridor. It seemed to spread and fasten itself to a number of other noises, and something made Polly feel queerly in her throat as if she should choke. She looked up in her mother's eyes, as they sped through the room.

"Yes, Polly," said Mother Fisher, "it is fire. The hotel is on fire; you will be brave, my child, I know."

"Phronsie!" gasped Polly. They were now in the corridor and hurrying along.

"She is safe; her father took her."

"Oh, Mamsie, Jasper and Grandpapa!"

"They know it; your father ran and told them. Obey me, Polly; come!"

Mrs. Fisher's firm hand on her arm really hurt Polly, as they hurried on through the dense waves of smoke that now engulfed them.

"Oh, Mamsie, not this way; we must find the stairs." But Mrs. Fisher held her with firmer fingers than ever, and they turned into a narrower hall, up toward a blinking red light that sent a small bright spark out through the thick smoke, and in a minute, or very much less, they were out on the fire-escape, and looking down to hear — for they couldn't see — Jasper's voice calling from below, "We are all here, Polly," and "Be careful, wife, how you come down," from Dr. Fisher.

"Oh," cried Polly, as the little group drew her and Mamsie into their arms, "are we all here?"

"Yes, Polly; yes, yes," answered Jasper. And "Oh, yes," cried old Mr. King, his arm around Phronsie, "but we shouldn't have been but for this doctor of ours."

"And Mr. and Mrs. Henderson?" cried Polly, shivering at Grandpapa's words.

"We are here, dear child," said the parson's wife, pressing forward, and then the crowd surged up against them this way and that, and more people came down the fire-escape, and some were screaming and saying they had lost everything, and they must go back for their jewels, and one woman brought down a big feather pillow, and set it carefully on the grass, she was so crazed with fright.

"O dear, dear, can't we help them?" cried Polly, wringing her hands, "Look at that girl!"

She was about as old as Polly, and she rushed by them plunging into the thickest of the crowd surging up against the fire-escape. "I'm going up," she kept screaming.

Polly remembered her face as she flashed by. She sat at the next table to theirs in the dining room, with a slender, gentle, little old lady whom she called "Grandmamma." "O dear!" groaned Polly, "we *must* help her!"

Jasper dashed after the girl, and Polly ran, too. He laid his hand on the arm of the flying figure as she broke through the crowd, but she shook him off like a feather. "She's up there," pointing above, "and I must get her."

One of the firemen seized her and held her fast. Jasper sprang for the fire-escape. "*Jasper!*" called Polly, hoarsely, "it will kill Grandpapa if you go — oh!" She turned at a cry from the girl, whose arms were around a bent, shaking, little figure, and they had both sunk to the ground.

"I brought her down long ago," said another fireman, who could speak English, pointing to the white-haired old lady, who, on hearing her granddaughter's voice, had pushed her way through the crowd, as Dr. Fisher hurried up.

And then Mr. King and his party gathered his group, and they hurried to another hotel close by, Jasper and Mr. Henderson and Mother Fisher waiting to see to the belongings of the party; for the fire was now subdued, although the guests had to go elsewhere for shelter, and the little doctor was in his element, taking care of the old lady, and then he rushed off to look after a score or more of other fainting women.

But nobody was really hurt — the smoke and the panic had been the worst, only the poor thing who had dragged down the feather pillow sat by it till the little doctor, discovering her, called two stout men, who took her up in their arms — she screaming all the while for her treasure — and bore her to a neighboring house that kindly opened its doors to some of the people so suddenly thrown out of shelter. And it wasn't till near breakfast time that the little doctor came to the hotel that was now their home.

"Brain-fever patient," he said briefly. "Wife, I must get a cold plunge, or I'll be having it next." And when breakfast was really set before their party, he appeared with the others fresh from his bath, and as cheery as if nothing had happened to break his good night's rest.

"O dear me! How did you ever get so many things over here, in all this world, and why didn't you let me stay with you?" Polly had exclaimed in one breath, looking at the array of dresses, sacks, and hats disposed around the room. And Mamsie was kneeling before an open trunk to take out more.

"It wasn't best, Polly," said her mother, who had longed for Polly as no one knew better than did Mother Fisher herself. "You were really needed here with Grandpapa and Phronsie. You truly were, my dear."

"I know," said Polly. "Well, do let me take those out, Mamsie; you're tired to death, already. Oh, and you've brought my dear little American flag!" She seized it and hugged it with delight.

"Did you suppose I could come back without that flag," exclaimed Mother Fisher in a reproving tone, "when you've put it up in your room every place where we've stopped? — why, Polly!"

"No, Mamsie, I really didn't think you could," answered Polly, quickly, and running to her, little silk flag and all, to throw her arms around her neck, "only it's so good to see the dear thing again."

"You may take the things from me, and hang them up somewhere," said her mother; "that will help me the most," giving her an armful. "I don't see how you ever thought of so many things, Mamsie!" exclaimed Polly going off with her armful.

"I brought all I thought we needed just at first," said Mother Fisher, diving into the trunk depths again.

"How did you ever do it?" cried Polly, for the fiftieth time, as she sorted, and hung the various garments in their proper places.

"Oh, Jasper helped me pack them, and then he got the hotel porter to bring over the trunks," answered Mother Fisher, her head in the trunk. "I've locked up our rooms, and got the keys, so I can get the rest by and by."

"But how did you first hear of the fire?" asked Polly, when they were all finally seated around the breakfast table, little Mrs. Gray — for so the white-haired old lady was called — and her granddaughter Adela being invited to join, "do tell me, Mamsie, I don't understand," she added in a puzzled way.

"No, you were talking about Marken in your sleep," said Mother Fisher, "when I went to call you, and how you would be ready in the morning."

"Marken?" repeated old Mr. King, looking up from the egg he was carefully breaking for Phronsie so that she might eat it from the shell. "So we were going there this morning. Well, we won't see that island now for a good many days; at least, till we get over this fright. Beside, we have things to settle here, and to get comfortably fixed. But we'll have that excursion all in good time, never fear."

"Well, how did you, Mamsie," Polly begged again, "first hear of the fire? Do tell me."

"Somebody made a good deal of noise down in the corridor," said Mother Fisher, "and your father went out to see what was the matter, and then he came back and told me what to do, and he took Phronsie and went for old Mr. King. But he had sent a porter to warn them in 165, and they would tell the Hendersons in the next room, before he ran upstairs to me." It was a long speech for Mother Fisher.

"Mamsie," asked Polly, suddenly, after she had leaned across her mother and beamed at the little doctor, which so delighted him that his big spectacles nearly fell off in his plate, "how *did* you know where the fire-escape was?"

"Oh, that was your father's doings, too," said Mother Fisher. She couldn't help but show her pride. "He told me all about it the first day we got to the hotel. He always does; he says it's better to know these things."

"Wife — wife," begged the little doctor, imploringly.

"I'm going to tell, Adoniram," said Mother Fisher, proudly, "the whole story; they ought to know."

"Indeed we had; and so you shall," commanded Mr. King, from the head of the table.

"I can't help it! I really must!" exclaimed Polly, hopping out of her chair, — there were no other people in the breakfast room beside their party, so really it wasn't so very dreadful after all, — and she ran back of her mother's chair, and threw her arms around the little doctor's neck. "Oh, Papa Fisher," she cried, setting ever so many kisses on his cheeks under the big spectacles, "you've saved all our lives."

"There — there, Polly," cried the little doctor, quite overcome.

"And ours, too," said little Mrs. Gray, in a shaking voice.

XI

THE TWO BIRTHDAYS IN OLD HOLLAND

And Polly never knew about a certain shelf in Grandpapa's closet, nor how full it was getting, when Jasper ran every now and then to add the gifts as fast as the different members of the party picked up pretty things in the shops for the coming birthday — now very near. And she actually forgot all about the birthday itself; all her mind being set on the Henderson box, so soon to sail off over the sea.

And Mother Fisher would look over at her absorbed face, and smile, to watch her in the shops, picking out things for the Henderson boys; and old Mr. King would send many a keen glance at her, and Jasper had hard work not to exclaim, "Oh, Polly, father has got you a —" And then he'd pull himself up, and rush off into some great plan to buy Peletiah Henderson something that a Badgertown boy ought to have. And Phronsie was carefully guarded on all sides these days, lest she should let out the great secret, for, of course, she ought to be in the very center of all these preparations to celebrate Polly's birthday in Old Amsterdam, so she knew everything just as soon as it was planned. But sometimes, with all this care, the whole thing nearly popped out.

"Mr. King!" It was Mother Fisher who called after him, and her voice didn't sound like hers, for it had an excited little ring. "Oh, are you going out?" for she didn't see that he held his hat in his hand till he turned in the corridor.

"I can wait just as well if it's anything you want, Mrs. Fisher," he said gladly, controlling his surprise at her unusual manner. "I was only about to run down to the Kalver-straat for a little matter I just thought of for the birthday. Can I do anything for you?" he begged.

"Yes, it's just that," said Mrs. Fisher, hurriedly; "it's about the birthday — I must speak quickly — I've just found out, —" she glanced up and down the corridor as if fully expecting to see Polly dash around a corner, — "that Adela Gray's birthday is tomorrow —"

"The dickens! You don't say so!" exploded Mr. King. "Well, now, I call that very clever on your part to have found it out. Very clever indeed, Mrs. Fisher," he repeated, beaming at her. "And just in time, for it would have been a dreadful thing, indeed, to have had that poor little girl left out, and her birthday too! Dear me!"

"It would, indeed," said Mrs. Fisher, heartily, with a shiver at the mere thought.

"And we might as well have had no celebration in such a case, for Polly wouldn't have enjoyed a single bit of it — not an atom!" declared old Mr. King, bringing his walking stick heavily down on the floor.

"What is it — oh, Grandpapa, what is it?" and Polly came hurrying along the corridor, and Jasper after her.

"Here she comes!" exclaimed Grandpapa, in a fright. "Glad you told me — Hush — O dear me — I'll take care of the gifts."

"And I'm to do the rest — just the same — Doctor Fisher and I. Remember!" It was all Mrs. Fisher had time to utter. Even then, Polly caught the last words in the flurry.

"Oh, what is it, Mamsie — Is anything the matter with Papa-Doctor?" And her brown eyes filled with alarm at her mother's unusual manner.

"Polly," Mrs. Fisher looked into the brown eyes with a steady glance, and all the hurry was gone out of her voice, "your father is all right. And now, run away, you and Jasper." She looked over Polly's shoulder at him as she spoke. "No, not another word, child." And away Mrs. Fisher hurried, while old Mr. King slipped off in the opposite direction.

"How funnily they act," said Polly, looking first after one and then another, with a puzzled face. "What can it be, Jasper?"

"Oh, well, I suppose they are in a hurry," said Jasper, as carelessly as he could. "Never mind, Polly, everything is all right. Oh, I say, let's fix our stamp books."

"But I was going to ask Grandpapa to go out with us, and now he's gone by himself," and Polly's face grew more puzzled than ever.

"Polly," said Jasper, desperately, "I really think we ought to fix our stamp books. I really do," and he took her hand. "My stamps are all in heaps in the envelopes, and in a mess generally. Come, let's begin now — do." And he led her back down the corridor.

"I suppose so," said Polly, with a reluctant little sigh, as they went off.

And that afternoon, there was another narrow escape, when it seemed as if the secret really must pop out. Polly, rushing along to the reading room opposite the big dining room, saw Mother Fisher in consultation with the head waiter, and he was saying "cake," and then he stopped suddenly, and Mrs. Fisher turned and saw her. And Mamsie came across the hall, and into the reading room, and sat there a bit, while Polly tossed off a letter to Alexia Rhys, that had been worrying her for days. And there was a funny little smile tucked away in the corners of Mother Fisher's mouth, and Polly thought that things were getting queerer than ever.

"I am glad you are writing that letter," said Mrs. Fisher, with an approving smile that chased the funny little one all around the strongly curved mouth, "for Alexia will feel badly not to hear often from you, Polly."

"I know it," said Polly, wrinkling her brows, "and I didn't mean to let this wait so long," scribbling away as fast as she could.

"Take care, Polly," warned her mother; "a carelessly written letter is no compliment, and it gets you in a bad way. Don't hurry so, child," as Polly's pen went scratching across the paper at a fearful rate.

"But there are so many letters to write to all the girls," said Polly, stopping a minute to look at her mother, "and I've only just got all the letters in my steamer mailbag answered. I *must* write to Cathie and Philena, and Amy Garrett too, today, Mamsie," she added, in distress.

"Polly," said Mother Fisher, looking into the flushed face, "I tell you what would be the best way for you to do. All the letters in your mailbag are answered, you said?"

"Yes, indeed," declared Polly. "Oh, Mamsie, you didn't think I could put those off?" she asked reproachfully.

"No, Polly, I really didn't," Mrs. Fisher made haste to assure her. "Well, now, mother will tell you what will be the best way for you to do. Write as good a letter as you can to Alexia, and tell her to send it around to all the girls, for a kind of a bulletin, and —"

"Oh, Mamsie Fisher," cried Polly, not stopping to hear the rest, but deserting the writing table to run and throw her arms around her mother's neck, "you're the bestest, dearest mother in all this world — oh — oh! Now I shan't have but one letter to write! How fine!"

"And you must write that one letter very nicely, Polly, and take ever so much pains with it," said Mother Fisher, her black eyes shining at the happy solution; "and that is much better than to hurry off a good many slovenly ones. Besides, it is not well to take your time and strength for too much letter writing, for there are the boys, and Mrs. Whitney and —"

"Grandma Bascom and dear Mrs. Beebe," finished Polly. "Oh, I couldn't ever forget them, Mamsie, in all this world." She stopped cuddling Mother Fisher's neck, to peer into the black eyes.

"No, you mustn't ever forget them," repeated Mrs. Fisher, emphatically, "in all this world, Polly. Well, get to work now over your one letter that's to be a bulletin!"

"I shall tear this one up," declared Polly, running back to get into her chair again. "O dear me, what a horrible old scrawl," she cried, with a very red face. "I didn't know it did look so bad" And she tore it clear across the page, and then snipped it into very little bits.

"That's the result of hurry," observed Mother Fisher, wisely, "and I would begin all over again, Polly."

So Polly took a fresh sheet and set to work; and Mrs. Fisher, seeing her so busily occupied, soon stole out. And there was the head waiter waiting for her in the dining room, and Polly never heard a word they said, although "cake" was mentioned a great many times, and several other things too.

But the next morning Polly Pepper woke up to the fact that it was her birthday. For there was Mamsie leaning over her pillow, the first thing she saw the minute her eyes were opened. And Phronsie was sitting on the end of the bed with her hands folded in her lap.

When she saw Polly's eyes open, she gave a little crow and darted forward. "Oh, I thought you never would wake up, Polly," she said, throwing her arms around Polly's neck.

"Yes, this child has been sitting there a whole hour, Polly." Mother Fisher gave a merry little laugh, and then she began to drop kisses on Polly's rosy cheek — ever so many of them.

Polly's dewy eyes opened wide.

"It's your birthday, don't you know!" exclaimed Phronsie, trying to drop as many kisses and as fast, on Polly's other cheek, and to talk at the same time.

"Mamsie Fisher!" cried Polly, springing up straight in the middle of the bed, nearly knocking Phronsie over. "Why, so it is. Oh, how could I forget — and sleep over. And I'm fifteen!"

"You're fifteen," repeated Mother Fisher, setting the last little kiss on Polly's cheek, — "and it's the best thing you could possibly do, to sleep over, child. Now, then, Phronsie, let us help her to get dressed."

Wasn't there a merry time, though, for the next half-hour, till Polly had had her bath, and was arrayed, Mother Fisher and Phronsie here, there, and everywhere, helping to tie and to hook Polly's clothes — Phronsie bringing her little silver button-hook that Auntie Whitney gave her, declaring that she should button Polly's boots.

"Oh, no, child," protested Polly. "I'll button them myself," flying off for the boots.

But Phronsie piped out, hurrying after her, "I have them, Polly," and, sure enough, there they were, one under each arm; "do let me, Polly — do, please!" she begged.

"I would, Polly," advised Mrs. Fisher, "for Phronsie really has set her heart on doing it."

So Polly sat down in the low chair, and put out her foot, feeling very queer indeed, and as if she ought to be doing up Phronsie's boots instead. And Phronsie curled up on the floor, and patiently drew every one of the buttons into place, and buttoned them fast. And then on with the other boot.

"There, now, I did do them all by myself," she announced, getting up from the floor, and smoothing down her gown with much importance. "I did truly, Polly."

"So you did, Pet," cried Polly, sticking out both feet to look at them. "You buttoned every single one of those buttons up splendidly, Phronsie Pepper. Now my toes will be just as happy all day; oh, you can't think how happy they'll be." And she seized her, half smothering her with kisses.

"Will they?" cried Phronsie, coming out of the embrace to peer up into Polly's face, in a transport. "Will your toes really and truly be happy, Polly?"

"They'll be so happy," declared Polly, with a little wriggle of each foot, "that they'll want to sing, only they can't," and she burst out into a little laugh.

"Put on your blue dress, Polly," said Mother Fisher, coming out of the closet to hurry operations a bit.

"Oh, Mamsie," begged Phronsie, "mayn't Polly wear her white one? Do, Mamsie, please!" She ran up to her mother pleadingly.

"Polly will wear a white gown tonight," said Mother Fisher, her eyes shining, and the same funny little smile hiding in the corners of her mouth; "but this morning she would better put on her blue gingham."

"Yes, that's best," said Polly, reassuringly, running off to get it out of the big bureau drawer. "It's all done up spick and span," drawing it out. "Mamsie, don't these Dutch women do up things well, though?"

"They do, indeed," assented Mrs. Fisher, with a critical eye for the blue gingham; "but I really suppose the Swiss beat them, Polly."

"Well, they must be just perfect, then," said Polly, putting the blue gown carefully over her head. "Mamsie, I just love this dress."

"Yes, it is pretty," said Mother Fisher, with an approving eye for the dainty ruffles, "and you keep your clothes cleaner than you used to, Polly; you're improving."

"I used to get them all mussed up just as soon as could be," mourned Polly, her cheeks rosy at the remembrance. "Mamsie, how much trouble I've made you." She stopped dressing, and sprang over to Mrs. Fisher. Phronsie, trying to button on the waistband, and clinging to it, went stumbling after.

"Take care," warned Mrs. Fisher, "don't muss it; it looks so nice now."

"There, there, Phronsie, I'll do that," said Polly, a trifle impatiently, looking over her shoulder.

"Oh, I want to, Polly," said Phronsie, fumbling for the button. "Do let me; I want to."

"No, I can do it myself," said Polly, trying to whirl off from the busy little fingers.

"Polly," began Mother Fisher, who saw what Polly couldn't, Phronsie's little face very red with her exertion, and the brown eyes filling with tears.

"Well, I declare," cried Polly, at sound of her mother's tone; "so you shall, Phronsie. Now I'll stand just as still as a mouse, and you shall make that old button fly into its hole."

"So he shall, old button fly into his hole," laughed Phronsie through her tears. And presently she declared it was done. And with a final pat, this time from Mother Fisher's fingers, Polly was released, and the rest of the dressing was soon done.

And there, waiting at the end of their corridor, was Jasper, in every conceivable way trying to get the better of his impatience. When he did finally see Polly, he dashed up to her. "Well, are you really here?"

"Yes," cried Polly, scampering on, with Phronsie clinging to her hand, "I really believe I am, Jasper. But don't let's go faster than Mamsie," looking back for her.

"You all run on," said Mother Fisher, laughing, "I shall get there soon; and really, Mr. King has waited long enough," she added to herself.

And, indeed, Mr. King thought so too, and he couldn't control his delight when the three danced into the little private parlor, opening out from his bedroom, and came up to his side.

"I slept over," said Polly, in a shamefaced little way; "I'm sorry, Grandpapa dear."

"You needn't be; not a bit of it," declared Grandpapa, holding her off at arm's length to scan her rosy face; "the best thing you could possibly do" — Mamsie's very words. So Polly felt relieved at once. "And now we will wait for Mrs. Fisher," he added, with a glance at the door.

"Here she is," piped Phronsie, who had been regarding the door anxiously.

"Yes, here she is," repeated old Mr. King, in great satisfaction, holding Polly fast. "Well, now, Mrs. Fisher, that you have come, we'll begin our festivities. Our Polly, here, is fifteen years old today — only think of that!" Still he held her fast, and bent his courtly white head to kiss her brown hair.

Polly clung to his other hand. "It can't be a house celebration, Polly, my dear, with a party and all that, but we'll do the best we can. And to add to our pleasure, and to be company for you" (not a suggestion of the pleasure he was to give), "why, we've another little girl with us who has chosen this very day for her birthday, too. Adela, come here."

Adela Gray, who had been standing silently, looking on with a sad heart at finding herself with a birthday on her hands, and no one to celebrate it with her, though for that matter all her birthdays had been rather dismal affairs at the best, in the Paris school, now shrank back at Mr. King's sudden summons, and hid behind her grandmother's black gown.

"Come, Adela," commanded Mr. King, in a tone that brooked no further delay. So she crept out, and stood in front of him.

"Oh, Adela!" exclaimed Polly, in a transport, drawing her up by her other hand, for still Grandpapa held her fast. "Is it your birthday too? How perfectly elegant! oh, oh!"

And everybody said, "How fine!" And they all were smiling at her. And Adela found herself, before she knew it, coming up out of her old despair into brightness and warmth and joy. And she never knew when old Mr. King proclaimed her fourteen years old, and dropped a kiss — yes, he actually did — on her head. And then she found herself on his other side, by the big center table, that was covered with a large cloth. And Polly made her put her hand under it first, saying, "Oh, no, Grandpapa, please let Adela pull out the first parcel." And lo, and behold — she held a neat little white-papered bundle tied with a blue ribbon.

"Open it," cried Jasper, as she stood stupidly staring at it, in her hand. "Don't you see it's got your name on it?" But Adela didn't see anything, she was so dazed. So Jasper had to open it for her. "We may thank our stars the first parcel happened to be for her," he was thinking busily all the time he was untying the ribbon. And there was just what she had wanted for, oh, so long — Mrs. Jameson's little books on Art — her very own, she saw as soon as her trembling fingers opened the cover.

After that, the skies might rain down anything in the shape of gifts, as it seemed to be doing for Polly and for her; it didn't matter to Adela; and she found herself, finally, looking over a heap of white papers and tangled ribbons, at Polly Pepper, who was dancing about, and thanking everybody to right and to left.

"Why don't — why don't — you — thank him?" old Mrs. Gray mumbled in her ear, while the tears were running down her wrinkled cheeks.

"Let her alone," said old Mr. King, hearing her. "She's thanked me enough. Now then, to breakfast, all of us! Come, Polly — come, Adela — Jasper, you take Mrs. Gray," and the others falling in, away they all went down to the big dining room, to their own special table in the center.

"I do so love what Joey sent me, and Ben and Davie," breathed Polly, for about the fiftieth time, patting her little money-bag which she had hung on her belt. Then she looked at the new ring on her finger very lovingly, and the other hand stole up to pinch the pin on her trim necktie, and see if it were really there. "Oh, Jasper, if the boys were only here!" she whispered, under cover of the chatter and bustle around the table.

"Don't let us think of that, Polly," Jasper made haste to say; "it will make father feel so badly if he thinks you are worrying."

"I know it," said Polly, pulling herself out of her gloom in an instant, to be as gay as ever, till the big somber dining room seemed instinct with life, and the cheeriest place imaginable.

"What good times Americans do have!" exclaimed a lady, passing the door, and sending an envious glance within.

"Yes, if they're the right kind of Americans," said her companion, wisely.

All that wonderful day the sun seemed to shine more brightly than on any other day in the whole long year. And the two girls who had the birthday together, went here and there, arm in arm, to gladden all the tired, and often discontented, eyes of the fellow-travelers they chanced to meet. And when finally it came to the dusk, and Polly and Adela were obliged to say, "Our birthday is almost all over," why then, that was just the very time when Mother Fisher and the little doctor (for he was in the plan, you may be very sure, only he wanted her to make all the arrangements, "It's more in a woman's way, my dear," he had said), — well, then, that was their turn to celebrate the double birthday!

"Where are those girls?" cried the little doctor, fidgeting about, and knocking down a little table in his prancing across the room. Jasper ran and picked it up. "No harm done," he declared, setting the books straight again.

"O dear, did I knock that over?" asked Dr. Fisher, whirling around to look at the result of his progress. "Bless me, did I really do that?"

"It's all right now," said Jasper, with a laugh at the doctor's face. "Lucky there wasn't anything that could break on the table."

"I should say so," declared the little doctor; "still, I'm sorry I floored these," with a rueful hand on the books. "I'd rather smash some other things that I know of than to hurt the feelings of a book. Dear me!"

"So had I," agreed Jasper, "to tell you the truth; but these aren't hurt; not a bit." He took up each volume, and carefully examined the binding.

When he saw that this was so, the little doctor began to fidget again, and to wonder where the girls were, and in his impatience he was on the point of prancing off once more across the room, when Jasper said, "Let us go and find them — you and I."

"An excellent plan," said Dr. Fisher, hooking his arm into Jasper's and skipping off, Jasper having hard work to keep up with him.

"Here — where are you two going?" called Mr. King after them. And this hindered them so that Polly and Adela ran in unnoticed. And there they were on time after all; for it turned out that the little doctor's watch was five minutes ahead.

Well, and then they all filed into the big dining room, and there, to be sure, was their special table in the center, and in the middle of it was a tall Dutch cake, ornamented with all sorts of nuts and fruits and candies, and gay with layers of frosting, edged and trimmed with colored devices, and on the very tip-top of all was an elaborate figure in sugar of a little Dutch shepherdess. And around this wonderful cake were plates of mottoes, all trimmed in the Dutch fashion — in pink and green and yellow — while two big bunches of posies, lay one at each plate, of the two girls who had a birthday together in Old Amsterdam.

"Oh — oh!" cried Polly, seizing her bunch before she looked at the huge Dutch cake, and burying her nose deep among the big fragrant roses, "how perfectly lovely! Who did do this?"

But no one said a word. And the little doctor was as sober as a judge. He only glared at them over his spectacles.

"Grandpapa," gasped Polly, "you did."

"Guess again," advised Grandpapa. "Mamsie —" Polly gave one radiant look at Mother Fisher's face.

Then Dr. Fisher broke out into a hearty laugh. "You've guessed it this time, Polly, my girl," he said, "your mother is the one."

"Your father really did it," corrected Mother Fisher. "Yes, Adoniram, you did, — only I saw to things a little, that's all."

"Which means that pretty much the whole business was hers," added the little doctor, possessing himself of her hand under cover of the table. "Well, girls, if you like your birthday party fixings, that's all your mother and I ask. It's Dutch, anyway, and what you won't be likely to get at home; there's so much to be said for it."

XII

THE HENDERSON BOX

*A*nd as Mother Fisher observed, they would all enjoy Marken better for the delay, for there would be more time to anticipate the pleasure; and then there was the Henderson box to get ready, for Grandpapa King had not only approved the plan; he had welcomed the idea most heartily. "It will be a good diversion from our scare," he said, when Polly and Jasper laid it before him.

"And give us all something to do," he added, "so go ahead, children, and set to work on it." And Polly and Jasper had flown off with the good news, and everyone did "set to work" as Grandpapa said, diving into the shops again.

Phronsie tried to find the mate to her china cat, that was by this time sailing over the sea to Joel; and it worried her dreadfully, for, try as she would, she never could see another one. And she looked so pale and tired one night that Mr. King asked her, in consternation, as they were all assembled in one corner of the drawing room, what was the matter.

"I wish I could find a cat," sighed Phronsie, trying not to be so tired, and wishing the prickles wouldn't run up and down her legs so. "We've walked and walked, Grandpapa, and the shop wouldn't come, where it must be."

"What kind of a cat is it you want?" asked Adela Gray.

"It was just like Joey's," said Phronsie, turning her troubled blue eyes on Adela's face.

"Well, what color?" continued Adela.

"It was yellow," said Phronsie, "a sweet little yellow cat."

"With green eyes?"

"No, I don't think it's eyes were green," said Phronsie, slowly trying to think, "but they were so pretty; and she had a pink ribbon around her neck, and —"

"Oh, that settles it," declared Adela, quite joyful that she could help the little Pepper girl in any way, "at least the pink ribbon round its neck does, for I know where there is a cat exactly like that — that is, the one I saw had green eyes, but everything else is like it — it's sitting upon a shelf in a shop where I was just this very day, Phronsie Pepper."

"Oh!" Phronsie gave a little gurgle of delight, and, slipping out of her chair, she ran over to Adela. "Will you show me that shop tomorrow?" she begged, in great excitement.

"To be sure I will," promised Adela, just as happy as Phronsie; "we will go in the morning right after breakfast. May we, Mrs. Fisher?" looking over to her, where she sat knitting as cozily as if she were in the library at home. "For I think people who travel, get out of their everyday habits," she had said to her husband, before they started, "and I'm going to pack my knitting basket to keep my hands out of mischief."

And old Mr. King had smiled more than once in satisfaction to glance over at Mother Fisher in her cozy corner of an evening, and it made him feel at home immediately, even in the dreariest of hotel parlors, just the very sight of those knitting needles.

And so, in between the picture galleries and museums, to which some part of every day was devoted, the Peppers and Jasper and Adela, and old Mr. King, who always went, and Mother Fisher, who sometimes was of the party, the ransacking of the lovely shops took place. And it really seemed as if everything that the Henderson boys could possibly want, was in some of those places — no matter how out-of-the-way — and waiting to be bought to fly over the sea to Badgertown. At last off that box went. Then Polly was quite happy, and could enjoy things all the more, with a mind at rest.

"Now we are all ready for Marken," she cried that night, after dinner, when the box was on its way to the steamer, "and I do hope we are going tomorrow." Jasper and she had a little table between them, and they were having a game of chess.

"Yes, we are, I think," said Jasper, slowly considering whether he would better bring down one of his knights into the thick of the battle, or leave it to protect his queen.

"Oh, how fine!" exclaimed Polly, unguardedly moving the pawn that held at bay a big white bishop, who immediately swooped down on her queen, and away it went off the board; and "oh, how perfectly dreadful!" all in one and the same breath.

"You may have it back," said Jasper, putting the black queen in place again.

"No, indeed — it's perfectly fair that I lost it," said Polly; "oh, I wouldn't take it back for anything. I was talking; it was all my own fault, Jasper."

"Well, you were talking about Marken, and I don't wonder, for we have been so long trying to go there. Do take it back, Polly," he begged, holding it out.

"No, indeed!" declared Polly again, shaking her brown head decidedly, "not for the world, Jasper."

"What is going over in that corner?" called Grandpapa's voice, by the big reading table. He had finished his newspaper, and was now ready to talk. So Jasper and Polly explained, and that brought out the subject of Marken, and old Mr. King said yes, it was perfectly true that he had made all the arrangements to go the following day if the weather were fine. So Polly and Jasper swept off the remaining pieces on the chessboard, and packed them away in their box, and ran over to hear all the rest of it that he was now telling to the family.

"So you see it didn't make any difference about that old queen anyway," said Polly, as they hurried over to him, "for nobody has beaten."

"I'm glad I didn't beat," declared Jasper. "I've that satisfaction, anyway, because you wouldn't have moved that pawn, Polly, if you hadn't been talking of Marken."

The next day was fine enough to warrant the trip, though not absolutely sunshiny. Old Mr. King wisely deciding that the fun of the expedition would lose its edge if postponed again, said, "Start!" So after breakfast they all went down to the Wester dock and embarked on the little steamer bound for the island of Marken in the Zuyder Zee.

"Oh, Polly, look," said Jasper, "doesn't Amsterdam look fine?" as the little steamer slowly put forth.

Polly leaned over the rail and drew in long breaths of delight. "Come, Adela," she called, "here is a good place;" for the little old lady was still too much shaken up to make much attempt at traveling, so Polly had begged Mother Fisher and Grandpapa to ask Adela to come with them on their sightseeing trips.

And this was done, and the young girl was happy as a bird. So here she was, going down to Marken too.

Adela ran and kneeled down on the seat by Polly's side and hung over the rail too. "Don't the houses lean over queerly?" she said, pointing to the long narrow buildings they were leaving behind. "They look worse from the water than when we are in the midst of them."

"It's just as if they were holding each other up," said Polly. "Dear me, I should think they'd tumble over some fine day.

"What makes them sag so?" asked Adela, intently regarding them.

"That's because the city is built on piles, I suppose," said Jasper. "It's mostly sand in Holland, you know, particularly around Amsterdam, and so they had to drive down piles to get something strong enough to put their houses on. That's what — who was it? — oh I know — Erasmus — meant when he said, 'I know a city whose inhabitants dwell on the tops of the trees like rooks.'"

"O dear me," said Adela, quite impressed; "well, what makes them not sag anymore?" she asked at length.

"Because they've sagged all they want to, I suppose'" said Jasper, laughing. "Anyway they've stood so for years on years — probably, so it's fair to believe they're all right."

"And I think they're ever so much prettier leaning every which way," declared Polly. "We can see plenty of straight houses at home, so it's nice to see crooked ones over here. Oh, Jasper, there's the King's palace!"

"Yes and there is the dome of the Lutheran Church," said Jasper.

"Look at that woman with the boy," said Adela, "on the wharf. She's got a little black bonnet tied on top of her white cap."

"That's nothing to what we shall see at Marken, I suppose," said Polly. "I'm going to take ever so many photographs." She tapped her Kodak lovingly, as it hung from the strap on her shoulder.

"I wish I'd brought mine," said Adela.

"Why didn't you?" cried Polly, whirling around to scan Adela.

"I forgot it," said Adela. "I put it on the table last night close to my hat and gloves, and then walked off this morning without it."

"Now that's too bad!" exclaimed Polly in sympathy. Then she turned back uncomfortably, and began to talk of something else. "I'm not going to," she said to herself; "it isn't my fault she forgot her Kodak, and I want every one of my films myself. And I care a great deal more for Marken than for almost any other place." The next moment Mamsie seemed to say, "Is that my Polly?" and although she was at the other end of the boat, Polly's head drooped as if she had heard the words.

"O dear me — and Adela hasn't anyone but a sick grandmother — and I have just — everybody," she thought "You shall use my Kodak," cried Polly, aloud, "one-half the time, Adela."

"Oh, no," protested Adela; but she looked hungrily at Polly's Kodak swinging over her shoulder.

"Yes, you shall too," declared Polly, cheerily. "I can take all the pictures I want in that time, and I have lots of films."

"I'll divide with you, Polly," said Jasper. "I brought ever so many, and will go shares with my Kodak, too." But Polly made up her mind that Jasper's Kodak was to be used for his own special pictures, for she knew he had set his heart on taking certain ones, and a good many of them, too.

"Isn't that water just perfectly lovely!" she exclaimed; "such a bluish grey."

"I think it's a greyish blue," said Adela, squinting along its surface critically.

"Well, what's the difference?" asked Polly, laughing.

"Not much," said Jasper, "I should think."

"Well, anyway, it's lovely," declared Polly; "I just wish I could paint it."

"Do you paint?" asked Adela, suddenly.

"No," said Polly, "not a bit"

"Polly is all for music," said Jasper, quickly. "You ought to hear her play."

"Oh, I can't play much now," said Polly, "but I mean tot some time. Jasper, how long it is since we have had a duet." Her face dropped its cheery curves and a sad little look crept into her eyes.

"That's the bother of traveling about; one can't play in a hotel," said Jasper. "But wait till we get to Dresden, Polly."

"Oh, I can't bear to wait," said Polly. "I don't want to hurry on, Jasper — but oh, I do wish we could play on a piano." Her fingers drummed on the rail in her eagerness.

"Why, you are playing now," said Adela, bursting into a laugh, "or pretending to, Polly Pepper."

"I know it," said Polly, laughing too; "well, that's what I always used to do in the little brown house, — drum on the table."

"In the little brown where?" demanded Adela in astonishment.

"The little brown house," answered Polly, and her eyes lightened as she seemed to see it before her. "That's where we used to live, Adela — oh, the sweetest place, you can't think!" Polly's fingers stopped drumming now, and the color flew up to her cheek; she forgot all about Adela.

"Oh, I suppose it had everything beautiful about it," said Adela, delighted to make Polly talk, "big gardens, and terraces, and —"

"Oh, no," said Polly, "it didn't have gardens at all, Adela, only a little bit of a green grass-plot in front. But there was an apple tree at the back."

"Apple tree at the back?" echoed Adela, faintly.

"Yes, and we had beautiful plays under it," cried Polly, rushing on in remembrance; "and sometimes when all the work was finished, Mamsie would let us spend the whole afternoon out there. You can't think what perfectly splendid times we had there, Adela Gray!"

Adela by this time was beyond words, but stared up at Polly's face speechlessly. "And what fun it was on baking days, Polly," cried Jasper, unable to keep quiet any longer; "do you remember when I burned all my cakes around the edges?"

"Well, that was because the old stove acted so," said Polly; "one minute it wouldn't bake at all, and the next it burned things black."

"And the washing the dishes and things up afterward," said Jasper, reflecting; "I think I liked that just as well as the baking, Polly."

"It was good fun," said Polly; "and how funny you looked with one of Mamsie's aprons tied round under your chin, Jasper."

"I know it," said Jasper, bursting into a laugh. "I must have looked like — I don't know what. But it was good fun, Polly."

And then Phronsie came running up, and after her came Grandpapa to see that she got there all right.

"Oh, Polly, do you see the windmills?" she cried, clapping her small hands.

"Yes, Pet," said Polly, looking all along the soft curves of the shore, "there are hundreds of them, aren't there?"

"There was a girl coming out of the door of one of them," announced Phronsie, climbing up on the seat and putting her arm around Polly's neck. "Polly, I'd like to live in a windmill; I would," she whispered close to her ear.

"Would you, Pet?"

"Yes, I would truly," she said. "Why couldn't I, Polly, just like that girl I saw coming out of the door?" she asked, looking back wistfully.

"Well, that girl never had a little brown house to live in," said Polly; "think of that, Phronsie."

XIII

"THE CLEANEST PLACE IN ALL HOLLAND"

"Oh, Polly, see the cunning little doll-houses!" exclaimed Phronsie in a little scream, flying about from Grandpapa at the head of his party on their way up from the boat-landing, and then back to the rear of the procession, which happened to be Polly and Jasper.

"Hush, Phronsie, don't talk so loud; they are not doll-houses," said Polly. "People live in them."

"People live in them!" echoed Phronsie, standing quite still on the paved road, that shone as if just freshly scoured.

"Yes, yes; come along, child, the people will hear you," said Polly, seizing her hand.

Phronsie suffered herself to be piloted along, but she stumbled more than once over the cobbles, her eyes were so busy.

"Take care, Phronsie," warned Polly, "you came near falling on your nose that time."

"I'll go on the other side," said Jasper; "there, now, Phronsie, give us your hand. Well, I don't wonder you are surprised. I never saw such a place as this Broek is."

"They've just washed it all up, haven't they, Jasper?" asked Polly, her brown eyes scanning the little walks along each tiny garden they passed. Everything shone alike.

"They're always washing up, I believe," answered Jasper, with a laugh. "I suppose they live in a pail of water, so to speak."

"Oh, Jasper, in a pail of water!" exclaimed Phronsie, between them, poking her head out to look for such a strange and unwarrantable sight provided by the inhabitants of Broek.

"I mean they're always scrubbing, so they can never be separated from their pails of water," said Jasper.

"It seems almost too bad to step on such clean roads," said Polly, getting up on her tiptoes, and stepping gingerly off. When Phronsie saw

Polly do that, she got up on her tiptoes too, and tried to get over the ground with her.

"You can't do that long," said Jasper, with a laugh for both, "and it wouldn't do any good, Polly, if you could, for these Broek women will have to come out and scrub up after us all the same."

"I suppose they will," said Polly, with a sigh of relief, coming down on to the rest of her feet, which proceeding, Phronsie was very glad to copy. "And it isn't as nice as it looks to walk on the tips of your toes. Jasper, do see those cunning little windows and those china images inside!"

"It seems as if they were all windows," said Jasper, scanning the tiny panes shining at them from all the cottages. "Dear me, the Broek women have something to do, don't they, to keep everything so shiny and clean?"

"Haven't they!" cried Polly. "Well, I don't wonder it is the cleanest place in all Holland. They must have to sit up all night and wash and scrub."

"It's the cleanest place on the whole earth, I imagine," laughed Jasper.

"But I should love to see some boys playing with mud pies," sighed Polly, running her glance up and down the immaculate road, and compassing all the tiny gardens possible to her range of vision.

"Mud pies!" exclaimed Jasper, in mock surprise. "Polly, how can you mention such a thing as dirt or mud here!"

"Jasper, do you suppose the children can have a good time here?" pursued Polly, anxiously, willing to give up the mud pies, if only reassured on the latter point, which seemed to her a very doubtful one.

"We'll hope so," answered Jasper. "See the klompen outside that door, Polly. Well, here we are at the dairy, Polly."

"And can I see the cows?" cried Phronsie. "Oh, Grandpapa is calling me," and off she ran.

And so he was calling her, as he and the parson had now reached the dairy door, under cover with the dwelling, which seemed much less an object of painstaking care than the house where the cows resided and the cheeses were made.

But everything was as neat as a pin in the house, though, and Polly and Jasper concluded they would explore the two rooms, as everybody seemed to be expected to do, after the main object of the visit was accomplished and the dairy inspected.

"Dear me, do they have to take their shoes off before they go in the house?" cried Polly.

"I suppose so," said Jasper. "Well, it isn't much trouble to get out of those sabots, that's one comfort for them."

"Dear me," Mrs. Fisher was saying, "if they haven't a carpet on the floor for the cows to walk on!" And there, surely, were strips of carpeting all down the walks between the rows of stalls, and something that looked like braided hemp in the bottom of the stalls themselves. And everything was tiled where it could be, with little tiles, and all these and every bit of the woodwork itself shone beautifully — it was so clean and polished.

Mrs. Fisher's black eyes shone, too. "It's beautiful," she said to her husband, "to see everything so clean for once in the world."

"What are those hooks for?" asked Jasper of the stolid Dutchman, who showed them about, and who spoke English fairly well.

"We hook the cows' tails up so they won't shake any dirt on their sides," said the Dutchman.

"O dear me!" exclaimed Polly Pepper, and everybody laughed — but she didn't.

"I think that is cruel," she said. "What do the poor things do to beat off the flies, pray tell?"

"Flies?" said Mother Fisher. "I don't suppose they ever see a fly here, Polly."

"They'd chase one worse than the dirt, I guess," said the little doctor.

"Oh," said Polly, with a sigh of relief.

"Come, Polly, let us go into the cheese room," suggested Jasper, peering in, for everything was connected and under one roof. "There's a man in there, and he is telling something;" so they skipped in, while Phronsie was bewailing that there were no cows there, and where were they?

"Why, Phronsie, they are all out in the fields. You wouldn't have them shut up this hot day," said Grandpapa.

"No," said Phronsie, swallowing the lump in her throat, "I wouldn't, Grandpapa; I'd much rather know they are having a nice time. I don't want them in here, I truly don't."

"That's a nice child," said old Mr. King, approvingly. "Well, now, we'll see how they make these wonderful Edam cheeses, Phronsie."

"I shall call this place the Cheesery," announced Polly, running about between the vats and the big press.

"Oh, Polly, that's a capital name," said Jasper. "So shall I call it the 'Cheesery' in my journal. Look at the rows and rows of them, Polly."

"And how round and yellow they are," said Polly; "just like pumpkins, aren't they? Wouldn't it be fine if we could take some home, to send to Badgertown? Dear Mrs. Beebe is so fond of cheese, Jasper."

"It is a pity; but we couldn't take cheeses very well. Fancy our trunks, Polly!" He wrinkled up his face; at sight of it Polly laughed merrily.

"No, of course not," she said; "but oh, how fine they look!"

"Grandpapa, I'd like to buy one," said Phronsie, overhearing a bit of this, and opening her little bag that hung on her arm, to get her purse.

"What in the world can you do with a Dutch cheese, child?" exclaimed old Mr. King.

"But I would like to buy one," persisted Phronsie. And after much diving Phronsie produced the little silk purse — "Polly wants one, Grandpapa," she got up on her tiptoes to whisper confidentially.

"Oh, is that it?" said Mr. King. "Well, now, Phronsie, I don't really believe Polly wants one. You would better ask her. If she wants one you shall buy it for her."

So Phronsie ran off. "Do you, Polly? Do you?" then she gently pulled Polly's sleeve to make her hear, for Polly and Jasper were hanging on the description that the man in attendance was pouring forth.

"Do I what?" cried Polly, only half understanding, and lost in the thought of how much fun it must be to make little yellow cheeses, and set them up in rows to be taken to market.

"— want one of those dear sweet little cheeses?" finished Phronsie.

"Yes, indeed," answered Polly, bobbing her head, and listening to the man with all her might.

"Yes, she does, Grandpapa," declared Phronsie, flying back, "she told me so her very own self."

"The goodness, she does!" exclaimed old Mr. King, "Well then, she shall have one. But pick out a small one, Phronsie, the very smallest you can find."

This was so much a work of time, Phronsie laying aside one selection after another, each yellow cheese looking so much better on comparison, that at last old Mr. King was almost in despair, and counseled the purchase of the last one that Phronsie set her eyes on. But meantime she had spied one on the upper shelf of all.

"There it is, Grandpapa," she cried, clapping her hands in delight, "the very littlest of all, and isn't it beautiful, Grandpapa, dear?"

"Indeed it is," assented Grandpapa, and he had the man lift it down and do it up; a piece of a Dutch newspaper again doing duty, when Phronsie held out her arms to receive it. "You can't carry it, child; give it to me. What in the world shall we do with the thing?" all this Grandpapa was uttering in one breath.

"Oh, Grandpapa, dear, I do so want to carry Polly's little yellow cheese," said Phronsie, the tears beginning to come in her eyes.

Grandpapa, who had taken the round parcel from her arms, looked from it to her with increasing perplexity. "Have the goodness to put a string around it, will you?" he said to the man who was regarding him stolidly, after satisfying himself that the coin Phronsie had drawn out of her purse and put in his hand was a good one.

"Yah, yah," said the man, and he brought out of one of his pockets a long piece of thick twine. This with much hard breathing accompanying the work, he proceeded to twist and interlace around the paper containing the little yellow cheese in such a way that when it was completed, Phronsie was carrying what looked like a little net basket, for there was a good strong twine handle sticking up, into which she put her small hand in great satisfaction.

When they all gathered in the living room of the house that had open doors into the cow-house and dairy, all being under one roof, they found a huge pile of photographs displayed of various views of the premises indoors and out.

"But they aren't half as nice as ours will be," whispered Jasper; "how many did you take, Polly?"

"Three," said Polly.

"Oh, Polly, didn't you get more than that?" said Jasper, quite disappointed for her, for Polly dearly loved to take photographs. "Oh, you've let Adela Gray take your Kodak," he added; "it's a shame I didn't give you mine. Take it now, Polly," he begged, slinging off the leather strap from his shoulder.

"No, no," said Polly, "I don't want to, Jasper, and I wanted Adela to take it, and don't let her hear us, she may come back from the other room;" — for Adela had disappeared with the Kodak; "and it's all right, Jasper," she finished up incoherently.

"Aren't these queer beds, Mrs. Fisher?" the parson's wife was saying, peering into the shelves against the side of the wall, boarded up, with doors swung open inviting inspection.

"The idea of sleeping in one of them!" exclaimed Mrs. Fisher, inspecting the interior with a sharp eye. "They're clean enough and as neat as a pink" — with a critical glance along the white lace spread and the immaculate pillow — "but to be shut up in a box like that. I should as soon go to bed in a bureau drawer."

"So should I," laughed the parson's wife; "and look at the artificial flowers hanging up over the head, and that picture pinned, above the foot. Well, well, well, and so that is a Dutch bed!"

"There are a good many kinds and sorts of Dutch beds, I suppose," observed Mrs. Fisher, turning away, "just as there are a good many American ones; but I hope there aren't many of this particular kind."

"Jasper," exclaimed Polly, as they all filed decorously out of the "Model Farm," "how I do wish you and I could race down to the boat-landing!"

Jasper looked longingly down the washed and shining road. "So do I, Polly," he said, "but I suppose it wouldn't do; we should shock these natives."

"I suppose so," assented Polly, ruefully. Just then Phronsie came up holding with both hands her paper-covered, twine-netted little round yellow cheese.

"What in the world has Phronsie got!" exclaimed Polly, catching sight of her. "Come here, Pet," she called.

Phronsie hesitated. On Polly's calling her again she drew near, but more slowly than was her wont.

"What have you got, Phronsie?" asked Polly, wondering and not a little hurt by her manner. "A little basket of string; isn't it funny, and where did you get it?"

"It isn't a basket," corrected Phronsie, "and I cannot tell you now, Polly," said Phronsie, shaking her head.

"Why, Phronsie," began Polly in surprise; and she couldn't help it, her voice quavered in spite of her.

When Phronsie heard that, she was equally distressed, and at once decided to present the gift then instead of carrying it back to the hotel for Polly as she had at first intended. So she cast her burden into Polly's hands and piped out, "It's for you, Polly, a sweet little yellow cheese; you said you wanted it," and stood smiling and triumphant.

"Oh, my goodness me!" exclaimed Polly Pepper, standing quite still. Then she did shock the natives, for she sat right down in the road, with the cheese in her hands.

XIV

THE ISLAND OF MARKEN

*W*hen the boat was nearing the island of Marken, the little yellow cheese had been presented with all due formality to one of the sailors who had been specially kind in the matter of securing good seats for Mr. King's party, Polly and Phronsie having held a whispered conference in a retired nook, to come out of it bright and smiling.

"And now it has made two people happy, Phronsie," Polly had said, when the presentation was well over, and she ended up with a kiss. "It made me happy in the first place because you thought of me, and then, just think, Pet, that poor sailor, how glad he will be to take it home."

"Will he, Polly?" asked Phronsie, in a rapture; "and do you think he has got any little girls?"

"Perhaps so," said Polly, "and at any rate, he can eat it himself. And he looks hungry enough."

"I'd rather he had some little girls, Polly," said Phronsie, thoughtfully, "and have him give them each a piece."

"Well, maybe he has some; we'll think so, anyway," Polly answered. "Oh, see, Jasper is calling us."

To be sure, there he was on the other side of the boat nearest Marken, with a big group of passengers, intently watching the Marken children running along in their clacking sabots, on the high bank, and holding out their arms, singing something all the while in a shrill, high key.

"They want some stuivers," cried Jasper. "Come, Polly and Phronsie, let us toss them some."

Whiz — spin — went the coins, to fall into the thick stubby grass on the bank. The children, stopping their song in mid-air, scrambled and sprawled all over each other in their efforts to secure the coveted money. So Jasper and Polly threw the bits next time in the other direction. Then there was a shout and a rush, and the same thing was repeated till only a tangle of arms and legs could be seen. But someone of them always got the money.

"Dear me! they've eyes just like birds!" exclaimed Parson Henderson; "to think of finding anything in that thick grass."

"Let them alone for that," laughed old Mr. King; "their wits are sharpened by practice."

"Look out, Phronsie!" exclaimed Jasper. "Your stuivers went into the water. Here, I'll hold you up, then you can throw it farther. There you go," swinging her to his shoulder. "Now, then" — he guided her hand, and away spun the coin.

"It did, it did," crowed Phronsie, from her high perch. "It did, Jasper, go right straight down in the grass just like yours and Polly's."

"So it did, Pet. Well, now, here is another."

"There's a little girl back there and she hasn't any," mourned Phronsie. "Oh, dear, I want to give her some."

"To be sure," said Jasper. "Well, we must give her some, and that's a fact." The small girl kept on at a dog-trot along the bank, her eyes fixed on the wonderful people who tossed out such magic wealth, and holding out her arms and singing her shrill song. But when the money was thrown, she was always a bit too late, and the other children, scrambling and scuffling, had pounced upon it, and had made off with it.

"Here, you boys, keep away; you've had enough; we're going to give this to the little girl," Jasper shouted to them as they threw coin after coin.

"They don't know what you are saying, my boy," said old Mr. King, laughing heartily at the performance, "and they wouldn't mind you in the least if they did."

"I suppose not," said Jasper in chagrin. "Oh, the mean little beggars!"

"Hold up your apron," screamed Polly to the little girl.

"That's a good idea," said Jasper. "Why didn't we think of it before?"

"She won't understand any better than the boys," said old Mr. King. "You forget, children, that these youngsters don't know our language."

"What a bother," exclaimed Jasper, "it is to have so many different languages, anyway!"

"And she hasn't any apron, Polly," corrected her mother; "that is her brown gown."

Polly was already going through the motions of holding up an imaginary apron. And at last the little girl understood by gestures what she could not possibly get into her head by words, so she picked up the skirt of her gown in her sturdy little fists, and one, two, three clinking coins fell safely into it. But the boys racing along in advance soon discovered this successful trick, and completely swarmed around her, howling dreadfully, so she hastened off, happy in her prize, which she huddled up in her gown as she ran.

"Isn't this just richness?" exclaimed Polly, gazing all about her in an ecstasy. "Oh, Jasper, what pictures we'll take — and do see that woman's cap! and those pot-hooks of hair over her eyes, and that funny, long dangling curl!"

"Take care, Polly, you almost stepped off backward down the bank," warned Adela, pulling her back, as they got off the steamboat and stopped a bit to look around.

"Dear me, did I?" said Polly. "Well, it's enough to make anyone step backward to see such funny clothes; and they are hay-making, Adela Gray, as sure as you live."

"Didn't you suppose they would be?" answered Adela, composedly. "Why, that's one of the things I specially wanted to see."

"Yes, so did I," said Polly. "Well, it's too, too splendid for anything. I'm going to begin to take pictures right straight off." Then she stopped and looked at Adela. "You may first," she said.

"No, I'm not going to," declared Adela.

"Yes, yes," said Polly, "I'd rather you did first; I truly had, Adela." She ran after her, for Adela had retreated down the bank, and made as if she were going to follow the party. "Now, Adela, be good and listen to reason."

But Adela ran off.

"Now that's too bad," mourned Polly, "for I'm afraid she'll keep away from me all the while we're on this island, and then I can't get a chance to give her my Kodak at all."

"She had it at the 'Model Farm,'" said Jasper, by way of comfort, for Polly's face fell.

"Oh, that was nothing," said Polly, "such a little bit of a while doesn't count."

"Well, let us take pictures as fast as we can," suggested Jasper, "and then when we do come up with Adela, why you'll have yours done."

So Polly roused out of her dejection and set to work, and presently the hay-makers, and the Marken boys and girls, the funny little houses that looked as if they dropped down pell-mell from the clouds and settled where they had dropped — the high ridges along which the men and boys, walking in their full baggy trousers, looked as if they were blown up, and formed a Dutch perspective perfectly awful — all these queer, delightful things were presently imprisoned in the two Kodaks.

Jasper looked up. "There, that's my last picture," he declared. "At any rate, for now."

"Oh, one more! I must get a good picture of those girls raking hay." Polly ran off a few steps and sat down on a log to focus. The Marken girls happened to look up, and immediately whirled around and presented their backs to her.

"Oh, dear, how hateful!" she exclaimed; "that would have been a splendid picture."

"Never mind," said Jasper; "you can catch them unawares, and have another try at them."

"Not so good as that," said Polly, sorrowfully. "Well, it can't be helped." So she was just going to get up from her log, when the girls, thinking from her attitude that she had given up the idea of taking a picture of them, turned back to their work. As quick as a flash Polly focused again, and was just touching the button, when a hand came in front of her Kodak, and she saw the grinning face of a Marken girl under its pot-hook of hair and with the long, dangling curl on one side, close to her own.

"Too late!" exclaimed Polly. "And don't you ever do that again." And the hand was withdrawn, and the girl clattered off as fast as she could run in her wooden shoes.

"I got them," said Polly, running back in triumph to Jasper.

"Yes, and I took a picture of the saucy girl while she was trying to stop yours," said Jasper. "So she didn't do much harm, after all. Oh, here is a splendid group! See them standing by that old tumble-down house, Polly," he added excitedly.

"I thought you had taken your last picture, Jasper," said Polly, bursting into a laugh.

"Well, I had then, but I've begun again," said Jasper, recklessly. He walked up to the group and held out his hand, then pointed to his Kodak. They smiled and nodded, showing all their teeth, and the mother took the littlest baby, for there seemed to be a very generous number of the smaller members of the family, and sat down with it in her lap on the rickety step. Then they all drew up stiff as sticks, and didn't even wink.

"That's capital," said Jasper, in huge satisfaction, pouring the coins into the mother's lap, where they rolled underneath the fat baby. Polly and he hurried on.

"Oh, Polly, I'm so very glad you've come," said Phronsie, as Polly and Jasper ran up to a doorway through which they could see their party. Phronsie stood just inside, and appeared to be watching for them. "There's a woman here who's been showing us things." There was Mrs. Fisher up by the tiny window, bending over an old woman who had spread out in her lap some white embroidered garments, while a young woman hovered near, smiling and blushing, and very happy at all this notice. And the rest of the party crowded up as close as they could.

"They are her daughter's wedding clothes," said Mrs. Fisher, "I do believe." For, the old woman was working fearfully hard to make them understand, and pointing first to the white garments and then to the young woman. "Wedding clothes?" asked Mrs. Fisher, speaking very slowly.

The old woman seemed to understand the one word "wedding," for she nodded furiously and smiled well pleased; and then devoted her whole time and energy to the display of the garments. And she even laughed aloud when old Mr. King put some coins in her hard hand.

Polly took the time to study her headgear. "I think there is a round board under the cap," she confided to Jasper when once out of doors; "how else could they be pulled so tight? And they look as hard as a drum."

"I didn't investigate," he said, laughing. "I'll leave that to you, Polly."

"Well, it's funny anyway," she said, "that all the women and girls dress alike in those queer gowns in two parts, and those embroidered jackets over their waists, and those caps and horrible pot-hooks and long curls."

"It's well that we've got so many pictures, for the people at home would never believe our stories without them."

"And these houses," continued Polly, squinting up at a crooked row, "all colors — green stripes and black stripes — and, O dear me! Jasper King, just look at Phronsie!"

Jasper followed the direction of Polly's finger. There sat Phronsie on a grassy bank a little above them, with one of the fattest Marken babies in her lap. A variegated group of natives was near by, watching her intently. But Phronsie didn't appear to notice them.

"Polly, I wish we had a baby just like this," sighed Phronsie, giving motherly pats to the stout little legs dangling down from her lap.

"Come, children," — Grandpapa emerged from the little old house, — "we must hurry on, else we shan't get through this island. Come, Phronsie — goodness me!" as he saw how she was occupied.

"May I carry her?" begged Phronsie, staggering to her feet — "she's mine" — and dragging the Marken baby up with her.

"Goodness me! no, child!" exclaimed Grandpapa, in horror. "Put her down, Phronsie; she's ever so much too heavy for you, dear." He put forth a protesting hand, but the tears ran down Phronsie's cheeks and fell on the baby's stiff white cap. At that old Mr. King was quite gone in despair.

"Phronsie," Polly bent over and whispered close to the wet little cheek, "don't you see Grandpapa is feeling badly? I'm afraid he will be sick, Phronsie, if he is unhappy."

Phronsie dropped the pudgy little hand, and threw herself into old Mr. King's arms. "Don't be sick, Grandpapa," she wailed, struggling with her tears. "I'd rather not have my baby, please; I don't want her. Please be all well, Grandpapa, dear."

XV

MR. KING DOES HIS DUTY

*P*olly's face appeared over Adela's shoulder. "Don't!" said Adela, shrinking away into the corner of the big sofa, and putting her hands over something she held in her lap.

"Excuse me!" exclaimed Polly, tumbling back in amazement. "I wasn't looking. I don't want to see. I only meant to surprise you." She kept backing off toward the door, the color all over her round cheek.

"You mustn't get mad, Polly," cried Adela, flying up straight to look at her, but still keeping her lap well covered.

Jasper, running in, heard the words. "Polly never gets mad," he said slowly, standing quite still.

"Well, she is now — just as mad as can be," said Adela, in a fretful little voice; "look at her."

"Oh, I'm not mad, Adela," began Polly, "only sorry. And it's my fault, Jasper," seeing his face darken, "for I looked over her shoulder. I only wanted to surprise her; and Adela, of course, thought I wanted to see what she was doing."

"Yes," said Adela, "I did think so, Polly Pepper, and I don't want anybody to see it." With that she huddled the thing, whatever it was, down by her side, and ran out of the room as fast as she could go.

"A disagreeable creature," began Jasper, hotly; "and she's been a perfect nuisance all along to take her everywhere. Now we drop her, Polly." He looked more like his father at this moment than Polly had ever seen him before.

"Oh, no, Jasper," she remonstrated in dismay.

"Yes, we drop her like a hot cake," said Jasper, decidedly; "that would be my opinion, Polly."

"But we can't, she's so alone," went on Polly; "and, besides, she's troubled about something. That's what makes her feel so."

"It's a queer way to bear trouble, I should think, to abuse you," said Jasper, "when you've been bothering yourself about her all this time."

"Oh, I don't mind," said Polly, brightening up, "if only you won't talk of our dropping her, Jasper."

Jasper turned on his heel, and walked to the window. When he looked back, the annoyance had dropped out of his face, and he was just saying, "All right, Polly, it ought to be as you say, I'm sure," when Adela Gray rushed into the room and up to Polly, and flung her arms around her neck. "There, and there, and there!" and something tumbled into Polly's hands.

"I didn't want anybody to see it," mumbled Adela, "for I've spoiled it; and I was trying to rub out the spots when you came in, and I made it worse than ever. But I'll give it to you now, Polly; and please tear it up, and I'll make you another."

When this long speech was all mumbled out, Polly was looking at a little sketch of Phronsie holding the fat Marken baby, and the Marken people looking on.

"Oh, Jasper!" screamed Polly, "do come here! Oh, Adela, did you draw this? And oh! how perfectly beautiful!" all in one breath.

"It *is* a good thing," said Jasper, taking the drawing from Polly's hand and examining it critically, while Polly threw her arms around Adela, and oh-ed and ah-ed her delight at finding that she could draw and sketch so beautifully; and now to think of having this lovely picture of Phronsie!

"But, you must tear it up," said Adela, in alarm, "else I'm sorry I gave it to you, Polly."

"Tear it up!" repeated Polly, in astonishment; "tear up this lovely picture of Phronsie! What do you mean, Adela Gray?"

"Oh, I've a copy, of course," said Adela, carelessly; "and I'm going to do you another better one."

"Where did you learn to draw so well?" asked Jasper, in admiration of the bold, accurate lines, and the graceful curves.

"In school, at Paris," said Adela, quietly.

Polly looked over Jasper's arm, and scanned the sketch. "I never saw anything so lovely!" she exclaimed. "And it's just alive! Isn't it, Jasper?"

"Yes, it is splendid," he said enthusiastically; "and that's the best part of it — it's alive, Polly, as you say."

"I'd give anything in all this world, Adela, if I could draw like that," mourned Polly.

"I'd rather play on the piano," said Adela, "than do all the drawing in the world. But I can't learn; the music master said there was something the matter with my ear, and I never could tell one note from another by the sound. I do so wish I could play on the piano, Polly Pepper!" she added discontentedly.

"Well, Jasper can do both, — play on the piano, and draw, too," said Polly.

"I can't draw like this," said Jasper, holding the sketch off at arm's length to view it again. "I couldn't if I were to try a thousand years."

"Oh, Jasper!" exclaimed Polly, who couldn't bear to think there was anything that he could not do.

"Well, I can't," said Jasper.

"Let me see some of your sketches," begged Adela. "It's so nice to find someone else who can draw. Do show me some."

"Oh, no," protested Jasper, in dismay, "not after this," pointing to Adela's drawing.

"Do, Jasper," begged Polly, imploringly, "get your portfolio."

"Oh, I couldn't bring them all in," said Jasper. "I wouldn't show those old things for the world, Polly."

"Well, bring some of them, do," she begged, while Adela said, "I showed mine, and I didn't want to, I'm sure." So Jasper ran up to his room, and pretty soon he came back with his portfolio.

"You did bring it, after all," exclaimed Polly, in satisfaction, patting the brown leather cover. "Oh, how nice of you, Jasper," as they ran over and ensconced themselves in a cozy corner.

"I took out the worst ones," said Jasper, with a laugh. "And I'm awfully sorry I didn't leave behind more of the others."

"I hope you brought that woman with a basket of vegetables we saw at the market the other day," said Polly, as he opened the portfolio. "Do tell me, Jasper, you did bring that, didn't you?" beginning to fumble through the pile.

"Yes, I did, Polly," said Jasper; "she's in there all safe and sound."

So for the next hour, there was great turning over and comparing of sketches, and much talk about vertical lines and graceful curves, and shading and perspective, and expression, and dear knows what all, as the three heads bent over the portfolio. So intent were they all, that no one heard Grandpapa come in, and he sat there in a farther corner, for a good quarter of an hour. At last Polly looked up and saw him.

"Oh, Grandpapa!" she cried, flying off from the group, and carrying Adela's sketch in her hand. "Just see what a perfectly beautiful picture of Phronsie! Adela Gray made it. She draws splendidly, Grandpapa."

Old Mr. King took the little sketch and fairly beamed at it.

"It's very like, — it is excellent," he declared, caring nothing for its merits as a drawing, but only seeing Phronsie as she sat with the big Marken baby in her lap on the stubbly bank.

"Isn't it, Grandpapa?" cried Polly, overflowing with happiness; "and she has given it to me, Grandpapa. Oh, isn't she good!"

"She is, indeed," assented old Mr. King, just as well pleased as Polly. "A very good girl, indeed. Come here, Adela."

Adela, whose sharp ears had caught most of this dialogue at the other end of the room, — although Jasper was keeping a steady fire of talk to drown it if possible, — was looking in dismay at him.

"O dear me, I wish they'd stop," she breathed in distress.

"I thought you said you had no ear," said Jasper, laughing at her face.

"I can't tell music notes," she said, "but I can hear things."

"Yes, I should think you could," he said. And then came old Mr. King's "Come here, Adela," so she had to go across the room, shaking every step of the way, and stand in front of him.

"I didn't know we had such a good little artist among us," said Grandpapa, wonderfully well pleased and smiling kindly at her.

"That is nothing," said Adela, in despair at ever stopping the flow of praise. "I spoiled it, and I'm going to do Polly a better one."

"Nothing could be better, my dear," said Grandpapa, blandly; "it is a fine likeness of Phronsie." And then he questioned her as to her training in the art, and what she meant to do in the future, and where she intended to study and all that, getting an immense amount of information so artfully that Adela never for an instant suspected his reason. All the time he was holding the sketch of Phronsie in his hand, and intently gazing on it most of the time.

"Well," he said at last, "I won't keep you young people any longer," — for Jasper had thrown down the portfolio and joined the group, — "so run back to your own corner. Dear me," pulling out his watch, "it's only twenty minutes to luncheon. How time does fly, to be sure! Tomorrow morning, remember, we are off for Antwerp."

"O dear, dear!" exclaimed Polly, as they ran back and bent over the portfolio again, "we haven't half seen Amsterdam, Jasper."

"No, and you wouldn't if you stayed a year," observed Jasper, wisely.

"We must go over to the Ryks Museum once more," said Polly.

"Yes, let us go there directly after luncheon," proposed Jasper. "I know what you want to do, Polly, — sit in front of 'The Night Watch' again."

"Yes, I do," said Polly. "I couldn't go away without seeing that picture once more, Jasper."

"I don't like that 'Night Watch,'" said Adela, "it's too dark and too smutty. I don't see why people like it so much."

"Well, I do like it very much," reiterated Polly. "I know it's dreadfully dark, but the people in front seem to be stepping right out of the shadows, and to be alive. It seems to me they are just going to come right up toward me, as I sit there."

"And that, after all, I suppose is the best thing one can say of a picture," said Jasper. "And it is always the finest time to look at that picture in the afternoon, you know, so we will go there, Polly, after luncheon."

"And then Phronsie will want to see that picture of a woman with a cat, I suppose," said Polly. "Dear me, who was it that painted that, Jasper? I never can remember the artists' names."

"Metsu was it — Jan — no, Gabriel — Metsu," answered Jasper, wrinkling his brows. "Neither can I remember all those fellows' names. Yes, indeed, you'll find Phronsie won't let us go there without paying respects to her special picture."

"And then I suppose Grandpapa will take us for a last drive in Vondel Park. Oh, what nice times we have had, Jasper King!" exclaimed Polly, leaning back against the sofa, and clasping her hands restfully. "I just love Amsterdam! And I hate to leave it!"

"So you said about The Hague, Polly," observed Jasper, turning to her with a little laugh.

"Well, wasn't it perfectly beautiful?" asked Polly, flying up straight again. "Just think of that dear 'House in the Wood,' Jasper."

"I know it; you wanted to go there day after day," laughed Jasper.

"Why, we only went there three times," said Polly, "I'm sure, Jasper. And the picture-gallery —"

"That is in the Maurit — rit, whatever is the rest of it? Oh, I know," said Jasper, guilty of interrupting, "Mauritshuis, that is where the picture-gallery is, Polly."

"Yes, that's it," echoed Polly; "it's fine — Paul Potter's 'Bull' is there."

"Oh, I want to see that picture very much!" exclaimed Adela. "I've never been to The Hague."

"Well, you'll go, perhaps, sometime," said Polly, with an uncomfortable feeling that she ought not to enjoy the things that Adela hadn't seen. "And you are going to Antwerp with us tomorrow, anyway," she added, brightening up.

"Yes," said Adela, "Grandmamma is really going there. But that's all; for we go straight over to England then, and I shan't see you ever again, Polly Pepper," she finished gloomily.

And that evening Grandpapa sat down by little old Mrs. Gray in the parlor after dinner, and though he began about something as far distant as possible, before long he was talking about Adela, and her wonderful talent. And the most surprising thing about it all was, that the little old lady, not intending to do it in the least, nor really comprehending how much she was telling, soon had him informed on all that he had set his heart on learning — how Adela had just been taken from the Paris school, because the little fortune her father had left, had somehow shrunk up, and there was no more money to keep her there. "I can't tell how it is, sir," she mourned, raising her faded eyes under the widow's cap to the kind old face above her, "I thought there was enough to educate my grandchild; it wasn't a big sum, but I supposed it was quite sufficient; but now it appears to be almost gone, and I have only just enough to keep me." She didn't add that the curate, her husband, when he crept into his grave, in the English churchyard, had left her nothing but the memory of his good name, her small means coming as a legacy from some of his grateful friends, they, too, long since dead.

Old Mr. King made no comment, only passed on with a few little leading remarks when the information seemed to be on the wane. And then he said he thought he would like a game of backgammon, and he challenged the parson to come on and be beaten. And at an early hour the party broke up. "For remember," said Grandpapa, for about the fiftieth time that day, "it's Antwerp tomorrow!"

So it was at Antwerp that the whole splendid business was concluded. And when the story of it came out, there was a regular jubilee all around. For were not Adela and Adela's grandmother going with the King party around a bit more on the continent, and then off to Paris again, and back to the beloved school — Grandpapa's gift to the girl with the talent, to keep it alive!

And the little widow, stunned at first by the magnitude of the gift, could do nothing but feebly protest, "Oh, no, sir!" and put up both shaking hands to ward off the benefaction.

"It's your duty, Madam," said Mr. King, sternly, at which she shrank down farther in her chair. "Who knows what such talent will do in the world? and it's my duty to see that it is kept alive, — nothing more nor less than a question of duty."

He stamped up and down the room vehemently, and the little old lady protesting that she wanted to do her duty, — she was sure she always did, — the hardest part was over, and old Mr. King chuckled to himself triumphantly.

"And now," cried Polly, in a transport, when the first surprise was over, and everybody had settled down to the quiet enjoyment of it all, "we've really and truly got a celebrated artist all to ourselves," and she drew herself up in pride.

"I'm not celebrated yet," said Adela, with two little red spots on her cheeks, and with happy eyes on her grandmother. "You had better wait till I am."

"Oh, well; you will be," said Polly, confidently, "sometime, and then we can say 'yes, we knew her when she was a girl,' and we'll go to picture-galleries the same as we do here, and see your name stuck up in the corners of the very best ones, Adela."

XVI

"LET US FLY AT THOSE BOOKS"

"Now, Polly, in Antwerp," said Jasper, "we can see Rubens to perfection. Won't we just revel in his paintings, though!"

"Won't we!" ejaculated Polly. "I'm so glad Grandpapa came here to this hotel." She leaned out of the window as she spoke.

"Under the very eaves of the Cathedral, almost, isn't it?" said Jasper, in satisfaction.

The chimes just then pealed out. Indeed, it seemed as if they did nothing but ring, so short were the intervals. But to Polly and Jasper they brought only echoes of delight.

"There are forty of those bells, aren't there?" asked Polly, resting her elbows on the windowsill.

"I believe so," answered Jasper, absently. Polly looked at him curiously.

"Polly," he said abruptly, "do you know what I mean to do?"

"No," said Polly; "tell me, do, Jasper."

"Well, I mean to sit right down and finish my book. I'm ashamed to confess that it's not up to date."

"Neither is mine," confessed Polly.

"Well, now, that won't do," said Jasper, decidedly. "You see if we once let those books get behindhand, we're lost. We never can catch up, in all this world."

"We've had so much to do and to see," began Polly.

"That won't be any excuse that will amount to anything," said Jasper, shaking his head. "Let's fly at them and tackle them now, Polly."

"I say so, too," she cried, and deserting the window, they surrounded the center-table, and soon had the big journals, photographs, and pictures, of every sort and size, the ink bottle, and library paste, scissors, and all the rest of the paraphernalia, spread out on it.

"It's good that Grandpapa is lying down and doesn't wish to go out," remarked Polly, snipping away at a fearful rate, and pausing only to write down the dates and other bits of information around each picture, as she pasted it in. "Now we'll have all this morning to finish these books up to today."

"And none too much for the job," said Jasper, sagely. "I declare I shall feel like enjoying myself twice as well, when once they're up to date. They've been hanging round my conscience every day since I slackened work on them."

"And I am so glad you made me come away from that window, and set to work," said Polly, "or I never would have commenced on mine today."

"Oh, yes, you would, I think, Polly," said Jasper. "Well, we are at it now, and that's enough. Now says I, I'm on book No. 2!" And he flapped down the cover of the completed one. "That's done, thank fortune!"

"Oh, Jasper, have you the green one done?" asked Polly. "Why, I have three more pages of mine to do."

"Well, you'll catch up on the red one, I dare say," said Jasper, opening No. 2. "We are getting on famously, aren't we, Polly?" glancing over at her work.

"Yes, and I'm so glad you proposed this way to keep a journal," said Polly, "to have them labeled 'My Notes on My European Journey,' and to have No. 1 green, and No. 2 red, and so on all through the rest of the colors."

"That will help us to find them in a hurry," said Jasper, "and keep them distinct; but I didn't propose it, Polly, about the books. It was your plan as much as mine."

"No." Polly was guilty of contradicting. "I never should have thought of having the books of different colors and labeling them in that way, Jasper."

"Well, you first thought of cutting out pictures and all sorts of items, and then writing the dates and whatever else we wanted to around the pictures," said Jasper. "I'm sure that's more important than the title of the book, Polly."

"Well, won't the boys love to see them," asked Polly, suddenly, with a light in her eyes, ignoring the question as to her claim to the idea, "when we get home, Jasper?"

"Won't they, though!" he responded, falling to work with a will.

And so Antwerp was entered with clear consciences as to journals, and a strict determination not to fall behind again on them.

But Polly slipped in so many of the beautiful photographs of the "Descent from the Cross," and the other two famous pictures by Rubens, that her red book was closed the third day of their stay in the old town of Antwerp; and the photographs had even overflowed into the yellow book, No. 3.

They had a habit, most of their party, of dropping into the Cathedral once a day at least, usually in the morning, and sometimes before service. And then when it was quiet, and before the ordinary throng of sight-seers trailed through, Jasper would hire some chairs of one of the old women who always seem to be part and parcel of European cathedrals; and they would sit down before the painting, its wings spread over the dingy green background, and study what has made so many countless travelers take long and oftentimes wearisome journeys to see.

And Polly always wanted to go after that to see the "Assumption," which is the altar-piece, and then the "Elevation of the Cross," both by Rubens. "And I am sure, Grandpapa," she would always say, "I like them as well as I do the famous painting."

"And so do I, Polly, in a way," Grandpapa would invariably reply. "They are all marvelous, and that is all we can say, for no expressions could give the truth about them."

After the Cathedral, which they loved all the more, — "for being perched under its eaves" (as Polly always said when speaking of the hotel that was for the time being their home), — Polly and Jasper set next in their regard the Musée Plantin-Moretus. They were never tired of running down there to the Marché du Vendredi, until it became a regular question every day at dinner, "Well, what more have you discovered at the Musée Plantin?"

And old Mr. King would often answer, for he was as interested as the young people, "Marvelous things." And then he would expatiate on the antique furniture, the paintings, engravings, and tapestries, till the little doctor, fresh from his hospital visitations, would remark that it was just as good as if he had time to visit the place, to hear Grandpapa tell it all. And Adela would bring out her little sketches, which now she was not averse to showing, since everybody was so kind and sympathizing, and there would be some little nook or corner of corridor or court that Polly would fall upon and pronounce, "Just perfect, and how did you get it?"

"Oh, I just drew a bit now and then when you were looking at things," said Adela, carelessly.

"Everything just dances off your pencil," said Polly, wishing she could draw, and wondering if it was any use for her to try to learn.

And every afternoon they would go to drive as usual, very often around the docks, which gave them all a good idea of this wonderful port. They were never tired of watching the hydraulic cranes, of inspecting the dry docks; the intertwining railways by which all the docks, large and small, are connected, and the two basins, Le Petit and Le Grand Bassin.

"Dear me!" exclaimed Jasper, on one of these occasions, "I thought Amsterdam docks were huge affairs, but Antwerp!" And he left his sentence in mid-air, which was more impressive after all.

But Parson Henderson liked the church of St. Jacques best of all things in Antwerp, and he used to steal away mornings to go there again and again. And he asked Polly and Jasper to go there with him one day, and Polly begged to have Adela go too, and they all came home as enthusiastic as he was.

And then suddenly Mr. King would wrench them all off from this delightful study and put his foot down peremptorily. "No more cathedrals for a time," he would declare; "my old head cannot carry anymore just yet." And he would propose a little in-letting of fun. And then off they would go a-shopping, or to the Zoological Gardens; and they always had concerts, of course, wherever they were, for Polly and Jasper's sakes, if for no other reason. And by and by somebody announced, one fine morning, that they had been in Antwerp a fortnight.

And then one day Mother Fisher looked into Polly's brown eyes, and finding them tired, she calmly tucked Polly quietly in bed. "Why, Mamsie," declared Polly, "I'm not sick."

"No, and I'm not going to have you be," observed Mrs. Fisher, sensibly. "This running about sight-seeing is more tiresome, child, than you think for, and dreadfully unsettling unless you stop to rest a bit. No, Jasper," as he knocked at the door, "Polly can't go out today, at least not this morning. I've put her to bed."

"Is Polly sick, Mrs. Fisher?" called Jasper, in great concern.

"No, not a bit," answered Mrs. Fisher, cheerily, "but she's tired. I've seen it coming on for two or three days back, so I'm going to take it in time."

"And can't she come out, today?" asked Jasper, dreadfully disappointed, with a mind full of the host of fine things they had planned to do.

"No, Jasper," said Mother Fisher, firmly, "not to jaunt about." So Jasper took himself off, feeling sure, despite his disappointment, that Polly's mother was right.

And there was another person who wholly agreed with Mother Fisher, and that was old Mr. King. "If you can stop those young folks from killing themselves running about to see everything, you'll do more than I can, Mrs. Fisher," he observed. "It makes no difference how long I plan to stay in a town, so as to do it restfully, if they won't rest."

"That is a fact," said Mother Fisher. "Well, that's my part to see that they do rest."

"I don't envy you the job," said the old gentleman, dryly.

Polly fidgeted and turned on her pillow, knowing Mamsie was right, but unable to keep from thinking of the many beautiful plans that Jasper and she had formed for that very morning, till her head spun round and round. "I can't get to sleep," she said at last.

"Don't try to," said her mother, dropping the heavy wool curtains till the room was quite dark; "that's the worst thing in the world to do, if you want to rest. Just lie still and don't try to think of anything."

"But I can't help thinking," said poor Polly, feeling sure that Jasper was dreadfully disappointed at the upsetting of all the plans.

"Never say you can't help anything, Polly," said her mother, coming over to the bedside to lay a cool hand on Polly's hot forehead, and then to drop a kiss there; and somehow the kiss did what all Polly's trying had failed to accomplish.

"That's good, Mamsie," she said gratefully, and drew a long, restful breath.

Mother Fisher went out and closed the door softly.

It was just three o'clock that afternoon when Polly woke up.

"Oh, I'm dreadfully ashamed!" she exclaimed when she found it out. "I've slept almost this whole day!"

Mother Fisher smiled, "And it's the best day's work you've done in one long while, Polly," she said.

"And here's my girl, Polly," cried Grandpapa, when she ran down to him, and holding her at arm's length, he gazed into her bright eyes and on her rosy cheeks. "Well, well, your mother's a clever woman, and no mistake."

So Polly knew if she didn't take care and not get tired again, she would be tucked into bed another fine day.

It was a long summer morning, and they were sailing up the Rhine, with the delights of Brussels and Cologne behind them, and in between the covers of the purple book, No. 4, Polly had been looking at ruined castles and fortresses, at vine-clad terraces, and châlets, until she turned to Grandpapa with a sigh.

"Tired, Polly, little woman?" he said, cuddling her up against him.

"No, not tired, Grandpapa," said Polly, "but, oh, there's so very much of it over here in Europe."

"If you've found that out, you've learned the lesson early," said old Mr. King, with a laugh. "As many times as I've been over here, there's nothing that surprises me so much as the presumption with which we travelers all rush about, expecting to compass all there is."

"But we ought to see everything," said Polly, "oughtn't we, Grandpapa, when we've come so far to see it?" and she looked troubled.

"There's just where you are wrong, Polly, child," said old Mr. King. "And this 'ought to see,' why, it's an old dragon, Polly, lying in wait to destroy. Don't you let it get hold of you, but take my advice and see only what you can make your own and remember. Then you've got it."

XVII

POLLY WROTE A NICE LITTLE NOTE

"Polly," said Jasper, running down the stairs after her, on her way to the little garden on the terrace at Heidelberg, "here's something for you; just came in the mail."

"For me," said Polly, as he put a little parcel in her hand.

"Yes," said Jasper, "father just gave it to me."

"What can it be!" cried Polly, wonderingly; "oh, something from Alexia or one of the other girls, most likely," and she tore off the outer wrapper.

"It is registered," said Jasper, "and Mr. Henderson got it out for you, father said; that can't be from one of the girls, Polly," as the next layer of paper dropping off, disclosed the name of one of the biggest of big London jewelers across a wooden box.

"What can it be!" gasped Polly, tugging at the cover.

"Here — let me." Jasper essayed to open it, but it stuck fast in the slide. Another pull, and a little red leather case appeared in view.

"What in the world —" began Polly; "oh, it can't be for me!" and she stood staring at it, without any attempt to take it out.

"It must be for you, Polly," said Jasper. "There couldn't be any other Miss Mary Pepper, and besides it is addressed to father's care, and comes through our bankers, — see here." He stooped, and picked up the outer wrapper; it was torn almost in two, but the name and address was all there.

So Polly lifted out the little red leather case, still feeling very much as if she were opening a parcel belonging to someone else, and touching a spring at the end, the top flew up, and there on a white satin bed lay a little green enameled watch set with diamonds.

"O dear me!" exclaimed Polly, tumbling back in the utmost distress, "now I *have* got someone else's box, Jasper. How very dreadful!"

"Let us go to father," said Jasper, feeling this quite beyond him. "Shut the box up tight, Polly; it might tumble out on the way."

"You carry it, do, Jasper," begged Polly, with an eye askance at the little case; and snapping the cover down, she set it in his hand.

"All right, now, then," said Jasper. "We must carry these papers, and wooden box, and the whole business. Don't worry, Polly," seeing her face, "father will straighten it out."

"Give me the wrapper, Jasper, and the wooden box, if only you'll take the other," said Polly, feeling very much depressed at coming into possession of other people's property; and Jasper followed with the little enameled watch.

And Grandpapa was just as much astounded as was Polly herself; and all the family congregating in Mother Fisher's room, the little watch was handed about from one to the other, and everybody stared at everybody else, and the mystery thickened every moment. And the strangest thing about it was that no one opened the little back cover where anyone might have read: —

"Polly Pepper, from her grateful friend, Arthur Selwyn."

— until the middle of the night, when Jasper was awakened by a noise as if someone were prowling around in his father's room. He started up and listened.

"It's I," said old Mr. King's voice. So Jasper threw on his wrapper, and hurried in. There sat his father, in dressing gown and slippers, by the table, with the little enameled watch in his hand.

"Of all the idiots, Jasper," he exclaimed, "your father is the very worst. I've only just this moment thought to look in here." He flashed the little watch around in Jasper's face; it was now opened at the back.

"Dear me!" cried Jasper, for want of anything better to say, as he read the inscription. Then he looked helplessly at his father.

"Earl or no earl, this piece of foolishness goes back," fumed old Mr. King, getting out of his chair, and beginning to march back and forth across the floor as he always did when irritated. "Yes, sir, the very first thing in the morning," he repeated, as vehemently as if Jasper had contradicted him.

"But, father —" began the boy.

"Yes, sir, it goes back, I tell you," repeated his father, now well wrought up to a passion. "What right has he to send such a piece of foolishness to my Polly Pepper? I can give her all the watches she needs. And this trumpery," pointing to the jeweled gift still lying in Jasper's hand, "is utterly unfit for a schoolgirl. You know that yourself, Jasper."

"But Polly was kind to him," began Jasper, again.

"Kind to him!" snorted his father, "don't I know that? Of course she was. Polly Pepper would be kind to anyone. But that's no reason why the old idiot should presume to give her such a silly and expensive present as that. The man doesn't know anything who would do such a thing. And this one is queerer than the average."

"As you say, he is eccentric," observed Jasper, seeing here a loophole by which to get in a soothing word.

"Eccentric? That's a mild way to put it," fumed his father. "He's odder than Dick's hatband. Heaven save Old England if many of her earls are like him. Well, I shall just write the fellow a decent sort of a note, and then I'll pack the box off to him, and that'll be the end of the matter."

"I'm afraid Polly will be sorry," said Jasper, feeling at a standstill so far as finding the right word was concerned, for everything he uttered only seemed to make matters worse. So he said the best thing he could think of, and stopped short.

"Sorry?" Old Mr. King came to a dead stop and glared at him. "You can't mean that Polly Pepper would like me to keep that watch. It's the last thing on earth that she would want, such a gewgaw as that. Why, the child hates the sight of it already as much as I do."

"I don't think Polly would want the watch," said Jasper, quickly. "I know she doesn't like it, and I'm sure I wish I could smash it myself," he added in a burst.

"That's the most sensible thing you've said yet, Jasper," said his father, with a grim smile.

"But she would feel dreadfully for you to send it back, for don't you see, father, that would hurt his feelings? And Polly would worry awfully to have that happen."

Old Mr. King turned uneasily, took a few steps, then came back to throw himself into his chair again.

"And this old gentleman has such ill attacks," said Jasper, pursuing his advantage, "that it might be the very thing to bring one on if he should get that watch back."

"Say no more, say no more, Jasper," said his father, shortly; "put this thing up for tonight, and then get back to bed again." And Jasper knew that was the end of it.

And the next day Polly wrote a nice little note, thanking the old earl for his gift, and hoping that he was quite well; and with so many other pleasant things in it, that if she could have seen him when he received it, she would have been glad indeed. And then she handed the little red leather case to Mr. King. "Keep it for me, Grandpapa," she said simply.

"All right, Polly, my child," he said. And then everybody forgot all about the episode and proceeded to enjoy Heidelberg.

"I'm so sorry for people who are not going to Bayreuth, Adela!" exclaimed Polly, looking out of the compartment window, as the train steamed rapidly on from Nuremberg where they had passed several days of delight reveling in the old town.

Adela, with her mind more on those past delights, had less attention for thoughts of music, so she answered absently, "Yes. Oh, Polly, wasn't that Pentagonal Tower fine? What is it they call it in German?"

But Polly didn't hear, being absorbed in the Wagner festival of which her mind was full, so Jasper answered for her. "Alt-Nuenberg, you mean, the oldest building of all Nuremberg."

"Yes," said Adela, "well, I got two or three sketches of that tower."

"Did you?" cried Jasper, "now that's good."

"And I got that horrible old robber-knight, — what's his name? — sitting inside his cell, you know."

"Eppelein von Gallingen," supplied Jasper. "Well, he was a horrible-looking customer, and that's a fact."

"Oh, I liked him," said Adela, who rejoiced in ugly things if only picturesque, "and I got into one corner of the cell opposite him, so as to sketch it all as well as I could in such a dark place, and a lady came down the little stairs; you remember them."

"I rather think I do," said Jasper, grimly. "I was trying to get out of the way of a huge party of tourists, and I nearly broke my neck."

"Well, this lady came down the stairs. I could see her where I sat, but she couldn't see me, it was so dark in the cell; and she called to her husband — I guess he was her husband, because he looked so *triste.*" Adela often fell into French, from being so long at the Paris school, and not from affectation in the least. "And she said, 'Come, Henry, let us see what is in there.' And she took one step in, and peered into that robber-knight's face; you know how he is sitting on a little stool, his black hair all round his face, staring at one."

"Yes, I do," said Jasper; "he was uncanny enough, and in the darkness, his wax features, or whatever they were made of, were unpleasantly natural to the last degree."

"Well," said Adela, "the lady gave a little squeal, and tumbled right back into her husband's arms. And I guess she stepped on his toes, for he squealed, too, though in a different way, and he gave her a little push and told her not to be a goose, that the man had been dead a thousand years more or less and couldn't hurt her. So then she stepped back, awfully scared though, I could see that, and then she caught sight of me, and she squealed again and jumped, and she screamed right out, 'Oh, there's another in there, in the corner, and it glared at me.' And I didn't glare at all," finished Adela, in disdain. "And then I guess he was scared, too, for he said, 'That old cell isn't worth seeing, anyway, and I'm going down into the torture chamber,' and they hurried off."

"That torture chamber!" exclaimed Jasper; "how anyone can hang over those things, I don't see; for my part, I'd rather have my time somewhere else."

"Oh, I like them," said Adela, in great satisfaction, "and I've got a picture of the 'Iron Virgin.'"

"That was a good idea, to put the old scold into that wooden tub concern," said Jasper; "there was some sense in that. I took a picture of it, and the old tower itself. I got a splendid photograph of it, if it will only develop well," he added. "Oh, but the buildings — was ever anything so fine as those old Nuremberg houses, with their high-peaked gables! I have quantities of them — thanks to my Kodak."

"What's this station, I wonder?" asked Polly, as the train slowed up.

Two ladies on the platform made a sudden dash at their compartment. "All full," said the guard, waving them off.

"That was Fanny Vanderburgh," gasped Polly.

"And her mother," added Jasper.

"Who was it?" demanded old Mr. King.

His consternation, when they told him, was so great, that Jasper racked his brains some way to avoid the meeting.

"If once we were at Bayreuth, it's possible that we might not come across them, father, for we could easily be lost in the crowd."

"No such good luck," groaned old Mr. King, which was proved true. For the first persons who walked into the hotel, as the manager was giving directions that the rooms reserved for their party should be shown them, were Mrs. Vanderburgh and her daughter.

"Oh!" exclaimed Mrs. Vanderburgh, as if her dearest friends were before her, "how glad I am to see you again, dear Mr. King, and you all." She swept Mrs. Fisher and Mrs. Henderson lightly in her glance as if toleration only were to be observed toward them. "We have been perfectly *désolée* without you, Polly, my dear," she went on, with a charming smile. "Fanny will be happy once more. She has been disconsolate ever since we parted, I assure you."

Polly made some sort of a reply, and greeted Fanny, as of old times, on the steamer; but Mrs. Vanderburgh went on, all smiles and eagerness — so rapidly in her friendly intentions, that it boded ill for the future peace of Mr. King's party. So Mr. King broke into the torrent of words at once, without anymore scruple. "And now, Mrs. Vanderburgh, if you will excuse us, we are quite tired, and are going to our rooms." And he bowed himself off, and of course his family followed; the next moment Fanny and her mother were alone.

"If this is to be the way," said Mrs. Vanderburgh, with a savage little laugh, "we might much better have stayed in Paris, for I never should have thought, as you know, Fanny, of coming to this out-of-the-way place, seeing that I don't care for the music, if I hadn't heard them say on the steamer that this was their date here."

"Well, I wish that I was at home," declared Fanny, passionately, "and I never, never will come to Europe, Mamma, again as long as I live. You are always chasing after people who run away from you, and those who like me, you won't let me speak to."

"Well, I shall be thankful for the day when you are once in society," said her mother, every shred of self-control now gone; "and I shall sell my tickets for this old Wagner festival, and go back to Paris tomorrow morning."

At that, Fanny broke into a dismal fit of complaining, which continued all the time they were dressing for dinner, and getting settled in their room, and then at intervals through that meal.

Polly looked over at her gloomy face, three tables off, and her own fell.

"You are not eating anything, child," said Grandpapa, presently, with a keen glance at her. "Let me order something more."

"Oh, no, Grandpapa," and "yes, I will," she cried, incoherently, making a great effort to enjoy the nice things he piled on her plate.

Jasper followed her glance as it rested on the Vanderburgh table. "They will spoil everything," he thought. "And to think it should happen at Bayreuth."

"Yes, we are going," said Fanny Vanderburgh as they met after dinner in the corridor. Her eyes were swollen, and she twisted her handkerchief in her fingers. "And I did — did — did —" here she broke down and sobbed — "so want to hear the Wagner operas."

"Don't cry," begged Polly, quite shocked. "Oh, Fanny, why can't you stay? How very dreadful to lose the Wagner music!" Polly could think of no worse calamity that could befall one.

"Mamma doesn't know anybody here except your party," mumbled Fanny, "and she's upset, and declares that we must go back to Paris tomorrow. Oh, Polly Pepper, I hate Paris," she exploded. And then sobbed worse than ever.

"Wait here," said Polly, "till I come back." Then she ran on light feet to Grandpapa, just settling behind a newspaper in a corner of the general reading room.

"Grandpapa, dear, may I speak to you a minute?" asked Polly, with a woeful feeling at her heart. It seemed as if he must hear it beating.

"Why, yes, child, to be sure," said Mr. King, quite surprised at her manner. "What is it?" and he laid aside his paper and smiled reassuringly.

But Polly's heart sank worse than ever. "Grandpapa," she began desperately, "Fanny Vanderburgh is feeling dreadfully."

"And I should think she would with such a mother," exclaimed the old gentleman, but in a guarded tone. "Well, what of it, Polly?"

"Grandpapa," said Polly, "she says her mother is going to take her back to Paris tomorrow morning."

"How very fine!" exclaimed Mr. King, approvingly; "that is the best thing I have heard yet. Always bring me such good news, Polly, and I will lay down my newspapers willingly anytime." And he gave a pleased little laugh.

"But, Grandpapa —" and Polly's face drooped, and there was such a sad little note in her voice, that the laugh dropped out of his. "Fanny wanted above all things to hear the Wagner operas — just think of losing those!" Polly clasped her hands, and every bit of color flew from her cheek.

"Well, what can I do about it?" asked the old gentleman, in a great state of perturbation. "Speak out, child, and tell me what you want."

"Only if I can be pleasant to Fanny," said Polly, a wave of color rushing over her face. "I mean if I may go with her? Can I, Grandpapa, this very evening, just as if —" she hesitated.

"As if what, Polly?"

"As if we all liked them," finished Polly, feeling as if the words must be said.

There was an awful pause in which Polly had all she could do to keep from rushing from the room. Then Grandpapa said, "If you can stand it, Polly, you may do as you like, but I warn you to keep them away from me." And he went back to his paper.

XVIII

BAYREUTH AND OLD FRIENDS

*J*asper turned around to gaze at the vast audience filing into the Wagner Opera House before he took his seat. "This makes me think of Oberammergau, Polly," he said.

"To think you've seen the Passion Play," she cried, with glowing cheeks.

"That was when I was such a little chap," said Jasper, "ages ago, — nine years, Polly Pepper, — just think; so it will be as good as new next year. Father is thinking a good deal of taking you there next summer."

"Jasper," cried Polly, her cheeks all in a glow, and regardless of next neighbors, "what can I ever do to repay your father for being so very good to me and to all of us?"

"Why, you can keep on making him comfortable, just as you are doing now, Polly," replied Jasper. "He said yesterday it made him grow younger every minute to look at you. And you know he's never sick now, and he was always having those bad attacks. Don't you remember when we first came to Hingham, Polly?" as they took their seats.

"O dear me, I guess I do, Jasper, and how you saved Phronsie from being carried off by the big organ man," and she shivered even now at this lapse of years. "And all the splendid times at Badgertown and the little brown —"

Just then a long hand came in between the people in the seat back of them. "I'm no end glad to see you!" exclaimed a voice. It was Tom Selwyn.

"I'm going over into that vacant seat." Tom forgot his fear of Polly and his hatred of girls generally, and rushed around the aisle to plunge awkwardly into the seat just back of Jasper. "I'll stay here till the person comes." His long arms came in contact with several obstacles, such as sundry backs and shoulders in his progress, but he had no time to consider such small things or to notice the black looks he got in consequence.

"Now, isn't this jolly!" he exclaimed. Jasper was guilty of staring at him; there seemed such a change in the boy, he could hardly believe it was really and truly Tom Selwyn.

"My grandfather is well now, and he would have sent some message to you if he knew I was to run across you," went on Tom, looking at Jasper, but meaning Polly; "did you get a little trifle he sent you some weeks ago? He's been in a funk about it because he didn't hear."

Wasn't Polly glad that her little note was on the way, and perhaps in the old gentleman's hands at this very time!

"Yes," she said, "and he was very kind and —" Tom fumbled his tickets all the while, and broke in abruptly.

"I didn't know as you'd like it, but it made him sick not to do it, and so the thing went. Glad it didn't make you mad," he ended suddenly.

"He meant it all right, I'm sure," said Jasper, seeing that Polly couldn't speak.

"Didn't he though!" exclaimed Tom.

"And it didn't come till the day we left Heidelberg," said Polly, finding her tongue, and speaking rapidly to explain the delay; "that was a week ago."

"Whew!" whistled Tom; "oh, beg pardon!" for several people turned around and stared; so he ducked his head, and was mostly lost to view for a breathing space. When he thought they had forgotten him, he bobbed it up. "Why, Grandfather picked it out — had a bushel of things sent up from London to choose from, you know, weeks and weeks ago, as soon as he got up to London. That's no end queer."

"No," said Polly, "it didn't come till then. And I wrote to your grandfather the next morning and thanked him."

"Now you did!" exclaimed Tom, in huge delight, and slapping his knee with one long hand. "That's no end good of you." He couldn't conceal how glad he was, and grinned all over his face.

At this moment Mrs. Vanderburgh, who, seeing Fanny so happy again, concluded to stay on the strength of resurrected hopes of Polly Pepper's friendship, sailed into the opera house, with her daughter. And glancing across the aisle, for their seats were at the side, she caught sight of the party she was looking for, and there was a face she knew, but wasn't looking for.

"Fanny," she cried, clutching her arm, "there is Tom Selwyn! Well, now we *are* in luck!" And Tom saw her, and again he ducked, but for a different reason. When he raised his head, he glanced cautiously in the direction he dreaded. "There's that horrible person," he whispered in Jasper's ear.

"Who?" asked Jasper, in astonishment.

"That woman on the steamer — you knew her — and she was looking straight at us. Duck for your life, Jasper King!"

"Oh, that," said Jasper, coolly, following the bob of his head. "Yes, Mrs. Vanderburgh, I know; and she is at our hotel."

"The dickens! And you're alive!" Tom raised his head and regarded him as a curiosity.

"Very much so," answered Jasper, smothering a laugh; "well, we mustn't talk anymore."

Polly was sitting straight, her hands folded in her lap, with no thought for audience, or anything but what she was to see and hear on that wonderful stage. Old Mr. King leaned past Parson Henderson, and gazed with the greatest satisfaction at her absorbed face.

"I pity anybody," he said to himself, "who hasn't some little Peppers to take about; I only wish I had the boys, too. But fancy Joel listening to 'Parsifal'!"

This idea completely overcame him, and he settled back into his seat with a grim smile.

Polly never knew that Mamsie, with a happy look in her black eyes, was regarding her intently, too, nor that many a glance was given to the young girl whose color came and went in her cheek, nor that Jasper sometimes spoke a low word or two. She was lost in the entrancing world of mystery and legend borne upward by the grand music, and she scarcely moved.

"Well, Polly." Old Mr. King was smiling at her and holding out his hand. The curtains had closed for the intermission, and all the people were getting out of their chairs. Polly sat still and drew a long breath. "Oh, Grandpapa, must we go?"

"Yes, indeed, I hope so," answered Mr. King, with a little laugh. "We shall have none too much time for our supper, Polly, as it is."

Polly got out of her seat, very much wishing that supper was not one of the needful things of life.

"It almost seems wicked to think of eating, Jasper," she said, as they picked up their hats and capes, where he had tucked them under the seats.

"It would be more wicked not to eat," said Jasper, with a little laugh, "and I think you'll find some supper tastes good, when we get fairly at it, Polly."

"I suppose so," said Polly, feeling dreadfully stiff in her feet, and beginning to wish she could have a good run.

"And what we should do with you if we didn't stop for supper," observed Jasper, snapping the case to the opera-glasses, "I'm sure I don't know, Polly. I spoke to you three times, and you didn't hear me once."

"Oh, Jasper!" exclaimed Polly, in horror, pausing as she was pinning on her big, flowered hat, with the roses all around the brim; "O dear me, there it goes!" as the hat spun over into the next row.

"I'll get it," cried Tom Selwyn, vaulting over the tops of the seats before Jasper had a chance to try for it.

Just then Mrs. Vanderburgh, who hadn't heard anymore of the opera than could fit itself into her lively plans for the campaign she laid out to accomplish in siege of Tom Selwyn, pushed and elbowed herself along. "Of course the earl isn't here — and the boy is alone, and dreadfully taken with Jasper King, so I can manage him. And once getting him, I'll soon have the earl to recognize me as a relation." Then, oh! visions of the golden dream of bliss when she could visit such titled kin in Old England, and report it all when at home in New York, filled her head. And with her mind eaten up with it, she pushed rudely by a plain, somewhat dowdy-looking woman who obstructed her way.

The woman raised a quiet, yet protesting face; but Mrs. Vanderburgh, related to an earl, surveyed her haughtily, and pressed on.

"Excuse me," said the plain-looking woman, "but it is impossible for me to move; the people are coming out this way, Madam, and —"

"And I must get by," answered Mrs. Vanderburgh, interrupting, and wriggling past as well as she could. But the lace on her flowing sleeve catching on the umbrella handle of a stout German coming the other way, she tore it half across. A dark flush of anger rushed over her face, and she vented all her spite on the plain-looking person in her path. "If you had moved, this wouldn't have happened!" she exclaimed.

"It was impossible for me to do so," replied the woman, just as quietly as ever. Just then Tom Selwyn rushed up: "Mother!" to the plain-looking woman; "well, we *did* get separated! Oh!" and seeing her companion he plunged back.

Fanny Vanderburgh, well in the rear, a party of young German girls impeding the way, felt her mother's grasp, and looked around.

"Oh, you've torn your lace sleeve!" she exclaimed, supposing the black looks referred to that accident.

"Torn my sleeve!" echoed her mother, irately, "that's a trifle," while Fanny stared in surprise, knowing, by past experience, that much lesser accidents had made black days for her; "I'm the unluckiest person alive. And think of all the money your father has given me to spend, and it won't do any good. Fanny, I'm going straight back to Paris, as quickly as possible."

"Why, I'm having a good time now," said Fanny, just beginning to enjoy herself. "Polly Pepper is real nice to me. I don't want to go home a bit." All this as they slowly filed out in the throng.

"Well, you're going; and, oh, those Peppers and those Kings, I'm sick to death of their names," muttered her mother, frowning on her.

"Why can't we wait for Polly?" asked Fanny, not catching the last words, and pausing to look back.

"Because you can't, that's why. And never say a word about that Polly Pepper or any of the rest of that crowd," commanded her mother, trying to hurry on.

"Polly Pepper is the sweetest girl — the very dearest," declared Fanny, in a passion, over her mother's shoulder, "and you know it, Mamma."

"Well, I won't have you going with her, anyway, nor with any of them," answered her mother, shortly.

"Because you can't," echoed Fanny, in her turn, and with a malicious little laugh. "Don't I know? it's the same old story — those you chase after, run away from you. You've been chasing, Mamma; you needn't tell me."

"Oh, Jasper," Polly was saying, "did you really speak to me?"

"Three times," said Jasper, with a laugh, "but you couldn't answer, for you didn't hear me."

"No," said Polly, "I didn't, Jasper."

"And I shouldn't have spoken, for it isn't, of course, allowed. But I couldn't help it, Polly, it was so splendid," and his eyes kindled. "And you didn't seem to breathe or to move."

"I don't feel as if I had done much of either," said Polly, laughing. "Isn't it good to take a long stretch? And oh, don't you wish we could run, Jasper?"

He burst into another gay little laugh, as he picked up the rest of the things. "I thought so, Polly, and you'll want some supper yet. Well, here is Tom coming back again."

"Indeed I shall, and a big one, Jasper," said Polly, laughing, "for I am dreadfully hungry."

"Come to supper with us," Jasper said socially over the backs of several people, in response to Tom Selwyn's furious telegraphing.

"Can't," said Tom, bobbing his head; "must stay with my mother. Thought you never would turn around." Jasper looked his surprise, and involuntarily glanced by Tom. "Yes, my mother's here; we've got separated, she's gone ahead," said Tom, jerking his head toward the nearest exit. "She says we'll go and see you. Where?"

"Hotel Sonne," said Jasper.

Tom disappeared — rushed off to his mother to jerk himself away to a convenient waiting-place till the disagreeable woman on the steamer had melted into space. Then he flew back, and in incoherent sentences made Mrs. Selwyn comprehend who she was, and the whole situation.

The earl's daughter was a true British matron, and preserved a quiet, immovable countenance; only a grim smile passed over it now and then. At last she remarked coolly, as if commenting on the weather, "I don't believe she will trouble you, my son." Never a word about the lace episode or the crowding process.

Tom sniffed uneasily. "You haven't crossed on a steamer with her, mother."

"Never you mind." Mrs. Selwyn gave him a pat on the back. "Tom, let us talk about those nice people," as they filed slowly out with the crowd.

Not a word did Tom lisp about the invitation to supper, but tucked his mother's arm loyally within his own. "Sorry I forgot to engage a table!" he exclaimed, as they entered the restaurant.

"Why, there is Tom!" exclaimed Jasper, craning his neck as his party were about to sit down. "Father, Tom Selwyn is here with his mother, and they can't find places, I almost know, and we might have two more chairs easily at our table," he hurried it all out.

"What is all this about?" demanded old Mr. King; "whom are you talking about, pray tell, Jasper?"

So Jasper ran around to his father's chair and explained. The end of it all was, that he soon hurried off, being introduced to Tom's mother, to whom he presented his father's compliments, and would she do him the favor to join their party? And in ten minutes, everyone felt well acquainted with the English matron, and entirely forgot that she was an earl's daughter. And Tom acquitted himself well, and got on famously with old Mr. King.

But he didn't dare talk to Polly, but edged away whenever there was the least chance of matters falling out so that he would have to.

And then it came out that the Selwyns thought of going to Munich and down to Lucerne.

"And the Bernese Alps," put in Jasper, across the table. "How is that, Tom, for an outing? Can't you do it?" For it transpired that Mrs. Selwyn had left the other children, two girls and two smaller boys, with their grandfather, on the English estate. They all called this place home since the father was in a business in Australia that required many long visits, and Tom's mother had decided that he should have a bit of a vacation with her, so they had packed up and off, taking in the Wagner festival first, and here they were. "Yes," after she considered a bit, "we can do that. Join the party and then over to Lucerne, and perhaps take in the Bernese Alps."

Only supposing that Polly's letter hadn't gone to the little old earl, Jasper kept saying over and over to himself. Just for one minute, suppose it!

And in the midst of it all, the horn sounded; the intermission was over, chairs were pushed back hastily, and all flocked off. No one must be late, and there must be no noisy or bustling entrances into the opera house.

And if Polly Pepper sat entranced through the rest of the matchless performance, Tom Selwyn — three seats back and off to the left — was just as quietly happy. But he wasn't thinking so much of "Parsifal" as might have been possible. "It's no end fine of the little mother to say 'yes,'" he kept running over and over to himself, with a satisfied glance at the quiet face under the plain, English bonnet.

"It's funny we don't see Fanny Vanderburgh anywhere," said Polly, as they went through the corridor and up the hotel stairs that night.

"She and her mother probably came home earlier," said Mrs. Fisher; "you know we were delayed, waiting for our carriages. You will see her in the morning, Polly."

But in the morning, it was ten o'clock before Mr. King's party gathered for breakfast, for Grandpapa always counseled sleeping late when out the night before. And when Polly did slip into her chair, there was a little note lying on her plate.

"Fanny Vanderburgh has gone," she said, and turned quite pale.

It was too true. Mrs. Vanderburgh had sold her two tickets to the "Flying Dutchman," to be presented that evening, and departed from Bayreuth.

"It's no use, Polly," Fanny's note ran, "trying to make me have a good time. Mamma says we are to go back to Paris; and go we must. You've been lovely, and I thank you ever so much, and good-bye."

Mother Fisher found Polly, a half-hour later, curled up in a corner of the old sofa in her room, her face pressed into the cushion.

"Why, Polly," exclaimed her mother, seeing the shaking shoulders, and, bending over her, she smoothed the brown hair gently, "this isn't right, child —"

Polly sprang up suddenly and threw her arms around her mother's neck. Her face was wet with tears, and she sobbed out, "Oh, if I'd done more for her, Mamsie, or been pleasant to Mrs. Vanderburgh, she might have stayed."

"You haven't any call to worry, Polly, child," said Mother Fisher, firmly. "You did all that could be done — and remember one thing, it's very wrong to trouble others as you certainly will if you give way to your feelings in this manner."

"Mamsie," exclaimed Polly, suddenly wiping away the trail of tears from her cheek, "I won't cry a single bit more. You can trust me, Mamsie, I truly won't."

"Trust you," said Mother Fisher, with a proud look in her black eyes, "I can trust you ever and always, Polly; and now run to Mr. King and let him see a bright face, for he's worrying about you, Polly."

XIX

MR. KING HAS A LITTLE PLAN FOR POLLY

"Oh Jasper," exclaimed Polly, clasping her hands, "do you suppose we'll ever get to a piano where it's all alone, and nobody wants to play on it —"

"But just you and I," finished Jasper. "I declare I don't know. You see we don't stay still long enough in any one place to hire a decent one; and besides, father said, when we started, that it was better for us to rest and travel about without any practicing this summer. You know he did, Polly."

"I know it," said Polly; "but oh, if we could just play once in a while," she added mournfully.

"Well, we can't," said Jasper, savagely; "you know we tried that at Brussels, when we thought everybody had gone off. And those half a dozen idiots came and stared at us through the glass door."

"And then they came in," added Polly, with a little shiver at the recollection. "But that big fat man with the black beard was the worst, Jasper." She glanced around as if she expected to see him coming down the long parlor.

"Well, he didn't hear much; there didn't any of them," said Jasper; "that's some small satisfaction, because you hopped off the piano stool and ran away."

"You ran just as fast, I'm sure, Jasper," said Polly, with a little laugh.

"Well, perhaps I did," confessed Jasper, bursting into a laugh. "Who wouldn't run with a lot of staring idiots flying at one?" he brought up in disgust.

"And we forgot the music," went on Polly, deep in the reminiscence, "and we wouldn't go back — don't you remember? — until the big fat man with the dreadful black beard had gone, for he'd picked it up and been looking at it."

"Yes, I remember all about it," said Jasper; "dear me, what a time we had! It's enough to make one wish that the summer was all over, and that we were fairly settled in Dresden," he added gloomily, as he saw her face.

"Oh, no," exclaimed Polly, quickly, and quite shocked to see the mischief that she had done.

"We wouldn't have the beautiful summer go a bit faster, Jasper. Why, that would be too dreadful to think of."

"But you want to get at your music, Polly."

"I'll fly at it when the time comes," cried Polly, with a wise little nod, "never you fear, Jasper. Now come on; let's get Phronsie and go out and see the shops."

Old Mr. King in a nook behind the curtain, dropped the newspaper in his lap and thought a bit. "Best to wait till we get to Lucerne," he said to himself, nodding his white head; "then, says I, Polly, my child, you shall have your piano."

And when their party were settling down in the hotel at Lucerne, ending the beautiful days of travel after leaving Munich, Jasper's father called him abruptly. "See here, my boy."

"What is it, father?" asked Jasper, wonderingly; "the luggage is all right; it's gone up to the rooms — all except the portmanteau, and Francis will go down to the station and straighten that out."

"I'm not in the least troubled in regard to the luggage, Jasper," replied his father, testily; "it's something much more important than the luggage question about which I wish to speak to you."

Jasper stared, well knowing his father's views in regard to the luggage question. "The first thing that you must unpack — the very first," old Mr. King was saying, "is your music. Don't wait a minute, Jasper, but go and get it. And then call Polly, and —"

"Why, father," exclaimed Jasper, "there isn't a single place to play in. You don't know how people stare if we touch the piano. We can't here, father; there's such a crowd in this hotel."

"You do just as I say, Jasper," commanded his father. "And tell Polly to get her music; and then do you two go to the little room out of the big parlor, and play to your hearts' content." And he burst into a hearty laugh at Jasper's face, as he dangled a key at the end of a string, before him.

"Now I do believe, father, that you've got Polly a piano and a little room to play in," cried Jasper, joyfully, and pouncing on the key.

"You go along and do as I tell you," said Mr. King, mightily pleased at the success of his little plan. "And don't you tell Polly Pepper one word until she has taken her music down in the little room," as Jasper bounded off on the wings of the wind.

And in that very hotel was the big fat man with the dreadful black beard, resting after a long season of hard work.

But Polly and Jasper wouldn't have cared had they known it, as long as they had their own delightful little music room to themselves — as they played over and over all the dear old pieces, and Polly reveled in everything that she was so afraid she had forgotten.

"I really haven't lost it, Jasper!" she would exclaim radiantly, after finishing a concerto, and dropping her hands idly on the keys. "And I was *so* afraid I'd forgotten it entirely. Just think, I haven't played that for three months, Jasper King."

"Well, you haven't forgotten a bit of it," declared Jasper, just as glad as she was. "You didn't make any mistakes, hardly, Polly."

"Oh, yes, I made some," said Polly, honestly, whirling around on the piano stool to look at him.

"Oh, well, only little bits of ones," said Jasper; "those don't signify. I wish father could have heard that concerto. What a pity he went out just before you began it."

But somebody else, on the other side of the partition between the little music room and the big parlor, had heard, and he pulled his black beard thoughtfully with his long fingers, then pricked up his ears to hear more. And it was funny how, almost every day, whenever the first notes on the piano struck up in Mr. King's little music room, the big fat man, who was so tired with his season of hard work, never seemed to think that he could rest as well as in that particular corner up against that partition. And no matter what book or paper he had in his hand, he always dropped it and fell to pulling his black beard with his long fingers, before the music was finished.

And then, "Oh, Polly, come child, you have played long enough," from Mother Fisher on the other side of the partition; or old Mr. King would say, "No more practicing today, Miss Polly;" or Phronsie would pipe out, "Polly, Grandpapa is going to take us out on the lake; do come, Polly." And then it was funnier yet to see how suddenly the big fat man with the dreadful black beard seemed to find that particular corner by that partition a very tiresome place. And as the piano clicked down its cover, he would yawn, and get up and say something in very rapid German to himself, and off he would go, forgetting all about his book or newspaper, which, very likely, would tumble to the floor, and flap away by itself till somebody came and picked it up and set it on the sofa.

One morning old Mr. King, hurrying along with his batch of English mail to enjoy opening it in the little music room where Jasper and Polly were playing a duet, ran up suddenly against a fat heavy body coming around an opposite angle.

"Oh, I beg your pardon, sir," exclaimed Mr. King in great distress, the more so as he saw that the stranger's glasses were knocked off his nose by the collision. "I do trust they are not broken," he added, in a concerned tone, endeavoring to pick them up.

But the big man was before him. "Not a beet, not a beet," he declared, adjusting them on his nose again. Then he suddenly grasped old Mr. King's hand. "And I be very glad, sir, *very* glad indeed, dat I haf roon into you."

"Indeed!" exclaimed Mr. King, releasing his hand instantly, and all the concern dropping out of his face.

"*Very* glad indeed!" repeated the big man, heartily; then he pulled his black beard, and stood quite still a moment.

"If you have nothing more to remark, sir," said Mr. King, haughtily, "perhaps you will be kind enough to stand out of my way, and allow me to pass. And it would be as well for you to observe more care in the future, sir, both in regard to your feet, and your tongue, sir."

"Yes, I am *very* glad," began the big man again, who hadn't even heard Mr. King's tirade, "for now —" and he gave his black beard a final twitch, and his eyes suddenly lightened with a smile that ran all over his face, "I can speak to you of dis ting dat is in my mind. Your —"

"I want to hear nothing of what is on your mind," declared old Mr. King, now thoroughly angry. "Stand aside, fellow, and let me pass," he commanded, in a towering passion.

The big man stared in astonishment into the angry face, the smile dropping out of his own. "I beg to *ex*cuse myself," he said, with a deep bow, and a wave of his long fingers. "Will you pass?" and he moved up as tightly as possible to the wall.

Old Mr. King went into the little music room in a furious rage, and half an hour afterward Polly and Jasper, pausing to look around, saw him tossing and tumbling his letters and newspapers about on the table, fuming to himself all the while.

"Father has had bad news!" exclaimed Jasper, turning pale; "something about his agents, probably."

"O dear me! and here we have been playing," cried Polly in remorse, every vestige of color flying from her cheek.

"Well, we didn't know," said Jasper, quickly. "But what can we do now, Polly?" he turned to her appealingly.

"I don't know," she was just going to say helplessly, but Jasper's face made her see that something must be done. "Let's go and tell him we are sorry," she said; "that's what Mamsie always liked best if she felt badly."

So the two crept up behind old Mr. King's chair: "Father, I'm *so* sorry," and "Dear Grandpapa, I'm *so* sorry," and Polly put both arms around his neck suddenly.

"Eh — what?" cried Mr. King, sitting bolt upright in astonishment. "Oh, bless me, children, I thought you were playing on the piano."

"We were," said Polly, hurrying around to the side of the table, her face quite rosy now, "but we didn't know —" and she stopped short, unable to find another word.

"— that you felt badly," finished Jasper. "Oh, father, we didn't know that you'd got bad news." He laid his hand as he spoke on the pile of tumbled-up letters.

"Bad news!" ejaculated old Mr. King, in perplexity, and looking from one to the other.

"No, we didn't," repeated Polly, clasping her hands. "Dear Grandpapa, we truly didn't, or we wouldn't have kept on playing all this time."

Mr. King put back his head and laughed long and loud, as he hadn't done for many a day, his ill humor dropping off in the midst of it. "The letters are all right," he said, wiping his eyes, "never had better news. It was an impertinent fellow I met out there, that's all."

"Father, who has dared —" began Jasper, with flashing eyes.

"Don't you worry, my boy; it's all right, the fellow got his quietus; besides, he wasn't worth minding," said Mr. King, carelessly. "Why, here is your mother," turning to Polly. "Now then, Mrs. Fisher, what is it; for I see by your eye some plan is on the carpet."

"Yes, there is," said Mrs. Fisher, coming in with a smile, "the doctor is going to take a day off."

"Is that really so?" cried Mr. King, with a little laugh. "What! not even going to visit one of his beloved hospitals?" while Polly exclaimed, radiantly, "Oh, how perfectly elegant! Now we'll have Papa-Doctor for a whole long day!"

Phronsie, who had been close to her mother's gown during the delivery of this important news, clasped her hands in a quiet rapture, while Polly exclaimed, "Now, Grandpapa, can it be the Rigi?" Jasper echoing the cry heartily.

"I suppose it is to be the Rigi," assented old Mr. King, leaning back in his chair to survey them all, "that is, if Mrs. Fisher approves. We'll let you pick out the jaunting place," turning to her, "seeing that it is the doctor's holiday."

"I know that Dr. Fisher wants very much to go up the Rigi," said his wife, in great satisfaction at the turn the plans were taking.

"And we'll stay over night, father," cried Jasper, "won't we?"

"Stay over night?" repeated his father, "I should say so. Why, what would be the good of our going up at all, pray tell, if we didn't devote that much time to it and have a try for a sunrise?"

"We're to go up the Rigi!" exclaimed Polly, giving a little whirl, and beginning to dance around the room, repeating, "We're to go up the Rigi," exactly as if nobody knew it, and she was telling perfectly fresh news.

"Here — that dance looks awfully good — wait for me," cried Jasper. And seizing her hands, they spun round and round, Phronsie scuttling after them, crying, "Take me, too. I want to dance, Polly."

"So you shall," cried Polly and Jasper together; so they made a little ring of three, and away they went, Polly this time crying, "Just think, we're going to have the most beautiful sunrise in all this world."

And on the other side of the partition, in his accustomed nook in the big parlor, the big fat man with the black beard sat. He pulled this same black beard thoughtfully a bit, when Mr. King was telling about the impertinent fellow. Then he smiled and jabbered away to himself very hard in German; and it wasn't till the King party hurried off to get ready for the Rigi trip, that he got up and sauntered off.

And almost the first person that old Mr. King saw on getting his party into a car on the funicular railway, was the "impertinent fellow," also bound for the top of the Rigi.

"Oh, Grandpapa!" Polly got out of her seat and hurried to him with cheeks aflame, when midway up.

"I know — isn't it wonderful!" cried Grandpapa, happy in her pleasure, and finding it all just as marvelous as if he hadn't made the ascent several times.

"Yes, yes!" cried Polly. "It is all perfectly splendid, Grandpapa; but oh, I mean, *did* you hear what that lady said?" and she dropped her voice, and put her mouth close to Grandpapa's ear.

"I'm sure I didn't," said old Mr. King, carelessly, "and I'm free to confess I'm honestly glad of it. For if there is one thing I detest more than another, Polly, my girl, it is to hear people, especially women, rave and gush over the scenery."

"Oh, she didn't rave and gush," cried Polly, in a whisper, afraid that the lady heard. "She said, Grandpapa, that Herr Bauricke is at Lucerne; just think, Grandpapa, the great Herr Bauricke!"

She took her mouth away from the old gentleman's ear in order to look in his face.

"Polly, Polly," called Jasper from his seat on the farther end, "you are losing all this," as the train rounded a curve. "Do come back."

"Now, I'm glad of that," exclaimed Grandpapa, in a tone of the greatest satisfaction, "for I can ask him about the music masters in Dresden and get his advice, and be all prepared before we go there for the winter to secure the very best."

"And I can see him, and perhaps hear him play," breathed Polly, in an awestruck tone, quite lost to scenery and everything else. Jasper leaned forward and stared at her in amazement. Then he slipped out of his seat, and made his way up to them to find out what it was all about.

"How did she know?" he asked, as Polly told all she knew; "I'm just going to ask her." But the lady, who had caught snatches of the conversation, though she hadn't heard Mr. King's part of it, very obligingly leaned forward in her seat and told all she knew.

And by the time this was done, they all knew that the information was in the American paper printed in Paris, and circulated all over the Continent, and that the lady had read it that very morning just before setting out.

"The only time I missed reading that paper," observed old Mr. King, regretfully.

"And he is staying at our very hotel," finished the lady, "for I have seen you, sir, with your party there."

"Another stroke of good luck," thought old Mr. King, "and quite easy to obtain the information I want as to a master for Polly and Jasper."

"Now then, children," he said to the two hanging on the conversation, "run back to your seats and enjoy the view. This news of ours will keep."

So Polly and Jasper ran back obediently, but every step of the toilsome ascent by which the car pushed its way to the wonderful heights above, Polly saw everything with the words, "Herr Bauricke is at *our* hotel," ringing through her ears; and she sat as in a maze. Jasper was nearly as bad.

And then everybody was pouring out of the cars and rushing for the hotel on the summit; all but Mr. King's party and a few others, who had their rooms engaged by telegraphing up. When they reached the big central hall there was a knot of Germans all talking together, and on the outside fringe of this knot, people were standing around and staring at the central figure. Suddenly someone darted away from this outer circle and dashed up to them. It was the lady from their hotel.

"I knew you'd want to know," she exclaimed breathlessly; "that's Herr Bauricke himself — he came up on our train — just think of it! — the big man in the middle with the black beard." She pointed an excited finger at the knot of Germans.

Old Mr. King followed the course of the finger, and saw his "impertinent fellow who wasn't worth minding."

XX

"I SHOULD MAKE HIM HAPPY," SAID PHRONSIE

*P*olly got Jasper away into a side corridor by a beseeching little pull on his sleeve. "Oh, just to think," she mourned, "I called that great man such unpleasant things — that he was big and fat, and — oh, oh!"

"Well, he *is* big and fat," declared Jasper. "We can't say he isn't, Polly."

"But I meant it all against him," said Polly, shaking her head. "You know I did, Jasper," she added remorsefully.

"Yes, we neither of us liked him," said Jasper, "and that's the honest truth, Polly."

"And to think it was that *great* Herr Bauricke!" exclaimed Polly. Then her feelings overcame her, and she sank down on the cushioned seat in the angle.

Jasper sat down beside her. "I suppose it won't do to say anything about people after this until we know them. Will it, Polly?"

"Jasper," declared Polly, clasping her hands, while the rosy color flew over her cheek, "I'm never going to say a single —"

Just then the big form of Herr Bauricke loomed up before them, as he turned into the corridor.

Polly shrank up in her corner as small as she could, wishing she was as little as Phronsie, and could hop up and run away.

Herr Bauricke turned his sharp eyes on them for a moment, hesitated, then came directly up, and stopped in front of them. "I meant — I *in*tended to speak to your grandfader first. Dat not seem best *now.*" The great man was really talking to them, and Polly held her breath, not daring to look into his face, but keeping her gaze on his wonderful fingers. "My child," those wonderful fingers seized her own, and clasped them tightly, "you have great promise, mind you, you know only a leedle now, and you must work — *work — work.*" He brought it out so sharply, that the last word was fairly shrill. "But I tink you will," he added kindly, dropping his tone. Then he laid her fingers gently in her lap.

"Oh, she does, sir," exclaimed Jasper, finding his tongue first, for Polly was beyond speaking. "Polly works all the time she can."

"Dat is right." Herr Bauricke bobbed his head in approval, so that his spectacles almost fell off. "I hear dat, in de music she play. No leedle girl play like dat, who doesn't work. I will hear you sometime at de hotel," he added abruptly, "and tell you some tings dat will help you. Tomorrow, maybe, when we go down from dis place, eh?"

"Oh, sir," exclaimed Polly, springing off from her cushion before Jasper could stop her. "You are *so* good — but — but — I cannot," then her breath gave out, and she stood quite still.

"Eh?" exclaimed Herr Bauricke, and pushing up his spectacles to stare into her flushed and troubled face. "Perhaps I not make my meaning clear; I mean I *geef* you of my time and my best *ad*vice. Now you understand — eh?" He included Jasper in his puzzled glance.

"Yes, sir," Jasper made haste to say. "We do understand; and it is so very good of you, and Polly will accept it, sir." "For father will make it all right with him as to the payment," he reflected easily.

"Ah, now," exclaimed Herr Bauricke, joyfully, a light beaming all over his fat face, "dat is someting like — tomorrow, den, we —"

"But, oh, sir," Polly interrupted, "I cannot," and she twisted her hands in distress. "I — I — didn't like you, and I said so." Then she turned very pale, and her head drooped.

Jasper leaned over, and took her hand. "Neither did I, sir," he said. "I was just as bad as Polly."

"You not tink me nice looking — so?" said Herr Bauricke. "Well, I not tink so myself, eeder. And I scare you maybe, wid dis," and he twisted his black beard with his long fingers. "Ah, so; well, we will forget all dis, leedle girl," and he bent down and took Polly's other fingers that hung by her side. "And eef you not let me come tomorrow to your leedle music room, and tell you sometings to help you learn better, I shall know dat you no like me *now* — eh?"

"Oh, sir," Polly lifted her face, flooded with rosy color up to her brown hair, "if you only will forgive me?"

"I no forgeef; I not remember at all," said Herr Bauricke, waving his long fingers in the air. "And I go tomorrow to help you, leedle girl," and he strode down the corridor.

Polly and Jasper rushed off, they scarcely knew how, to Grandpapa, to tell him the wonderful news, — to find him in a truly dreadful state of mind. When they had told their story, he was as much worse as could well be imagined.

"Impossible, impossible!" was all he could say, but he brought his hand down on the table before him with so much force that Jasper felt a strange sinking of heart. What could be the matter?

"Why, children, and you all" (for his whole party was before him), exclaimed Mr. King, "Herr Bauricke is that impertinent person who annoyed me this morning, and I called him 'fellow' to his face!"

It was so very much worse than Jasper had dreamed, that he collapsed into the first chair, all Polly's prospects melting off like dew before the sun.

"Hum!" Little Dr. Fisher was the first to speak. He took off his big spectacles and wiped them; then put them on his nose and adjusted them carefully, and glared around the group, his gaze resting on old Mr. King's face.

Polly, who had never seen Jasper give way like this, forgot her own distress, and rushed up to him. "Oh, don't, Jasper," she begged.

"You see I can't allow Herr Bauricke to give any lessons or advice to Polly after this," went on Mr. King, hastily. "Of course he would be paid; but, under the circumstances, it wouldn't do, not in the least. It is quite out of the question," he went on, as if someone had been contradicting him. But no one said a word.

"Why don't some of you speak?" he asked, breaking the pause. "Dr. Fisher, you don't generally keep us waiting for your opinion. Speak out now, man, and let us have it."

"It is an awkward affair, surely," began the little doctor, slowly.

"Awkward? I should say so," frowned Mr. King; "it's awkward to the last degree. Here's a man who bumps into me in a hotel passage, — though, for that matter, I suppose it's really my fault as much as his, — and I offer to pick up his spectacles that were dropped in the encounter. And he tells me that he is glad that we ran up against each other, for it gives him a chance to tell me what is on his mind. As if I cared what was on his mind, or on the mind of anyone else, for that matter," he declared, in extreme irritation. "And I told him to his face that he was an impertinent fellow, and to get out of my way. Yes, I did!"

A light began to break on little Dr. Fisher's face, that presently shone through his big spectacles, fairly beaming on them all. Then he burst into a laugh, hearty and long.

"Why, Adoniram!" exclaimed Mother Fisher, in surprise. Polly turned a distressed face at him; and to say that old Mr. King stared would be stating the case very mildly indeed.

"Can't you see, oh, can't you see," exploded the little doctor, mopping up his face with his big handkerchief, "that your big German was trying to tell you of Polly's playing, and to say something, probably pretty much the same that he has said to her and to Jasper? O dear me, I should like to have been there to see you both," ended Dr. Fisher, faintly. Then he went off into another laugh.

"I don't see much cause for amusement," said old Mr. King, grimly, when this idea broke into his mind, "for it's a certain fact that I called him a fellow, and told him to get out of the way."

"Well, he doesn't bear you any malice, apparently," said the little doctor, who, having been requested to speak, saw no reason for withholding any opinion he might chance to have, "for, if he did, he wouldn't have made that handsome offer to Polly."

"That may be; the offer is handsome enough," answered Mr. King, "that is the trouble, it's too handsome. I cannot possibly accept it under the awkward circumstances. No, children," he turned to Polly and Jasper, as if they had been beseeching him all the while, "you needn't ask it, or expect it," and he got out of his chair, and stalked from the room.

Jasper buried his face in his hands, and a deep gloom settled over the whole party, on all but little Dr. Fisher. He pranced over to Polly and Jasper just as merrily as if nothing dreadful had happened. "Don't you be afraid, my boy," he said; "your father is a dreadfully sensible man, and there's no manner of doubt but that he will fix this thing up."

"Oh, you don't know father," groaned Jasper, his head in his hands, "when he thinks the right thing hasn't been done or said. And now Polly will miss it all!" And his head sank lower yet.

"Nonsense!" exclaimed Dr. Fisher. Yet he had a dreadful feeling coming over him, and he turned to Polly imploringly.

"Oh, I do believe it, Jasper," cried Polly, "what Papa-Doctor says. And just look at Mamsie!" she cried, beneath her breath.

And truly Mother Fisher was having a hard time to control herself. That Jasper could see as he lifted his head. And the little doctor also saw, and skipped back across the room to her side. And Phronsie, feeling plunged into the deepest woe by all this dreadful state of affairs, that had come too bewilderingly for her to rally to Grandpapa's side, first began to cry. And then, thinking better of it, went softly out of the door, and no one noticed her when she went — with the tears running down her cheeks.

Down the long corridor she hurried, not knowing which way Grandpapa went, but turning into the little reading room, she spied him sitting by the table. The apartment was otherwise empty. He wasn't reading, not even looking at a paper, but sitting bolt upright, and lost in thought.

"Grandpapa," she said, laying a soft little hand on his arm. "Oh, I'm so glad I found you." And she nestled up to his side.

"Eh? Oh, Phronsie, child." Old Mr. King put his arm around her, and drew her closely to him. "So you came after your old Grand-daddy, did you?"

"Yes, I did," said Phronsie, with a glad little cry, snuggling up tighter to him, while the tears trailed off down his waistcoat, but not before he had seen them.

"Now, Phronsie, you are not to cry anymore," he said, with a pang at the sight. "You won't, dear; promise me that."

So Phronsie promised; and he held her hands, and, clearing his throat, he began, "Well, now I suppose they felt pretty badly, back there in the room, your mother and all — eh, Phronsie?"

"Yes, Grandpapa," said Phronsie, her round face falling. Yet she had promised not to cry, and, although she had a hard time of it, every tear was kept back valiantly.

"And Polly, now —" asked old Mr. King, cautiously, "and Jasper — how were they feeling?"

"Grandpapa," Phronsie did not trust herself to reply, but, springing up, she laid her rosy little mouth close to his ear. "What does it all — the dreadful thing mean?" she whispered.

"It means," old Mr. King whispered back, but very distinctly, "that your old Granddaddy is an idiot, Phronsie, and that he has been rude, and let his temper run away with him."

"Oh, no, Grandpapa dear," contradicted Phronsie, falling back from him in horror. "You couldn't ever be that what you say." And she flung both arms around his neck and hugged him tightly.

"What? An idiot? Yes, I have been an idiot of the worst kind," declared Mr. King, "and all the rest just as I say; rude and — why, what is the matter, Phronsie?" for the little arms clutched him so tightly he could hardly breathe.

"Oh, Grandpapa," she wailed, and drawing away a bit to look at him, he saw her face convulsed with the effort not to cry. "Don't say such things. You are never naughty, Grandpapa dear; you can't be," she gasped.

"There, there, there," ejaculated old Mr. King, frightened at the effect of his words and patting her yellow hair, at his wits' end what to say. So he broke out, "Well, now, Phronsie, you must tell me what to do."

Thereupon Phronsie, seeing there was something she could really do to help Grandpapa, came out of her distress enough to sit up quite straight and attentive in his lap. "You see I spoke rudely to a man, and I called him a fellow, and he was a gentleman, Phronsie; you must remember that."

"Yes, I will, Grandpapa," she replied obediently, while her eyes never wandered from his face.

"And I told him to get out of the way and he did," said Mr. King, forcing himself to a repetition of the unpleasant truth. "O dear me, nothing could be worse," he groaned.

"And you are sorry, Grandpapa dear?" Phronsie leaned over and laid her cheek softly against his.

"Yes, I am, Phronsie, awfully sorry," confessed the old gentleman; "but what good will that do now? My temper has made a terrible mess of it all."

"But you can tell the gentleman you are sorry," said Phronsie. "Oh, Grandpapa dear, do go and tell him now, this very minute." She broke away from him again, and sat straight on his knee, while a glad little smile ran all over her face.

"I can't — you don't understand — O dear me!" Mr. King set her abruptly on the floor, and took a few turns up and down the room. Phronsie's eyes followed him with a grieved expression. When she saw the distress on his face, she ran up to him and seized his hand, but didn't speak.

"You see, child," — he grasped her fingers and held them closely, — "it's just this way: the gentleman wants to do me a favor; that is, to help Polly with her music."

"Does he?" cried Phronsie, and she laughed in delight. "Oh, Grandpapa, how nice! And Polly will be so happy."

"But I cannot possibly accept it," groaned old Mr. King; "don't you see, child, after treating him so? Why, how could I? The idea is too monstrous!" He set off now at such a brisk pace down the room that Phronsie had hard work to keep up with him. But he clung to her hand.

"Won't that make the gentleman sorry?" panted Phronsie, trotting along by his side.

"Eh — oh, what?" exclaimed old Mr. King, coming to a dead stop suddenly. "What's that you say, Phronsie?"

"Won't the gentleman feel sorry?" repeated Phronsie, pushing back the waves of yellow hair that had fallen over her face, to look up at him. "And won't he feel badly then, Grandpapa?"

"Eh — oh, perhaps," assented Mr. King, slowly, and passing a troubled hand across his brow. "Well, now, Phronsie, you come and sit in my lap again, and we'll talk it over, and you tell me what I ought to do."

So the two got into the big chair again, and Phronsie folded her hands in her lap.

"Now begin," said old Mr. King.

"I should make the gentleman happy, Grandpapa," said Phronsie, decidedly.

"You would — no matter what you had to do to bring it about?" asked Grandpapa, with a keen pair of eyes on her face. "Eh? think now, Phronsie."

"I should make the gentleman happy," repeated Phronsie, and she bobbed her head decidedly. "I really should, Grandpapa."

"Then the best way is to have it over with as soon as possible," said old Mr. King; "so come on, child, and you can see that the business is done up in good shape." He gathered her little fingers up in his hand, and setting her once more on the floor, they passed out of the apartment.

The door of the private parlor belonging to Mr. King's rooms was flung wide open, and into the gloomy interior, for Mother Fisher and Jasper were still inconsolable, marched old Mr. King. He was arm in arm, so far as the two could at once compass the doorway, with Herr Bauricke; while Phronsie ducked and scuttled in as she could, for the big German, with ever so many honorary degrees to his name, held her hand fast.

Old Mr. King continued his march up to Mother Fisher. "Allow me to introduce Herr Bauricke, Professor and Doctor of Music, of world-wide distinction," he said, bowing his courtly old head.

And then Mother Fisher, self-controlled as she had always been, astonished him by turning to her husband to supply the answering word.

"Glad to see you!" exclaimed the little doctor, bubbling over with happiness, and wringing the long fingers extended. "My wife is over-come with delight," which the big German understood very well; and he smiled his knowledge of it, as he looked into her black eyes. "She is like to mein Frau," he thought, having no higher praise. And then he turned quickly to Polly and Jasper.

XXI

ON THE RIGI-KULM

*F*or all that grand old Rigi's summit claimed them, it was some time before Mr. King's party left the little parlor. Herr Bauricke surely didn't want to until he had gotten it settled just what he did mean about Polly's music. That she showed great promise, that some faults in the way she had been taught were there, but it was by no means too late to mend them, that she had spirit and expression and love for the art.

"Ah, dat is eet, after all." Herr Bauricke clasped his long fingers and beamed at her, and then swept the entire party. "Lofe, ah, how one must lofe eet! Eef not, shame, shame!" His countenance darkened frightfully, and he fairly glared at them, as he unclasped his hands and swung one over his head, while his black beard vibrated with each word.

"Goodness me!" exclaimed Tom Selwyn, "it takes a musical man to sling around. I say, Jasper, I'd like to do a bit of boxing or cricketing with him." But Jasper didn't hear or see anything but Herr Bauricke and Polly; and, indeed, the whole room was given up to the "musical man" and his words.

At last Polly drew a long breath; Grandpapa was taking her hand. "Let us all go out and explore a bit," and off they went, the entire party. And the "musical man," as Tom still continued to call him in private, proved to be as expert in the use of his feet as his fingers, for he led them here, there, and everywhere that promised the least chance of a good view.

But Polly saw only the glorious future when, on the morrow, Herr Bauricke would really show her on the piano how best to study and to work! And the rosy glow of sunset wasn't one-half as bright as all her dreams.

"Polly," said Phronsie, pulling her hand gently, as she peered up into her face, "are you looking at it?"

"What, Pet? Oh, yes," said Polly, starting out of her reverie with a little laugh, "you mean the sunset?"

"Yes," said Phronsie, "I do mean that. Are you looking at it, Polly? Because if you are not looking, I wish you would, Polly."

"Well, I suppose I am looking at it, Phronsie," said Polly, with another little laugh, "but perhaps not in just the right way, for you see, Phronsie, I can't seem to see anything but just the splendid thing that is coming tomorrow. Oh, Phronsie Pepper, just think of that."

"I know," said Phronsie, with a little gurgle of delight at Polly's happiness, "and I am so glad, Polly."

"Of course you are," declared Polly, warmly, "just as glad as can be, Phronsie," and she threw her arm around her. "And now I'm going to look at the sunset in the right way, I hope. Isn't it beautiful, child?"

"Polly," declared Phronsie, suddenly wriggling away from Polly's arm, to stand in front of her with a beaming face, "I think it's just as beautiful as it can be up top here. I can see right in between that red cloud and that little pink teenty one. And I wish I could just go in, Polly."

"Wouldn't it be nice?" echoed Polly, enthusiastically.

"What?" asked Adela, hurrying up from a point of rocks below, where she had been sketching.

"Oh, to go in between those clouds there and see it all," said Polly.

"Dear me!" exclaimed Adela, "I shouldn't like it. I'd much rather stay down here, and sketch it."

"We could go sailing off, oh, ever so far," said Polly, swinging her arms to suit the action to the words. "And you'd be stuck to your rock here, Adela; while, Phronsie, you and I would sit on the edge of a cloud, and let our feet hang over; and oh, Adela, you could sketch us then as we went sailing by."

"How that would look!" exclaimed Adela, with such a face that Polly burst out into a merry laugh, and Phronsie, joining with her little crow of delight and clapping her hands at the idea of such fun, brought pretty much the whole party around them.

"What's up?" cried Tom to Jasper, on the way to the girls with some fear, for he didn't dare even yet to talk much to Polly. As for Adela, he let her severely alone.

"Don't know," said Jasper, "but we'll soon find out," and they did, by Phronsie's flying away from Polly and skipping down over the rocks to meet them.

"Oh, Jasper, Polly's telling how we would sail on that beautiful cloud," announced Phronsie, her yellow hair flying from her face as she sped along, heedless of her steps.

"Take care or you'll fall," warned Jasper. "See, your mother is looking worried." And, truth to tell, Mrs. Fisher, on a point of rocks a little way off with the others, was getting a bit alarmed as she saw the progress of her baby.

"I'll take care," said Phronsie, sobering down at thought of Mamsie's being troubled, and beginning to pick her way carefully. And Jasper gathered up her fingers in his, thinking of the time when she toiled up and down the long stairway, when she first came to what was now her home, blessed thought! and Polly and he sat down at the foot to watch her.

"And so Polly and you are going to try sailing on that cloud there," said Jasper, squinting up at the brilliant sky.

"We aren't really going, Jasper," said Phronsie, shaking her head, soberly, "because you see we can't. But Polly's pretending it all; and we're to sit on the edge and swing our feet. And Adela is going to make a picture of us."

"Whew!" whistled Jasper. "And I say, Polly," — for now they had scrambled up to the two girls, — "isn't there room for us on that cloud too?" While Tom kicked pebbles, and wished he knew how to talk to girls.

"Perhaps," said Polly, gaily. "Oh, I suppose that those who couldn't get on our cloud could take the next one."

"I'd rather have your cloud, Polly," said Jasper.

"And Grandpapa must come too," cried Phronsie, in alarm at the very thought of his being left out. "I want him on our cloud, Polly."

"Yes, and Mamsie and Papa-Doctor," finished Polly, ready for any nonsense, she was just bubbling over so with joy at thought of the morrow and what it would bring. "Well, it is good the cloud is big," squinting up at the radiant sky.

"And, Tom, you are coming on that cloud-boat."

Jasper pulled him forward with a merry laugh, giving him a clap on the back at the same time.

"Eh — oh, I can't — no, thank you," stammered Tom, thus suddenly brought into notice. "Excuse me," just as if the invitation had been a *bona fide* one.

Polly never smiled, but Adela giggled right out. Tom's face flushed, and he rushed off furiously, determined never to chance it again whereby he'd be mortified before girls — not he!

All the gay time was flown, and the red and pink and purple clouds looked down upon a sorry, uncomfortable little group. Jasper spoke first. "I must go after him," and he dashed down the rocks.

"O dear me, I couldn't help it," said Adela, twisting uncomfortably, "it was so silly in him to take it all in earnest."

"He didn't really think we meant it," said Polly, her brown eyes very grave. Would Jasper really persuade him to forget that laugh? "But he is shy, and he said the first thing that came into his head."

"Boys haven't any right to be shy," said Adela, fussing with her little sketching block and pencil, "they are so big and strong."

"Why did Tom run away so fast?" asked Phronsie, only half comprehending.

"Never mind, child," said Polly, with a reassuring pat on her head.

"And isn't Jasper coming back?" asked Phronsie, in great distress.

"Yes, oh, I guess so," said Polly. "Well, there, the pretty glow has all faded; see, Phronsie," pointing up to the leaden clouds that no one who had failed to see a few moments before could have imagined alive with color. "Now we ought to run over to the others, for they'll be going back to the hotel."

"It's all gone," said Phronsie, sadly, looking up at the darkening sky. "Polly, where has the pretty red and pink gone to?"

"Oh, I don't know," said Polly, thinking only of Tom, and what a hard time Jasper must be having with him. "Take care, Phronsie, don't look up now — you'll fall! There, take my hand; now come on."

"O dear me, I didn't mean to laugh," Adela was saying to herself as she fell back in the zigzag path down the rocks. "I wish I hadn't — I'll — I'll —" What she meant to do wasn't very clear in her mind; what she did do, was to run up to her grandmother's and her room, and toss her sketch-book on the table, and herself on the bed, for a good hearty cry.

Polly found her there, when they couldn't find her anywhere else, with much searching and running about. Little old Mrs. Gray was worrying dreadfully, so afraid she had been blown from the rocks; for the wind had now risen, and all the travelers were seeking the shelter and warmth of the hotel corridor and parlors.

"Oh, Adela, how *could* you?" Polly was going to say. And then she thought that would be the very worst thing in all the world, for Adela's shoulders were shaking, and it would only make her cry worse. And besides, Polly remembered how she had sometimes given way in just this fashion, and how much worse she would have been, had it not been for a wise, good mother. So she ran out in the hall. "I must tell her grandmother," she said to herself.

"Have you found her?" asked Jasper, looking up from the foot of the staircase.

"Yes," said Polly, "I have."

"All right." And Jasper vanished, and Polly went slowly back, wishing she could be downstairs with all the dear people, instead of trying to comfort this dismal girl. The next moment she was kneeling down by the side of the bed, and trying to get hold of one of Adela's hands. But Adela bounced over to the farther side, and she cried out angrily, "It's all very well for you to say so, because you didn't do it. And everybody likes you. O dear me — tee — hee — boo — hoo!"

"But I've often done things just as bad," confessed Polly, "and, Adela, I've cried like this, too. But Mamsie — oh, Adela! she made me see it was wrong; so I had to stop it, you know."

"How is it wrong?" asked Adela, rolling over, and taking the handkerchief away from one eye enough to see Polly Pepper's face. "I can cry, I guess, if I want to, without asking anybody."

"Oh, no, you can't," said Polly, decidedly. "I mean no one can."

"Why not, pray tell?" said Adela, sniffing very hard. "My eyes are my own, and I shall cry, too, whenever I want to."

"Well, I can't just tell you exactly why you can't cry when you want to," said Polly, afraid she wasn't going to say the right word, "but Mamsie could if she were here. I'll go and call her, Adela." And Polly sprang to her feet. "She'll come, I know."

"Oh, no — no," cried Adela, in mortal alarm. "I don't want her — I mean I'd rather have you. You're a girl; and a woman talking at me scares me."

"Then you mustn't cry if I stay," said Polly, stopping short, and seeing her advantage, "for I surely shall go, Adela," she added firmly, "unless you stop crying."

"O dear me." Adela squirmed all over the bed. "I can't stop — I've always cried as much as I wanted to. O dear me — boo-hoo-hoo! I mean — I'll stop, don't go —" sopping up her wet face with a nervous hand. "See, Pol-*ly!*" for Polly had slipped out of the room. Adela flew off from the bed. "Polly — Polly, Pol-*ly!*" she called, in a piteous little tone.

Polly, halfway down the stairs, looked back. "Oh, you are up," she said, with a smile. "Now that's fine; come." And she held out her hand.

"Mercy me, and O my!" cried Adela. "I can't go looking like this; why, I'm a perfect sight, I know, Polly Pepper! and my nose feels all bunged out of shape and as big!"

"Never mind," said Polly, as reassuringly, "just dash some water over it, and it'll be all right. I'll wait here for you."

So Polly stood on her stair while Adela, bemoaning all the way that she didn't look fit to be seen, and that she was a perfect sight, and she couldn't go down among them all, stumbled back into her room. And pretty soon Polly heard a big splash. "O dear me — oh, what shall I do?"

"What *is* the matter?" cried Polly, deserting her stair, to run in and up to the washstand.

"Just see what I've done," exclaimed Adela, holding out one arm. It was dripping wet, and the water was running off in a stream and down to meet a small puddle where the splash had struck on the floor.

"The pitcher slipped — O dear me — ugh —" cried Adela, wriggling all over.

"Stand still," said Polly, "do, Adela, till I wipe your sleeve dry." And she got the towel and began to sop and to pat Adela's arm.

"It never'll feel dry, it's perfectly awful — ugh — Polly Pepper," declared Adela, twisting away from Polly's fingers; "it's just like a wet snake — ugh — O dear me! and it gives me the creeps."

"You'll have to put on another waist, I do think," said Polly, hanging up the towel, aghast to find herself growing angry at all this delay, and with half a mind to run and leave Adela to herself.

"O dear me, and there's this water running all over the floor," cried Adela, stepping gingerly over the pool, and trying to pick off the wet sleeve from her arm at the same time.

"I'll fix it," said Polly, as cheerily as she could, "while you get your waist on." And she sopped the water up. "There, that's done," she announced with satisfaction; "now do hurry, Adela."

"I can't get out of this old, horrid, wet sleeve," said Adela, very red in the face, and pulling and twitching at it.

"Take care, you'll tear it," warned Polly.

"I don't care if I do," said Adela, peevishly. "O dear me, somebody's coming!" With that she flew into the closet and pulled to the door.

"Why, Polly!" exclaimed Mother Fisher, in surprise, "what is the matter? We are all waiting to go in to dinner."

"Oh, I'm so sorry," began Polly, feeling as if nothing would be so delightful as to have a good cry in Mamsie's arms and tell all the story.

"Well, you must come right away," said Mrs. Fisher. "Why, where is Adela?" looking around the room.

"I'm here," said Adela, from the closet.

"Come out here, Adela," said Mrs. Fisher. So Adela came out, the wet sleeve still on her arm; but she had gotten out of the rest of the waist.

"That's too bad," said Mrs. Fisher; and in a minute Adela's wet arm was free and nicely dried, and a clean waist being found, it was soon on, and then Mother Fisher took up the hairbrush. "We must have this all nice and smooth," she said. And Adela stood still, liking it all very much; and her hair was brushed, much as if she had been Phronsie, and then Mother Fisher released her with a smile. "There, now you are ready," she said.

"She didn't scold a bit," said Adela, going after her with Polly down the stairs, and forgetting her red eyes and swollen nose.

"Our mother never scolds," declared Polly, with her head very high, "never in all this world, Adela Gray."

And at dinner Tom Selwyn looked across the table, and when he caught sight of Adela's face, and saw that someone else could feel as badly as he could, and he guessed the reason, he made up his mind what he was going to do next. And as soon as the meal was over, without giving himself time to think, he marched up to Adela. "Say, I didn't much mind because you laughed, don't you know," and held out his hand.

"I've been crying ever since," said Adela, "and I didn't mean to laugh."

"I know it," said Tom to the first part of her sentence, and looking at her nose. "Well, never mind now, so it's quits, and shake hands."

"I don't know what quits is," said Adela, putting out her hand.

"Oh, it's when things are evened up somehow," said Tom; "not exactly that, but it will do well enough by way of explaining."

"And I'm never going to laugh again at anybody," said Adela, lifting her red eyes.

"Well, come on, don't you want a game of drafts?" said Tom, awkwardly.

"Drafts?" repeated Adela, very much puzzled. "I don't know it."

"Why, what a whopper!" Tom was going to say, but changed it to, "Why, I saw you playing it last night with Polly Pepper."

"Why, no, you didn't," said Adela, not very politely, "that was checkers."

"That's the same thing," said Tom, triumphantly, "only you Americans call it that funny name."

"Well, I think it's a great deal nicer name than drafts," said Adela; "that's silly."

"Well, checkers; that's senseless," retorted Tom, "and, besides, you Americans always say 'nice' at everything." Then he looked at her red eyes and poor little nose, and added kindly, "Well, never mind, call it checkers, then, I don't care; let's have a game," and he rushed for the board.

Mrs. Selwyn looked from her corner where she had taken a book, and smiled to see him playing a game with a girl. Then she nodded over to Jasper, and he smiled back.

And Adela never once thought how she looked. And she beat Tom twice, and that quite set her up. And then for the next three games he routed her men completely off the board. And, strange to say, she kept her temper, and even smiled at the disaster.

"That's a good game." Old Mr. King came up as the last one was going on. "Tom, my boy, you play a fine one."

"And she fights well," said Tom, generously. "She beat me twice."

"You don't say so," exclaimed Mr. King. "Well, that's doing pretty well, Adela, to get ahead of the English lad. But you don't stand much of a chance this time; Tom's got the game, sure." And so it proved in less time than it takes to write it.

And then everybody said "good night" to everybody else; for the Alpine horn would sound at the earliest dawn to waken the sleepers to see the sunrise.

"Mamsie," cried Polly, raising her head suddenly as she cuddled into bed, "supposing we shouldn't hear that horn — just supposing it! Oh, can't I stay awake? Do let me, Mamsie."

"Your Grandfather has made arrangements for us all to be called," said Mrs. Fisher, "so we won't have to depend on the horn, and now you must go to sleep just as fast as ever you can. Then you'll be as bright as a button in the morning, Polly."

"Mamsie," said Polly, "I don't think Grandpapa has kept from doing anything he could to make us happy, do you, Mamsie? not a single thing."

"No," said Mother Fisher, "I don't, Polly."

XXII

POLLY TRIES TO HELP

"Mamsie, what shall we do?" Polly clasped her hands in despair, and looked down on Phronsie, sleeping away as if she meant to take her own time to wake up, regardless of sunrise on the Rigi. "O dear me, and she went to bed so early last night on purpose."

"You go right along, Polly," said Mother Fisher. "Put on your golf cape over your jacket, child, it's dreadfully cold out there. I shall stay with Phronsie, for of course we wouldn't leave her alone with Matilda, and all go off for a nice time."

"No, of course not," cried Polly, in horror at the mere thought.

"And she's in such a nice sleep and so warm, that it's a pity to wake her up," finished Mrs. Fisher.

"O dear me," cried Polly, in distress, "I'd rather stay, Mamsie, and have you go."

"No," said Mrs. Fisher, firmly, "I shall stay, so that is all there is about it, Polly. Now run along, child, and tell Matilda to hurry out too, for she wants to see the sunrise."

Polly still lingered, until her mother looked up in surprise. "Why, Polly," she said, reprovingly.

"O dear me!" exclaimed Polly, "I didn't mean to disobey, Mamsie, I really didn't; I'll go." And setting a kiss on Mother Fisher's black hair, she ran out on unsteady feet, and with all her comfort gone.

When she joined her group it would have been rather hard to distinguish any of them, as everybody was wrapped up in shawls and rugs, if Jasper hadn't been a sort of scout in waiting for her and Mrs. Fisher and Phronsie. And Tom could easily be picked out, for he hung around in Jasper's wake, and besides, he was so very big.

"Where are they?" asked Jasper, looking down the corridor back of her.

"Oh, Mamsie isn't coming, nor Phronsie either, for she's asleep. And Mamsie made me come," finished Polly, dismally.

"O dear me," said Jasper, quite gone in sympathy. Tom Selwyn poked his head forward to hear, but, as it was something quite beyond his powers to help, he thrust his hands into his pockets, and kicked aimlessly on the floor.

"Well, come on, Polly," said Jasper, wishing he could lift the gloom from Polly's face, and feeling quite dismal himself.

Little Dr. Fisher, muffled up in a big plaid shawl so that only his spectacles gleamed in between the folds and his cap, suddenly edged up back of Polly, and dropped the folds away from his ears so that he could hear what was going on. And when the group hurried out of the door, into the cold grey dawn, he was skipping down to his wife's room, in the liveliest way imaginable.

Old Mr. King had gone on ahead with the parson, as he couldn't scramble so fast. And now he met them with, "Well, are you all here — where's Phronsie?"

"Oh, Jasper, I can't tell him," gasped Polly, up on the tiptop bunch of rocks, and trying to be glad of the promise of the beautiful sunrise to come, for everybody agreed that it was apparently to be the best one that had gladdened the hearts of travelers for years. Then she whirled around and stared with all her might, "If there isn't Mamsie coming!"

"As true as you live it is!" cried Jasper, with a good look, and springing down the rocks to help her up. Tom Selwyn plunged after him, getting there first. So in the bustle, nobody answered Mr. King. And he, supposing from the merry chatter that Phronsie was in the midst of it, concluded it best not to interrupt their fun, even if he could make them hear.

"Your father made me come, Polly," said Mrs. Fisher, coming up between the two boys. "But I'd so much rather that he saw it." And her downcast face looked so very much like Polly, that Jasper thought matters hadn't bettered themselves any.

"But, Mamsie," said Polly, creeping up to her with all the comfort she could, "it makes him happy, just as it made you happy to have me go."

"I know it," said Mother Fisher, with a sigh, "but he has so few pleasures, Polly, and he works so hard." And her gaze wandered off to the distant clouds, slowly beginning to break away.

Polly held her breath as they waited and looked, although her heart was sad when the wee little streak of light began to come over in the east.

"Isn't that just beautiful!" exclaimed Jasper, trying to enjoy it as much as he had expected; "see, Polly, the stars seem going out — daylight's coming!"

"I know," said Polly, "so it is." Sure enough, a little strip of gold touched up the leaden sky, and spread slowly.

"See, it's turning pink." Mrs. Selwyn's plain, quiet face glowed. "See, Polly, look at that peak bathed in color."

Just then a little voice said, "Oh, isn't that beautiful!" And whirling around on her rock, Polly saw little Dr. Fisher staggering along with a big bundle in his arms, out of which was peering Phronsie's face.

Mother Fisher had turned too. "Oh, Adoniram!" was all she said, as Polly sprang off to meet them.

"Give her to me," cried Tom Selwyn, of course reaching there first, before either Polly or Jasper; and before Dr. Fisher quite knew how, Phronsie was perched on the broad shoulder, and Tom was prancing up the rocky path as easily as if a bird had lighted on his arm.

"She woke up, luckily," said little Dr. Fisher, "and she's bundled up so there isn't a chance of her taking cold. Wife, this is grand!" He gained her side, and drew her hand under the big shawl.

"You've come just in time," cried Polly, skipping around on her rock to the imminent danger of falling on her nose, and varying the exercises by cuddling Phronsie's toes, done up in a big bundle.

"I declare if Papa Fisher hasn't tied them up in one of the blankets," she announced merrily.

"A blanket is just as good as anything when the sunrise is waiting for you," said the little doctor, coolly.

"Isn't it!" cried Polly, back at him, happily. "Oh – oh!"

Everybody echoed, "Oh-oh!" then stood hushed to silence. A rosy blush spread from peak to peak, and all the shadows fell away. Everything below, towns, villages, lakes, and forests, stood out in the clear cold dawn, and at last the sun burst forth in all his glory.

"I'm so glad that people don't chatter," said Polly, when at last they turned away, for the swift clouds had shut it all out. "Did you see Phronsie's face, Jasper, when that light burst out?"

"Yes, and father's," answered Jasper. "I expect he'd been looking for her; everybody is so bundled up you can hardly find your best friend. And then he saw her."

"Yes, and she saw him and called him," said Polly, "didn't you hear her?"

"Didn't I, though?" said Jasper; "who could help it? Wasn't father pleased when he got up to us, Tom, to think you had Phronsie in such good shape? Phronsie, you're in luck," pinching as much of her toes as the bundle of blanket would allow; "you've got the best place of any of us, up on that perch."

"I like it," said Phronsie, in grave delight, "very much, indeed," surveying them out of the depths of the shawl, "and I wish it needn't stop."

"Well, it must," said Polly, with a sigh. "Dear me, see those people run."

"Well, it's cold," said Jasper; "let's you and I race to the hotel, Polly."

"And the show is over," said Tom, "why shouldn't they run?" as Jasper and Polly set off, and he strode after, getting there nearly as soon.

An hour later, Polly, who couldn't get to sleep again, for a nap before breakfast, went out to the little balcony window just outside her door, where she might sit and write in her journal, and meantime catch any chance view that the grey scudding clouds might afford. In this way she strove to work off the impatience possessing her for the beautiful hour to come after breakfast. "I can hardly believe it now," she thought, and she gave herself a little pinch to see if she were really awake; "it seems too good to be true to think that the great Professor Bauricke is actually going to tell me how to learn to play well!"

"Say," a voice struck upon her ear, "oh, I'm in the most awful distress."

Polly clapped her book to, and looked up.

"O dear, dear!" It was a tall, spare woman with a face that had something about it like Grandma Bascom's. It must have been the cap-frills flapping around her cheeks.

"What can I do for you?" asked Polly, springing up. "Oh, do take my chair and sit down and tell me about it."

"Oh, will you help me? The land! I couldn't set when I'm in such trouble," declared the old woman. "My senses, I should fly off the handle!" Polly, feeling that she was in the presence of some dreadful calamity, stood quite still. "You see, me and my sister — she's in highstrikes now in there." The old woman tossed her head to indicate a room further down the hall, whereat the cap-frills flapped wilder than ever. "Bein' as it belonged to both of us, she feels as bad as I do, but as I was the one that lost it, why it stands to reason I've got to shake around and get it again. Say, will you help me? You've got a pair of bright eyes as ever I see in a head; and what's the good of 'em if you can't help in trouble like this?"

Polly, feeling that her eyes would never forgive her if she didn't let them help on such an occasion, promised.

"What is it you have lost?" she asked.

"Don't you know?" cried the old woman, impatiently. "Mercy me! how many times shall I tell you? My buzzom pin; it was took of Pa when he was a young man and awful handsome, and I didn't want to leave it in the room when we went out, cause somebody might get in, and they'd be sure to want it, so I pinned it on my nightcap strings and it's gone, and I a-gallivanting round on them rocks, a-looking at the sunrise, and I can see that to home all I want to. I must have been crazy."

"Oh, I see; and you want me to go out and help you look for it," said Polly, her brow clearing.

"Of course," assented the old woman, impatiently. "Land, your intellects ain't as bright as your eyes. My sakes! — how many times do you expect me to tell you? I've been a-looking and a-peeking everywhere, but my eyes are old, and I don't dare to tell anyone to help me, for like enough they'd pick it up when I warn't seein', and slip Pa in their pocket, and I never'd see him again."

Polly, feeling, if Pa were slipped in a pocket and carried off, it would be a calamity indeed, said heartily, "I'll get my jacket and cap and come right out."

"She looks honest; I guess I hain't done no harm to tell her about our buzzom pin," said the old woman to herself as Polly disappeared. Mamsie being asleep, Polly could say nothing to her, but feeling that she would allow it if she knew, she threw on her things and ran out to meet the old woman, with a shawl tied over her nightcap and a big long cape on.

"I tell you she's in highstrikes," said the old woman, going down the hall. "That's our room, 37, an' I've seen you an' your folks goin' by, so I feel in some ways acquainted. An' if I don't find Pa, I'll be flabbergasted myself."

"Do let us hurry," said Polly, her mind now only on Pa. So they went down the stairs and out by the door and up the rocky path just where the old woman said she and sister Car'line took when they went out to see the sunrise.

"An' I wish we'd kept in bed," ejaculated Polly's companion. "I most lost my teeth out, they chattered so; and so did Car'line hers. But that wouldn't 'a' been nothin' to losin' Pa, cause we could 'a' got more teeth; but how could we 'a' got him took when he was nineteen and so handsome? There! here we stopped, just at this identical spot!"

"Well, I think we shall find it," said Polly, consolingly. "How did the pin look?" she asked, for the first time remembering to ask, and beginning to poke around in the crevices.

"My land sakes! I never see such a girl for wanting to be told over and over," exclaimed the old woman, irritably, picking up first one ample gaiter and then another to warm her cold toes in her hands. "Haven't I told you he was awful handsome? Well, he had on his blue coat and big brass buttons for one thing, an' his shirt front was ruffled. And —"

"Was it gold around it?" asked Polly, poking away busily.

"Gold? I guess it was; and there was dents in it, where Car'line an' I bit into it when we were babies, 'cause mother give it to us when our teeth was comin' — 'twas better'n a chicken bone, she said."

"Oh," said Polly.

"Well, now you know," said Car'line's sister, "an' don't for mercy's sakes ask anymore useless questions. I'm most sorry I brung you."

"I might go down and get the boys, Jasper and Tom — they'd love to help," said Polly, feeling that she was very much out of place, and there was no hope of finding Pa under the circumstances.

The old woman clutched her arm and held her fast. "Don't you say a single word about any boys," she commanded. "I hate boys," she exploded, "they're the worry of our lives, Car'line and mine, — they get into our garden, and steal all our fruit, and they hang on behind our chaise when we ride out, and keep me a-lookin' round an' slashin' the whip at 'em the whole livelong time; O my — *boys!*"

"What in the world is Polly Pepper doing up on those rocks?" cried Jasper, just spying her. "Come on, Tom, and let's see." And they seized their caps, and buttoned their jackets against the wind which had just sprung up, and dashed off to see for themselves.

"Ugh — you go right away!" screamed Car'line's sister, as their heads appeared over the point of rocks, and shaking both hands fiercely at them.

"Whew!" whistled Jasper, with his eyes in surprise on Polly.

"And what old party are you?" demanded Tom, finding it easy to talk to her, as she was by no means a girl. "And do you own this mountain, anyway?"

"Oh, don't," begged Polly. "And Jasper, if you would go away, please, and not ask any questions."

"All right," said Jasper, swallowing his disappointment not to know. "Come on, Tom, Polly doesn't want us here."

"An' I won't have you here," screamed the old woman, harder than ever. "So get away as soon as you can. Why, you are boys!"

"I know it." Tom bobbed his head at her. "We've always been, ma'am."

"An' boys are good for nothing, an' lazy, an' thieves — yes, I wouldn't trust 'em." So she kept on as they hurried back over the rocky path.

"That's a tiger for you!" ejaculated Tom. Then he stopped and looked back a little anxiously. "Aren't you afraid to leave Polly with her?"

"No," said Jasper; "it would trouble Polly to have us stay." Yet he stopped and looked anxious too. "We will wait here."

And after a while, down came the two searchers — the old woman quite beside herself now, and scolding every bit of the way, — "that she didn't see what bright eyes were for when they couldn't find anything — an' now that Pa'd gone sliding down that mountain, they might as well give up, she an' Car'line" — when a sudden turn in the path brought the boys into view waiting behind the rocks. Then all her fury burst upon them.

"See here, now," cried Tom, suddenly squaring up to her and looking at the face between the nodding cap-frills, "we are ready to take a certain amount of abuse, my friend and I, but we won't stand more, I can tell you."

"Oh, don't," began Polly, clasping her hands. "Oh, Tom, *please* keep still. She doesn't know what she's saying, for she's lost her pin with her father on."

"Hey?" cried Jasper. "Say it again, Polly," while Tom shouted and roared all through Polly's recital.

"Was it an old fright with a long nose in a blue coat and ruffles, and as big as a turnip?" he asked between the shouts. While Polly tried to say, "Yes, I guess so," and Miss Car'line's sister so far overcame her aversion to boys as to seize him by the arm, Tom shook her off like a feather. "See here, old party," he cried, "that ancient pin of yours is reposing in the hotel office at this blessed moment. Jasper and I," indicating his friend, "ran across it on the rocks up there more than an hour ago, and —"

"Oh, Pa's found!" exclaimed the old woman, in a shrill scream of delight, beginning to trot down to the hotel office.

"Yes, it would have been impossible for Pa to have got off this mountain without making a landslide," said Tom, after her.

XXIII

IN THE SHADOW OF THE MATTERHORN

*T*hey had been days at dear Interlaken, walking up and down the *Hoheweg,* of which they never tired, or resting on the benches under the plane and walnut trees opposite their hotel, just sitting still to gaze their fill upon the *Jungfrau.* This was best of all — so Polly and Jasper thought; and Phronsie was content to pass hour after hour there, by Grandpapa's side, and imagine all sorts of pretty pictures and stories in and about the snow-clad heights of the majestic mountain.

And the throng of gaily dressed people sojourning in the big hotels, and the stream of tourists, passed and repassed, with many a curious glance at the stately, white-haired old gentleman and the little yellow-haired girl by his side.

"A perfect beauty!" exclaimed more than one matron, with a sigh for her ugly girls by her side or left at home.

"She's stunning, and no mistake!" Many a connoisseur in feminine loveliness turned for a last look, or passed again for the same purpose.

"Grandpapa," Phronsie prattled on, "that looks just like a little tent up there — a little white tent; doesn't it, Grandpapa dear?"

"Yes, Phronsie," said Grandpapa, happily, just as he would have said "Yes, Phronsie," if she had pointed out any other object in the snowy outline.

"And there's a cunning little place where you and I could creep into the tent," said Phronsie, bending her neck like a meditative bird. "And I very much wish we could, Grandpapa dear."

"We'd find it pretty cold in there," said Grandpapa, "and wish we were back here on this nice seat, Phronsie."

"What makes it so cold up there, Grandpapa, when the sun shines?" asked Phronsie, suddenly. "Say, Grandpapa, what makes it?"

"Oh, it's so far up in the air," answered old Mr. King. "Don't you remember how cold it was up on the Rigi, and that was about nine thousand feet lower?"

"Oh, Grandpapa!" exclaimed Phronsie, in gentle surprise, unable to compass such figures.

Mr. King's party had made one or two pleasant little journeys to the Lauterbrunnen Valley, staying there and at Mürren, and to Grindelwald as well; but they came back to sit on the benches by the walnut and the plane trees, in front of the matchless Jungfrau. "And this is best of all," said Polly.

And so the days slipped by, till one morning, at the breakfast table, Mrs. Selwyn said, "Tomorrow we must say good-bye — my boy and I."

"Hey — what?" exclaimed Mr. King, setting his coffee cup down, not very gently.

"Our vacation cannot be a very long one," said Tom's mother, with a little smile; "there are my father and my two daughters and my other boys in England."

Tom's face was all awry as Mr. King said, "And you mean to say, Mrs. Selwyn, that you really must move on tomorrow?"

"Yes; we really must," she said decidedly. "But oh," and her plain, quiet face changed swiftly, "you cannot know how sorry we shall be to leave your party."

"In that case, Mrs. Fisher," — old Mr. King looked down the table-length to Mamsie, — "we must go too; for I don't intend to lose sight of these nice traveling companions until I am obliged to." Tom's face was one big smile. "Oh, goody!" exclaimed Polly, as if she were no older than Phronsie.

Jasper clapped Tom's back, instead of wasting words.

"So we will all proceed to pack up without more ado after breakfast. After all, it is wiser to make the move now, for we are getting so that we want to take root in each place."

"You just wait till you get to Zermatt," whispered Polly to Phronsie, who, under cover of the talk buzzing around the table, had confided to her that she didn't want to leave her beautiful mountain. "Grandpapa is going to take us up to the Gorner Grat, and there you can see another mountain, — oh, so near! he says it seems almost as if you could touch it. And it's all covered with snow, Phronsie, too!"

"Is it as big as my mountain here?" asked Phronsie.

"Yes, bigger, a thousand feet or more," answered Polly, glad that she had looked it up.

"Is it?" said Phronsie. "Every mountain is bigger, isn't it, Polly?"

"It seems to be," said Polly, with a little laugh.

"And has it a little white tent on the side, just like my mountain here?" asked Phronsie, holding Polly's arm as she turned off to catch the chatter of the others.

"Oh, I suppose so," answered Polly, carelessly. Then she looked up and caught Mamsie's eye, and turned back quickly. "At any rate, Phronsie, it's all peaked on the top — oh, almost as sharp as a needle — and it seems to stick right into the blue sky, and there are lots and lots of other mountains — oh, awfully high, — and the sun shines up there a good deal, and it's too perfectly lovely for anything, Phronsie Pepper."

"Then I want to go," decided Phronsie. "I do so want to see that white needle, Polly."

"Well, eat your breakfast," said Polly, "because you know we all have ever so much to do today to get off."

"Yes, I will," declared Phronsie, attacking her cold chicken and roll with great vigor.

"It seems as if the whole world were at Zermatt," said the parson, looking out from the big piazza crowded with the hotel people, out to the road in front, with every imaginable tourist passing and repassing. Donkeys were being driven up, either loaded down to their utmost with heavy bags and trunks, or else waiting to receive on their patient backs the heavier people. Phronsie never could see the poor animals, without such distress coming in her face that everyone in the party considered it his or her bounden duty to comfort and reassure her. So this time it was Tom's turn to do so.

"Oh, don't you worry," he said, looking down into her troubled little face where he sat on the piazza railing swinging his long legs, "they like it, those donkeys do!"

"Do they?" asked Phronsie, doubtfully.

"Yes, indeed," said Tom, with a gusto, as if he wished he were a donkey, and in just that very spot, "it gives them a chance to see things, and to hear things, too, don't you know?" went on Tom, at his wits' end to know how he was going to come out of his sentences.

"Oh," said Phronsie, yet she sighed as she saw the extremely fat person just being hauled up to a position on a very small donkey's back.

"You see, if they don't like it," said Tom, digging his knife savagely into the railing, "they have a chance to kick up their heels and unsettle that heavy party."

"O dear me!" exclaimed Phronsie, in great distress, "that would hurt the poor woman, Tom."

"Well, it shows that the donkey likes it," said Tom, with a laugh, "because he doesn't kick up his heels."

"And so," ran on Tom, "why, we mustn't worry, you and I, if the donkey doesn't. Just think," — he made a fine diversion by pointing with his knife-blade up to the slender spire of the Matterhorn — "we're going up on a little jaunt tomorrow, to look into that fellow's face."

Phronsie got out of her chair to come and stand by his side. "I like that white needle," she said, with a gleeful smile. "Polly said it was nice, and I like it."

"I should say it was," declared Tom, with a bob of his head. "Phronsie, I'd give, I don't know what, if I could climb up there." He thrust his knife once more into the railing, where it stuck fast.

"Don't." begged Phronsie, her hand on his sleeve, "go up that big white needle, Tom."

"No, I won't; it's safe to promise that," he said grimly, with a little laugh. "Good reason why; because I can't. The little mother wouldn't sleep nights just to think of it, and I promised the granddaddy that I wouldn't so much as think of it, and here I am breaking my word; but I can't help it." He twitched his knife out suddenly, sprawled off from the railing, and took several hasty strides up and down the piazza.

"Well, that's all right, Phronsie," he said, coming back to get astride the railing again; this time he turned a cold shoulder on Phronsie's "white needle." "Now, tomorrow, we'll have no end of fun." And he launched forth on so many and so varied delights, that Phronsie's pleased little laugh rang out again and again, bringing rest to many a wearied traveler, tired with the sights, sounds, and scenes of a European journey.

"I wish we could stay at this nice place," said Phronsie, the next morning, poking her head out over the side of the car, as it climbed off from the Riffelalp station.

"Take care, child," said Grandpapa, with a restraining hand.

"You would want to stop at every place," said Polly, from the seat in front, with a gay little laugh. "And we never should get on at that rate. But then I am just as bad," she confessed.

"So am I," chimed in Jasper. "Dear me, how I wanted to get a chance to sketch some of those magnificent curves and rapids and falls in the Visp River coming up."

"Oh, that dear, delicious Visp River!" echoed Polly, while Adela began to bemoan that it was the best thing they had seen, and the car whizzed them by so fast, she couldn't do a thing — O dear!

"I got some snap-shots, but I don't believe they are good for anything," said Jasper, "just from the pure perversity of the thing."

"Take my advice," said Tom, lazily leaning forward, "and don't bother with a camera anyway."

"As if you expected anyone to take up with such a piece of advice," ejaculated Jasper, in high disdain. "Say something better than that, Tom, if you want to be heard."

"Oh, I don't expect to be heard, or listened to in the slightest," he said calmly. "Anybody who will trot round with a Kodak hanging to his neck by a villainous strap — can't be —"

"Who's got a villainous strap hanging to his neck?" cried Jasper, while the rest shouted as he picked at the fern-box thus hanging to Tom.

"Oh, that's quite a different thing," declared Tom, his face growing red.

"I know; one is a Kodak, and the other is a fern-box," said Jasper, nodding. "I acknowledge they are different," and they all burst out laughing again.

"Well, at least," said Tom, joining in the laugh, "you must acknowledge, too, that I go off by myself and pick up my wild flowers and green things, and I'm not bothering round focusing every living thing and pointing my little machine at every freak in nature that I see."

"All right," said Jasper, good-naturedly, "but you have the strap round your neck all the same, Tom."

And Phronsie wanted to stay at the Riffelberg just as much; and old Mr. King was on the point of saying, "Well, we'll come up here for a few days, Phronsie," when he remembered Mrs. Selwyn and her boy, and how they must get on. Instead, he cleared his throat, and said, "We shall see it after dinner, child," and Phronsie smiled, well contented.

But when she reached the Corner Grat station, and took Grandpapa's hand, and began to ascend the bridle path to the hotel, she couldn't contain herself, and screamed right out, "Oh, Grandpapa, I'd rather stay here."

"It *is* beautiful, isn't it?" echoed old Mr. King, feeling twenty years younger since he started on his travels. "Well, well, child, I'm glad you like it," looking down into her beaming little face.

"You are very much to be envied, sir. I can't help speaking to you and telling you so," said a tall, sober-looking gentleman, evidently an English curate off on his vacation, as he caught up with him on the ascent, where they had paused at one of the look-offs, "for having that child as company, and those other young people."

"You say the truth," replied old Mr. King, cordially; "from the depths of my heart I pity anyone who hasn't some children to take along when going abroad. But then they wouldn't be little Peppers," he added, under his breath, as he bowed and turned back to the view.

"There's dear Monte Rosa," cried Polly, enthusiastically. "Oh, I just love her."

"And there's Castor and Pollux," said Jasper.

"And there's the whole of them," said Tom, disposing of the entire range with a sweep of his hand. "Dear me, what a lot there are, to be sure. It quite tires one."

"Oh, anybody but a cold-blooded Englishman!" exclaimed Jasper, with a mischievous glance, "to travel with."

"Anything on earth but a gushing American!" retorted Tom, "to go round the world with."

"I wish I could sketch a glacier," bemoaned Adela, stopping every minute or two, as they wound around the bridle path, "but I can't; I've tried ever so many times."

"Wait till we get to the *Mer de Glace,*" advised Tom. "You can sit down in the middle of it, and sketch away all you want to."

"Well, I'm going to," said Adela, with sudden determination. "I don't care; you can all laugh if you want to."

"You can sketch us all," suggested Jasper, "for we shall have horrible old stockings on."

"I shan't have horrible old stockings on," said Adela, in a dudgeon, sticking out her foot. "I wear just the same stockings that I do at home, at school in Paris, and they are quite nice."

"Oh, I mean you'll have to put on coarse woolen ones that the peasant women knit on purpose, — we all shall have to do the same, on over our shoes," explained Jasper.

"O dear me!" cried Adela, in dismay.

"And I think we shall slip and slide a great deal worse with those things tied on our feet, than to go without any," said Polly, wrinkling up her brows at the idea.

"'Twouldn't be safe to go without them," said Jasper, shaking his head, "unless we had nails driven in our shoes."

"I'd much rather have the nails," cried Polly, "oh, much rather, Jasper."

"Well, we'll see what father is going to let us do," said Jasper.

"Wasn't that fun snowballing — just think — in July," cried Polly, craning her neck to look back down the path toward the Riffelberg station.

"Did you pick up some of that snow?" asked Adela.

"Didn't we, though!" exclaimed Jasper. "I got quite a good bit in my fist."

"My ball was such a little bit of a one," mourned Polly; "I scraped up all I could, but it wasn't much."

"Well, it did good execution," said Tom; "I got it in my eye."

"Oh, did it hurt you?" cried Polly, in distress, running across the path to walk by his side.

"Not a bit," said Tom. "I tried to find some to pay you back, and then we had to fly for the cars."

The plain, quiet face under the English bonnet turned to Mrs. Fisher as they walked up the path together. "I cannot begin to tell you what gratitude I am under to you," said Tom's mother, "and to all of you. When I think of my father, I am full of thankfulness. When I look at my boy, the goodness of God just overcomes me in leading me to your party. May I tell you of ourselves some time, when a good opportunity offers for a quiet talk?"

"I'd like nothing better," said Mother Fisher, heartily. "If there is one person I like more than another, who isn't of our family, or any of our home friends, it's Mrs. Selwyn," she had confided to the little doctor just a few days before. "She hasn't any nonsense about her, if she is an earl's daughter."

"Earl's daughter," sniffed the little doctor, trying to slip a collar button into a refractory binding. "Dear me, now that's gone — no, 'tisn't — that's luck," as the button rolled off into a corner of the bureau-top where it was easily captured.

"Let me do that for you, Adoniram," said Mother Fisher, coming up to help him.

"I guess you'll have to, wife, if it's done at all," he answered, resigning himself willingly to her hands; "the thing slips and slides like all possessed. Well, now, I was going to say that I wouldn't hate a title so much, if there was a grain of common sense went along with it. And that Mrs. Selwyn just saves the whole lot of English nobility, and makes 'em worth speaking to, in my opinion."

And after they had their dinner, and were scattered in groups in the bright sunshine, sitting on the wooden benches by the long tables, or taking photographs, or watching through the big glass some mountain climbers on one of the snowy spurs of the Matterhorn, "the good opportunity for a quiet talk" came about.

"Now," said Mother Fisher, with a great satisfaction in her voice, "may we sit down here on this bench, Mrs. Selwyn, and have that talk?"

Tom's mother sat down well pleased, and folding her hands in her lap, this earl's daughter, mistress of a dozen languages, as well as mistress of herself on all occasions, began as simply and with as much directness as a child.

"Well, you know my father. Let me tell you, aside from the eccentricities, that are mere outside matters, and easily explained, if you understood the whole of his life, a kinder man never lived, nor a more reasonable one. But it was a misfortune that he had to be left so much alone, as since my mother's death a dozen years ago has happened. It pained me much." A shadow passed over her brow, but it was gone again, and she smiled, and her eyes regained their old placid look. "I live in Australia with my husband, where my duty is, putting the boys as fast as they were old enough, and the little girls as well, into English schools. But Tom has always been with my father at the vacations, for he is his favorite, as of course was natural, for he is the eldest. And though you might not believe it, Mrs. Fisher, my father was always passionately fond of the boy."

"I do believe it," said Mother Fisher, quietly, and she put her hand over the folded ones. Mrs. Selwyn unclasped hers, soft and white, to draw within them the toil-worn one.

"Now, that's comfortable," she said, with another little smile.

"And here is where his eccentricity became the most dangerous to the peace of mind of our family," continued Mrs. Selwyn. "My father seemed never able to discover that he was doing the lad harm by all sorts of indulgence and familiarity with him, a sort of hail-fellow-well-met way that surprised me more than I can express, when I discovered it on my last return visit to my old home. My father! who never tolerated anything but respect from all of us, who were accustomed to despotic government, I can assure you, was allowing Tom! — well, you were with him on the steamer," she broke off abruptly. The placid look was gone again in a flash.

"Yes," said Mother Fisher, her black eyes full of sympathy; "don't let that trouble you, dear Mrs. Selwyn; Tom was pure gold down underneath — we saw that — and the rest is past."

"Ah," — the placid look came back as quickly — "that is my only comfort — that you did. For father told the whole, not sparing himself. Now he sees things in the right light; he says because your young people taught it to him. And he was cruelly disappointed because you couldn't come down to visit him in his home."

"We couldn't," said Mother Fisher, in a sorry voice, at seeing the other face.

"I understand — quite," said Tom's mother, with a gentle pressure of the hand she held. "And then the one pleasure he had was in picking out something for Polly."

"Oh, if the little red leather case *had* gone back to the poor old man!" ran through Mother Fisher's mind, possessing it at once.

"I don't think his judgment was good, Mrs. Fisher, in the selection," said Mrs. Selwyn, a small pink spot coming on either cheek; "but he loves Polly, and wanted to show it."

"And he was so good to think of it," cried Mother Fisher, her heart warming more and more toward the little old earl.

"And as he couldn't be turned from it, and his health is precarious if he is excited, why, there was nothing to be done about it. And then he insisted that Tom and I come off for a bit of a run on the Continent, the other children being with him. And as my big boy" — here a loving smile went all over the plain face, making it absolutely beautiful — "had worried down deep in his heart over the past, till I was more troubled than I can tell you, why, we came. And then God was good — for then we met you! Oh, Mrs. Fisher!"

She drew her hands by a sudden movement away, and put them on Mother Fisher's shoulders. And then that British matron, rarely demonstrative with her own children, even, leaned over and kissed Polly's mother.

"I can't see why it's so warm up here," said Polly, racing over to their bench, followed by the others. "Dear me, it's fairly hot." And she pulled off her jacket.

"Don't do that, Polly," said her mother.

"Oh, Mamsie, it's so very hot," said Polly; but she thrust her arms into the sleeves and pulled it on again.

"I know; but you've been running," said Mrs. Fisher, "and have gotten all heated up."

"Well, it's perfectly splendid to travel to places where we can run and race," said Polly, in satisfaction, throwing herself down on the rocks. The others all doing the same thing, Mr. King and the Parson and Mrs. Henderson found them, and pretty soon the group was a big one. "Well, well, we are all here together, no — where is Mrs. Gray?" asked Mr. King, presently.

"She is resting in the hotel," said Mother Fisher, "fast asleep I think by this time."

"Yes," said Adela, "she is. I just peeked in on her, and she hasn't moved where you tucked her up on the lounge."

"Grandpapa," asked Polly, suddenly, from the center of the group, "what makes it so very warm up here, when we are all surrounded by snow?"

"You ask me a hard thing," said old Mr. King. "Well, for one thing, we are very near the Italian border; those peaks over there, you know, — follow my walking-stick as I point it, — are in sunny Italy."

"Well, it is just like sunny Italy up here," said Polly, "I think," blinking, and pulling her little cap over her eyes.

"It's all the Italy you will get in the summer season," said Grandpapa. "You must wait for cold weather before I take one of you there."

XXIV

THE ROUND ROBIN

"*D*ear me, how the summer is going!" mourned Polly, as they caught on the return journey the last glimpse of the roaring, tumbling Visp, and not all the craning of the necks could compass another view, as the cars drew them away from the rushing river.

"Never mind, Polly," said Jasper, "there's all next summer; and after our winter in Dresden, and all our hard work over music, won't it be fine, though, to jaunt round again?" and his eyes glistened.

"Dresden!" echoed Polly, sitting quite straight with very red cheeks; — "oh, Jasper!"

The magic word, "Dresden," had unlocked visions of months of future delight, bringing back every word of dear Herr Bauricke; all the instruction he had given her, on those happy days at Lucerne, that Polly felt quite sure were engraven deep on her heart to last forever and ever.

"And won't I study, though!" exclaimed Polly, to herself, "and make the professor that Herr Bauricke has engaged for me, glad that he teaches me, oh, won't I!"

"Well, I'm sorry the summer is going," said Adela, "because then I've got to leave you at Paris, and go into school."

"But you like your school," said Polly, brightly, "you've said so a dozen times, Adela."

"Yes, I do," said Adela, "and I've got some sketches to take back, and Mademoiselle will be glad of that."

"And you'll go on drawing and painting until you get to be a great artist," ran on Polly, enthusiastically, "and then we'll see something you've done, in the Louvre, maybe."

"The Louvre!" cried Adela; "O dear me, Polly Pepper."

"I don't care," said Polly, recklessly, pushing back the little rings of brown hair from her brow, "they'll be good enough, the pictures you are going to do, to put into the Louvre, anyway, Adela Gray."

Tom Selwyn had been very sober during all this merry chatter; and now in his seat across the narrow aisle, he drummed his heels impatiently on the floor. His mother looked over at him, and slipping out of her seat, went over to him. "Any room here, Tom, for mother?" she said.

"Oh, – ah, – I should say so!" Tom slipped out, gave her the window seat, then flew back.

"Now, this is comfy," observed Mrs. Selwyn, as the train sped on. "Tom, see here!"

"What's up, little mother?" asked Tom, in surprise, at her unusual manner.

"It's just this, Tom. You know we are going to Chamonix and up the *Mer de Glace* with Mr. King's party."

Tom bobbed his head, not allowing himself to exclaim, "But that will be only a short journey, now, and we must soon say 'good-bye.'"

"Well, I've been thinking that I should like to go on to Geneva, and to Paris," continued Mrs. Selwyn, "only you dislike Paris so much, Tom," she added.

"Oh, you're the bulliest – I mean – excuse me – you're no end a brick – oh, I mean – I can't say what I mean," brought up Tom, in despair. And he ran one long arm around her neck very much to the detriment of her neat collar.

"Then you can overcome your dislike to Paris enough to go there?" asked his mother, with a little twinkle in her eye.

"My dislike!" roared Tom, "O dear me!" as everybody looked around. "Why, I just love Paris!" he finished in an awful whisper, close to the plain, black bonnet.

When the news was circulated, as it was pretty soon, that the party was not to be broken into at all till Paris was a completed story, the jubilation was such as to satisfy even Tom. And as this particular party had the car entirely to themselves, it wasn't so very dreadful as it seems, and the elder members allowed indulgent smiles at it all.

That night in the marketplace at Martigny, Jasper, who was ahead with his father, ran back to Polly, and the others lingering behind. "Oh, do hurry," he begged, "it's the prettiest sight!"

"Oh, what is it?" cried Polly, as they scampered off.

There, in the center of the marketplace, was a ring of little girls, hand-in-hand, singing a little French song, and going round and round in a circle. They were of all ages and sizes, the littlest one in a blue pinafore, being about three years of age, and so chubby she had to be helped along continually by a big girl, evidently her sister. This big sister stopped the ring game, every now and then, to kiss the round face by the side of her gown; an example that was followed by so many of the other girls, that the game seemed to be never quite finished. And once in a while, big sister would pick up the chubby, little, blue-pinafored maiden and carry her through a considerable portion of the game, then down she would put her on her two chubby feet, and away they all circled without any break in the proceedings at all.

"Oh! isn't it 'Oats, Peas, Beans, and Barley grow'?" cried Polly, as they watched them intently.

"Ever so much like it," said Tom. "See those boys; now they are going to make trouble."

"Oh, they shan't!" declared Polly. "O dear me!" as one boy drew near, on the side next to the travelers, and watching his chance, picked at a flying apron or two. But the ring of girls paid no more attention to him, than they had to any other outside matters, being wholly absorbed in the game. So Polly and the others breathed freely again.

But up came another boy. "O dear me!" cried Polly, aghast. When number three put in an appearance, she gave up all hope at once.

"They're jealous chaps," cried Tom, "and are vexed because they can't get into the game! Hear them jeer!" And his long arm went out and picked a jacket-end of an urchin, who, incautiously regarding such quiet travelers as not worth minding, had hovered too near, while trying to tease the girls.

"Here, you, sir," cried Tom, with a bit of a shake, and a torrent of remarkably good French not to be disregarded; then he burst into a laugh. And the urchin laughed too, thinking this much better fun to tussle with the tall lad, than to hang around a parcel of girls. And presently a woman came and took little blue pinafore off, and then the rest of the girls unclasped their hands, and the ring melted away, and the game was over.

"I'm glad the girls over here have fun," said Polly, as Grandpapa and his party moved off. "Isn't it nice to think they do?"

"It isn't much matter where you live, there's a good deal to be gotten out of life; if you only know how," said the parson, thinking busily of the little brown house.

Two or three days of rest at Martigny put everybody in good shape, and gave them all a bit of time to pick up on many little things that were behindhand. Tom looked over all his floral treasures, with their last additions made at the Riffelalp, and discarded such as hadn't pressed well. And Jasper and Polly rushed up to date with their journals, and wrote letters home; and Adela worked up her studies and sketches.

Tom looked on silently when Polly and Jasper were scraping their pens in a lively fashion in the little writing room of the hotel. "That's my third letter, Polly," announced Jasper, on the other side of the table. "Now, I am going to begin on Joel's."

"One, two," said Polly, counting, "why, I thought I'd written three; well, this one is most finished, Jasper."

"Yes," said Jasper, glancing over at her, "is that your last page, Polly?"

"Yes," said Polly, hurrying away. Then she thought of what Mamsie had said, and slackened her speed.

Tom cleared his throat, and tried to speak, but the words wouldn't come nicely, so he burst out, "I say, I wish you'd write to my granddaddy, both of you," and then he stood quite still, and very red in the face.

Polly looked up quickly, her pen dropping from her fingers, and Jasper deserted his fourth letter and stared.

"Why," said Polly, finding her tongue, "we wouldn't dare, Tom Selwyn."

"Dare!" said Tom, delighted to think that no terrible result had really ensued from his words, that after they were out, had scared him mightily. "Oh, if you knew granddaddy!" And he sank into a chair by the table, and played with the heap of picture postal cards that Polly was going to address next.

"We might," said Polly, slowly, "write a letter, all of us. A kind of a Round Robin thing, you know, and send that."

"So we could," cried Jasper; "how would that do, Tom?"

"The very thing!" exclaimed Tom, striking his hand so heavily on the table, that for a minute it looked as if the ink-bottle hopped.

"Take care, there's no reason you should knock things over because you are overjoyed," cried Jasper, gaily. "Well, let's leave our letters today, Polly, and set to on the Round Robin."

"All right," said Polly, glad to think there was anything she could really do to please the little old earl, "but would your mother like it, Tom?" She stopped slowly in putting her unfinished letter into the little writing-case, and looked at him.

"If you think there's a shadow of doubt on that score, I'd best run and ask her now." Tom got himself out of the chair, and himself from the room, and in an incredibly short space of time, back there he was. "My mother says, 'Thank Polly for thinking of it; it will do father more good than anything else could possibly do.'"

"I don't suppose you want anymore answer," said Tom, quite radiant, and looking down at Polly.

"No, only I didn't think first of it," said Polly, in a distressed little tone.

"Why, Polly Pepper!" exclaimed Tom, "I certainly heard you say 'Round Robin,' when I'll venture to say not a soul of us had even thought of it; we certainly hadn't said so."

"Well, you spoke of the letter first," said Polly, unwilling to take the credit for all the comfort going to the little old earl, "and I shall tell your mother so, Tom."

"But I didn't say 'Round Robin,'" persisted Tom, "wasn't smart enough to think of it."

"And let's get to work," cried Jasper, huddling up his three letters. "I'll post yours, too, Polly; give them here."

"O dear, my stamps are all gone," said Polly, peering into the little box in one corner of her writing-case.

"I've plenty," said Jasper, hurrying off; "I'll stick on two for you."

"Oh, no, Jasper," cried Polly, after him, "you know Mamsie would not allow me to borrow."

"It isn't borrowing," said Jasper, turning back slowly. "I'll give them to you, Polly."

"But Mamsie said when we started I should get my stamps when I needed them," said Polly. "You know she did, Jasper."

"Yes, she did," said Jasper, uncomfortably. Then his face brightened, and he said, "And she's right, Polly," while Polly fished a franc out of Joel's little money-bag that hung at her belt. "Do get the stamps, please, Jasper, and put them on," as he took up her two letters. And she gave the bag a little pat for Joel's sake, wishing it was his stubby black hair that her fingers could touch.

"Dear me, you are dreadfully particular about taking two postage stamps, seems to me," said Adela, who had taken that time, as she hadn't any letters to write, to work up one of her studies from memory of the Visp.

Tom's blue eyes flashed dangerously, then he cleared his throat, whistled, and walked to the window.

"I don't know where we are going to get nice white paper for our 'Round Robin,'" said Polly, leaning her elbows on the table, and her chin in her hands.

"I know!" ejaculated Tom, whirling on his heel, and dashing out. In he came, swinging three or four goodly sheets. "Filched 'em out of the old woman's room," he said.

"Oh, Tom!" began Polly.

"I mean, the housekeeper — matron — concièrgerie — whatever you call the gentle lady who runs this house — was fortunately at our desk where she has the pleasure of making up our bills, and I worked on her feelings till she parted with 'em," explained Tom.

"Oh!" said Polly; "well, I'm glad she gave them."

"Never you fear but what they'll be in our bills, Polly," said Tom, who couldn't believe by this time that he hadn't always known Polly Pepper.

"It's dreadfully thin paper," said Adela, critically, getting off from the sofa to pick at one corner of the sheet Polly was beginning to divide.

"I'm glad we have any," hummed Polly, happily.

"Thank your stars you have," said Tom, as gaily. And Jasper running in, the table was soon surrounded by the makers of the Round Robin, Adela deserting her sketch-book and pulling up a chair.

"And Phronsie must come," said Polly, snipping away to get the paper the right width. "O dear me, I can't cut it straight. Do you please finish it, Jasper."

"That's all right," said Jasper, squinting at it critically, "only — just this edge wants a little bit of trimming, Polly." And he snipped off the offending points.

"I'll fetch Phronsie," cried Tom, springing off.

"And hurry," cried Polly and Jasper, together, after him.

"Polly," said Phronsie, as Tom came careering in with her on his shoulder. "I want to write, too, I do," she cried, very much excited.

"Of course, you shall, Pet. That's just what we want you for," cried Polly, clearing a place on the table; "there, do pull up a chair, Jasper."

"Now, Phronsie, I think you would better begin, for you are the littlest," and she flapped the long strip down in front of her.

"Oh, Polly, you begin," begged Tom.

"No, I think Phronsie ought to," said Polly, shaking her head.

"I want Polly to," said Phronsie, wriggling away from the pen that Polly held out alluringly.

"But Polly wants you to," said Jasper. "I really would, Phronsie dear, to please her."

To please Polly, being what Phronsie longed for next to pleasing Mamsie, she gave a small sigh and took the pen in unsteady fingers.

"Wait a minute, Phronsie!" exclaimed Polly, in dismay, "I believe we've made a mistake, Jasper, and got the wrong sheet." And Polly turned off with him to examine the rest of the paper.

Phronsie, who hadn't heard what Polly said, her small head being full of the responsibility of beginning the important letter, and considering, since it was to be done, it was best to have it over with as soon as possible, fell to scribbling the letters as fast as she could, all of them running down hill.

"Well, I'm glad to see that we haven't made any mistake," cried Polly, turning back in relief. "Oh, Phronsie, you haven't begun!"

She spoke so sharply that Phronsie started, and a little drop of ink trembling on the point of her pen concluded to hop off. So it did and jumped down on the clean white paper to stare up at them all like a very bad black eye.

"Oh, see what she's written!" cried Polly, quite aghast, and tumbling into her chair, she pointed at the top.

"Deer Mister Erl," scrawled clear across the top.

"I didn't — mean — oh, you said do it, Polly." Phronsie threw herself out of her chair, and over into Polly's lap, burrowing and wailing piteously.

"O dear me, how could I say anything?" cried Polly, overcome with remorse and patting Phronsie's yellow hair; "but it is so very dreadful. O dear me! Phronsie, there, there, don't cry. O dear me!"

Tom's mouth trembled. "It's all right. Granddaddy'll like it," he said.

"Oh, Tom Selwyn," gasped Polly, looking up over Phronsie's head, "you don't suppose we'd let that letter go."

"I would," said Tom, coolly, running his hands in his pockets. "I tell you, you don't know my granddaddy. He's got lots of fun in him," he added.

"Phronsie," said Jasper, rushing around the table, "you are making Polly sick. Just look at her face."

Phronsie lifted her head where she had burrowed it under Polly's arm. When she saw that Polly's round cheeks were really quite pale, she stopped crying at once. "Are you sick, Polly?" she asked, in great concern.

"I shan't be," said Polly, "if you won't cry anymore, Phronsie."

"I won't cry anymore," declared Phronsie, wiping off the last tear trailing down her nose. "Then you will be all well, Polly?"

"Then I shall be all as well as ever," said Polly, kissing the wet little face.

When they got ready to begin on the letter again, it was nowhere to be found, and Tom had disappeared as well.

"He took it out," said Adela, for the first time finding her tongue. "I saw him while you were all talking."

While they were wondering over this and were plunged further yet in dismay, Tom came dancing in, waving the unlucky sheet of the Round Robin over his head. "My mother says," he announced in triumph, "that father will get no end of fun over that if you let it go. It will cheer him up."

So that ended the matter, although Polly, who dearly loved to be elegant, had many a twinge whenever her eye fell on the letter at which Phronsie was now laboring afresh.

"We must put in little pictures," said Polly, trying to make herself cheery as the work went busily on.

"Polly, you always do think of the best things!" exclaimed Jasper, beaming at her, which made her try harder than ever to smile. "I wouldn't feel so badly, Polly," he managed to whisper, when Phronsie was absorbed with her work; "he'll like it probably just as father did the gingerbread boy."

"But that was different," groaned Polly.

"Pictures!" Tom Selwyn was saying, "oh, there's where I can come in fine with assistance. I'm no good in a letter." And again he rushed from the room.

"That's three times that boy has gone out," announced Adela, "and he joggles the table awfully when he starts. And he made me cut clear into that edge. See, Polly." She was trimming the third strip of paper, for the Round Robin was to be pasted together and rolled up when it was all done.

"He seems to accomplish something every time he goes," observed Jasper, dryly. "Halloo, just look at him now!"

In came Tom with a rush, and turned a small box he held in his hand upside down on the table.

"O dear me!" exclaimed Adela, as her scissors slipped, "now you've joggled the table again!" Then she caught Polly's eye. "Aren't those pictures pretty?" she burst out awkwardly.

"Aren't they so!" cried Tom, in satisfaction, while Polly oh-ed and ah-ed, and Phronsie dropped her pen suddenly making a second blot; only as good fortune would have it, it was so near the edge that they all on anxious examination decided to trim the paper down, and thus get rid of it.

"I don't see how you got so many," said Jasper, in admiration, his fingers busy with the heap.

"Oh, I've picked 'em up here and there," said Tom. "I began because I thought the kids at home might like 'em. And then it struck me I'd make a book like yours."

"Well, do save them now," said Jasper, "and we'll give some of our pictures, though the prettiest ones are in our books," he added regretfully.

"Rather not — much obliged," Tom bobbed his thanks. "I want to donate something to granddaddy, and I tell you I'm something awful at a letter."

"All right, seeing you wish it so," said Jasper, with a keen look at him, "and these are beauties and no mistake; we couldn't begin to equal them."

When the letter was finally unrolled and read to Grandpapa, who strayed into the reading room to see what Phronsie was doing, it certainly was a beauty. Picture after picture, cut from railroad guide books, illustrated papers, and it seemed to Jasper gathered as if by magic, with cunning little photographs, broke up the letter, and wound in and out with funny and charming detail of some of their journey.

"I wrote that all myself," hummed Phronsie, smoothing her gown, in great satisfaction, pointing to the opening of the letter.

"O dear me!" exclaimed Polly, softly, for she couldn't even yet get over that dreadful beginning.

"The rest of it is nice," whispered Jasper, "and I venture to say, he'll like that the best of all."

Mr. King thought so, too, and he beamed at Phronsie. "So you did," he cried; "now that's fine. I wish you'd write me a letter sometime."

"I'm going to write you one now," declared Phronsie. Since Grandpapa wanted anything, it was never too soon to begin work on it.

"Do," cried old Mr. King, in great satisfaction. So he put down the Round Robin, Adela crying out that she wanted her grandmother to see it; and Polly saying that Mamsie, and Papa-Doctor, and the Parson and Mrs. Henderson must see it; "and most important of all," said Jasper, breaking into the conversation, "Mrs. Selwyn must say if it is all right to go."

At that Polly began to have little "creeps" as she always called the shivers. "O dear me!" she exclaimed again, and turned quite pale.

"You don't know my mother," exclaimed Tom, "if you think she won't like that. She's got lots of fun in her, and she always sees the sense of a thing."

"But she's so nice," breathed Polly, who greatly admired Mrs. Selwyn, "and so elegant."

Tom bobbed his head and accepted this as a matter of course. "That's the very reason she understands things like a shot — and knows how to take 'em," he said; "and I tell you, Polly," he declared with a burst of confidence that utterly surprised him, "I'd rather have my mother than any other company I know of; she's awful good fun!"

"I know it," said Polly, brightly, with a little answering smile. "Well, I hope she'll like it."

"Never you fear," cried Tom, seizing the Round Robin; and waving it over his head, it trailed off back of him like a very long and broad ribbon. "Come on, now, all fall into line!"

"Take care!" cried Jasper, as he ran after with Polly and Adela, "if you dare to tear that, sir!" while Phronsie at the big table labored away on her letter, Grandpapa sitting by to watch the proceedings, with the greatest interest.

And one look at Mrs. Selwyn's face, as she read that Round Robin, was enough for Polly! And then to post it.

"Dear me," said Polly, when that important matter was concluded, "suppose anything should happen to it now, before it gets there!"

XXV

ON THE 'MER DE GLACE'

"Well, we can't all get into one carriage," said Polly, on the little brick-paved veranda of the hotel, "so what is the use of fussing, Adela?"

"I don't care," said Adela, "I'm going to ride in the same carriage with you, Polly Pepper, so there!" and she ran her arm in Polly's, and held it fast.

Jasper kicked his heel impatiently against one of the pillars where the sweetbrier ran; then he remembered, and stopped suddenly, hoping nobody had heard. "The best way to fix it is to go where we are put," he said at last, trying to speak pleasantly.

"No, I'm going with Polly," declared Adela, perversely, holding Polly tighter than ever.

"I'm going with you, Polly," cried Phronsie, running up gleefully, "Grandpapa says I may."

"Well, so am I," announced Adela, loudly.

Tom Selwyn gave a low whistle, and thrust his hands in his pockets, his great and only comfort on times like these.

"Anything but a greedy girl," he sniffed in lofty contempt.

Meanwhile the horses were being put in the carriages, the stable men were running hither and thither to look to buckle and strap, and a lot of bustle was going on that at any other time would have claimed the boys. Now it fell flat, as a matter of interest.

"Halloo — k-lup!" The drivers gave the queer call clear down in their throats, and hopped to their places on the three conveyances, and with a rattle and a flourish the horses now spun around the fountain in the little courtyard to come up with a swing to the veranda.

"Now, then," said Grandpapa, who had been overseeing every detail, "here we are," running his eyes over his party; "that's right," in great satisfaction. "I never saw such a family as I have for being prompt on all occasions. Well then, the first thing I have to do is to get you settled in these carriages the right way."

Adela, at that, snuggled up closer than ever to Polly, and gripped her fast.

"Now, Mrs. Fisher," said old Mr. King, "you'll ride with Mrs. Selwyn in the first carriage, and you must take two of the young folks in with you."

"Oh, let Polly and me go in there!" cried Adela, forgetting her wholesome fear of the stately old gentleman in her anxiety to get her own way.

"Polly is going with me and Phronsie," said Mr. King. "Hop in, Adela, child, and one of you boys."

Tom ducked off the veranda, while Adela, not daring to say another syllable, slowly withdrew her arm from Polly's and mounted the carriage step, with a miserable face.

"Come on, one of you boys," cried Mr. King, impatiently. "We should have started a quarter of an hour ago — I don't care which one, only hurry."

"I can't!" declared Tom, flatly, grinding his heel into the pebbles, and looking into Jasper's face.

"Very well," — Jasper drew a long breath, — "I must, then." And without more ado, he got into the first carriage and they rattled off to wait outside the big gate till the procession was ready to start.

Old Mrs. Gray, the parson's wife and the parson, and little Dr. Fisher made the next load, and then Grandpapa, perfectly delighted that he had arranged it all so nicely, with Polly and Phronsie, climbed into the third and last carriage, while Tom swung himself up as a fourth.

"They say it is a difficult thing to arrange carriage parties with success," observed Mr. King. "I don't find it so in the least," he added, complacently, just on the point of telling the driver to give the horses their heads. "But that is because I've such a fine party on my hands, where each one is willing to oblige, and —"

"Ugh!" exclaimed Tom Selwyn, with a snort that made the old gentleman start. "I'm going to get out a minute — excuse me — can't explain." And he vaulted over the wheel.

"Bless me, what's come to the boy!" exclaimed Mr. King; "now he's forgotten something. I hope he won't be long."

But Tom didn't go into the hotel. Instead, he dashed up to carriage number one. "Get out," he was saying to Jasper, and presenting a very red face to view. "I'm going in here."

"Oh, no," said Jasper; "it's all fixed, and I'm going to stay here." And despite all Tom could say, this was the sole reply he got. So back he went, and climbed into old Mr. King's carriage again, with a very rueful face.

Old Mr. King viewed him with cold displeasure as the driver smacked his whip and off they went to join the rest of the party.

"You must go first," sang out the little doctor, as Grandpapa's carriage drove up; "you are the leader, and we'll all follow you."

"Yes, yes," shouted the parson, like a boy.

And the occupants of carriage number one saying the same thing, Grandpapa's conveyance bowled ahead; and he, well pleased to head the procession, felt some of his displeasure at the boy sitting opposite to him dropping off with each revolution of the wheels.

But Tom couldn't keep still. "I didn't want to come in this carriage, sir!" he burst out.

"Eh! what?" Old Mr. King brought his gaze again to bear upon Tom's face.

"Well, you are here now," he said, only half comprehending.

"Because Jasper won't take the place," cried Tom, setting his teeth together in distress. "That's what I got out for."

"Oh, I see," said Mr. King, a light beginning to break through.

Tom wilted miserably under the gaze that still seemed to go through and through him, and Polly looked off at her side of the carriage, wishing the drive over the *Tête Noire* was all ended. Old Mr. King turned to Phronsie at his side.

"Well, now," he said, taking her hand, "we are in a predicament, Phronsie, for it evidently isn't going to be such an overwhelming success as I thought."

"What is a predicament?" asked Phronsie, wrenching her gaze from the lovely vine-clad hills, which she had been viewing with great satisfaction, to look at once into his face.

"Oh, a mix-up; a mess generally," answered Grandpapa, not pausing to choose words. "Well, what's to be done, now, — that is the question?"

Tom groaned at sight of the face under the white hair, from which all prospect of pleasure had fled. "I was a beastly cad," he muttered to himself.

Phronsie leaned over Mr. King's knee. "Tell me," she begged, "what is it, Grandpapa?"

"Oh, nothing, child," said Grandpapa, with a glance at Polly's face, "that you can help, at least."

Polly drew a long breath. "Something must be done," she decided. "Oh, I know. Why, Grandpapa, we can change before we get to the halfway place," she cried suddenly, glad to think of something to say. "Can't we? And then we can all have different places."

"The very thing!" exclaimed Mr. King, his countenance lightening. "Come, Tom, my boy, cheer up. I'll put Jasper and everyone else in the right place soon. Here you, stop a bit, will you?" — to the driver.

"K-lup!" cried the driver, thinking it a call to increase speed; so the horses bounded on smartly for several paces, and no one could speak to advantage.

"Make him hold up, Tom!" commanded Mr. King, sharply. And Tom knowing quite well how to accomplish this, Grandpapa soon stood up in the carriage and announced, "In half an hour, or thereabout, if we come to a good stopping-place, I shall change some of you twelve people about in the carriages. Pass the word along."

But Adela didn't ride with Polly. For rushing and pushing as the change about was effected, to get her way and be with Polly, she felt her arm taken in a very light but firm grasp.

"No, no, my dear," — it was old Mr. King, — "not that way. Here is your place. When a little girl pushes, she doesn't get as much as if she waits to be asked."

"It had to be done," he said to himself, "for the poor child has had no mother to teach her, and it will do her good." But he felt sorry for himself to be the one to teach the lesson. And so they went over the *Tête Noire* to catch the first sight of Mont Blanc.

"I'm going to have a donkey for my very own," confided Phronsie, excitedly, the next morning, to Jasper, whom she met in the little sun-parlor.

"No!" cried Jasper, pretending to be much amazed, "you don't say so, Phronsie!"

"Yes, I am," she cried, bobbing her yellow head. "Grandpapa said so; he really did, Jasper. And I'm going to ride up that long, big mountain on my donkey." She pointed up and off, but in the wrong direction.

"Oh, no, Phronsie, that isn't the way we are going. The Montanvert is over here, child," corrected Jasper.

"And I'm going to ride my donkey," repeated Phronsie, caring little which way she was going, since all roads must of course lead to fairyland, "and we're going to see the water that's frozen, and Grandpapa says we are to walk over it; but I'd rather ride my donkey, Jasper," confided Phronsie, in a burst of confidence.

"I guess you'll be glad enough to get off from your donkey by the time you reach the top of Montanvert," observed Jasper, wisely.

"Well, now, Phronsie, we are not going for a day or two, you know, for father doesn't wish us to be tired."

"I'm not a bit tired, Jasper," said Phronsie, "and I do so very much wish we could go today."

"O dear me!" exclaimed Jasper, with a little laugh, "why, we've only just come, Phronsie! It won't be so very long before we'll be off. Goodness! the time flies so here, it seems to me we shan't hardly turn around before those donkeys will be coming into this yard after us to get on their backs."

But Phronsie thought the time had never dragged so in all her small life; and, although she went about hanging to Grandpapa's hand as sweet and patient as ever, all her mind was on the donkeys; and whenever she saw one, — and the street was full, especially at morning and in the late afternoon, of the little beasts of burden, clattering up the stony roads, — she would beg to just go and pat one of the noses, if by chance one of the beasts should stand still long enough to admit of such attention.

"Oh, no, Phronsie," expostulated old Mr. King, when this pleasing little performance had been indulged in for a half a dozen times. "You can't pat them all; goodness me, child, the woods are full of them," he brought up in dismay.

"Do they live in the woods?" asked Phronsie, in astonishment.

"I mean, the place — this whole valley of Chamonix is full of donkeys," said Grandpapa, "so you see, child, it's next to impossible to pat all their noses."

"I hope I'm going to have that dear, sweet little one," cried Phronsie, giving up all her mind, since the soft noses couldn't be patted, to happy thoughts of tomorrow's bliss. "See, Grandpapa," she pulled his hand gently, "to ride up the mountain on."

"Well, you'll have a good one, that is, as good as can be obtained," said the old gentleman; "but as for any particular one, why, they're all alike to me as two peas, Phronsie."

But Phronsie had her own ideas on the subject, and though on every other occasion agreeing with Grandpapa, she saw good and sufficient reason why every donkey should be entirely different from every other donkey. And when, on the next morning, their procession of donkeys filed solemnly into the hotel yard, she screamed out, "Oh, Grandpapa, here he is, the very one I wanted! Oh, may I have him? Put me up, do!"

"He's the worst one of the whole lot," groaned Grandpapa, his eye running over the file, "I know by the way he puts his vicious old feet down. Phronsie, here is a cunning little fellow," he added, artfully trying to lead her to one a few degrees better, he fondly hoped. But Phronsie already had her arms up by her particular donkey's neck, and her cheek laid against his nose, and she was telling him that he was her donkey, for she thought Grandpapa would say "Yes." So what else could he do, pray tell, but say "Yes?" And she mounted the steps, and was seated, her little brown gown pulled out straight, and the saddle girth tightened, and all the other delightful and important details attended to, and then the reins were put in her overjoyed hands.

She never knew how it was all done, seeing nothing, hearing nothing of the confusion and chatter, of the mounting of the others, her gaze fixed on the long ears before her, and only conscious that her very own donkey was really there, and that she was on his back. And it was not until they started and the guide who held her bridle loped off into an easy pace, by the animal's head, that she aroused from her dream of bliss as a sudden thought struck her. "What is my donkey's name?" she asked softly.

The man loped on, not hearing, and he wouldn't have understood had he heard.

"I don't believe he has any name," said old Mr. King just behind. "Phronsie, is your saddle all right? Do you like it, child?" all in one breath.

"I like it very much," answered Phronsie, trying to turn around.

"Don't do that, child," said Grandpapa, hastily. "Sit perfectly still, and on no account turn around or move in the saddle."

"I won't, Grandpapa," she promised, obediently, and presently she began again, "I want to know his name, Grandpapa, so that I can tell my pony when I get home."

"Oh, well, we'll find out," said Grandpapa. "Here you, can't you tell the name of that donkey?" he cried to the guide holding Phronsie's bridle. "Oh, I forgot, he doesn't understand English," and he tried it in French.

But this was not much better, for old Mr. King, preferring to use none but the best of French when he employed any, was only succeeding in mystifying the poor man so that he couldn't find his tongue at all, but stared like a clod till the old gentleman's patience was exhausted.

At last Jasper, hearing what the trouble was, shouted out something from his position in the rear, that carried the meaning along with it, and Phronsie the next minute was delighted to hear "Boolah," as the guide turned and smiled and showed all his teeth at her, his pleasure was so great at discovering that he could really understand.

"Why, that's the name of my donkey," said Polly, patting the beast's rough neck. "He told me so when he helped me to mount."

"So it is mine," announced Jasper, bursting into a laugh. "I guess they only have one name for the whole lot."

"Well, don't let us tell Phronsie so," said Polly, "and I shall call mine 'Greybeard' because he's got such a funny old stiff beard and it is grey."

"And I shall christen mine 'Boneyard,'" declared Jasper, "for he's got such a very big lot of bones, and they aren't funny, I can tell you."

And so with fun and nonsense and laughter, as soon as they wound around by the little English church and across the meadows, and struck into the pine wood, the whole party of twelve, Grandpapa and all, began to sing snatches from the newest operas down to college songs. For Grandpapa hadn't forgotten his college days when he had sung with the best, and he had the parson on this occasion to keep him company, and the young people, of course, knew all the songs by heart, as what young person doesn't, pray tell! So the bits and snatches rolled out with a gusto, and seemed to echo along the whole mountain side as the procession of sure-footed animals climbed the steep curves.

"Oh, Polly, your donkey is going over," exclaimed Adela, who rode the second in the rear after Polly; "he flirts his hind legs right over the precipice every time you go round a curve."

"Well, he brings them round all right," said Polly, composedly; and, with a little laugh, "Oh, isn't this too lovely for anything!" she cried, with sparkling eyes.

"Well, don't let him," cried Adela, huddling up on her donkey, and pulling at the rein to make him creep closer to the protecting earth wall.

"Na — na," one of the guides ran up to her, shaking his head. Adela, fresh from her Paris school had all her French, of the best kind too, at her tongue's end, but she seemed to get on no better than Mr. King.

"My French is just bad enough to be useful," laughed Jasper. So he untangled the trouble again, and made Adela see that she really must not pull at her bridle, but allow the donkey to go his own gait, for they were all trained to it.

"Your French is just beautiful," cried Polly. "Oh, Jasper, you know Monsieur always says —"

"Don't, Polly," begged Jasper, in great distress.

"No, I won't," promised Polly, "and I didn't mean to. But I couldn't help it, Jasper, when you spoke against your beautiful French."

"We've all heard you talk French, Jasper, so you needn't feel so cut up if Polly should quote your Monsieur," cried Tom, who, strange to say, no matter how far he chanced to ride in the rear, always managed to hear everything.

"That's because we are everlastingly turning a corner," he explained, when they twitted him for it, "and as I'm near the end of the line I get the benefit of the doubling and twisting, for the front is always just above me. So don't say anything you don't want me to hear, old fellow," he sang out to Jasper on the bridle path "just above," as Tom had said.

"Now, don't you want to get off?" cried Jasper, deserting his donkey, and running up to Phronsie, as they reached the summit and drew up before the hotel.

"Oh, somebody take that child off," groaned old Mr. King, accepting the arm of the guide to help him dismount, "for I can't. Every separate and distinct bone in my body protests against donkeys from this time forth and forevermore. And yet I've got to go down on one," he added ruefully.

"No, I don't want to get down," declared Phronsie, still holding fast to the reins; "can't I sit on my donkey, Jasper, while you all walk over on the frozen water?"

"Oh, my goodness, no!" gasped Jasper. "Why, Phronsie, you'd be tired to death — the very idea, child!"

"No," said Phronsie, shaking her yellow hair obstinately, "I wouldn't be tired one single bit, Jasper. And I don't want to get down from my donkey."

"Well, if you didn't go over the *Mer de Glace*, why, we couldn't any of us go," said Jasper, at his wits' end how to manage it without worrying his father, already extremely tired, he could see, "and that's what we've come up for —"

Phronsie dropped the reins. "Take me down, please, Jasper," she said, putting out her arms.

"How are you now, father?" cried Jasper, running over to him when he had set Phronsie on the ground.

"It's astonishing," said old Mr. King, stretching his shapely limbs, "but all that dreadful sensation I always have after riding on one of those atrocious animals is disappearing fast."

"That's good," cried Jasper, in delight. "Well, I suppose we are all going to wait a bit?" he asked, and longing to begin the tramp over the *Mer de Glace*.

"Wait? Yes, indeed, every blessed one of us," declared his father. "Goodness me, Jasper, what are you thinking of to ask such a question, after this pull up here? Why, we shan't stir from this place for an hour."

"I supposed we'd have to wait," said Jasper, rushing off over the rocks, feeling how good it was to get down on one's feet again, and run and race. And getting Polly and Tom and Adela, they ran down where the donkeys were tethered and saw them fed, and did a lot of exploring; and it didn't seem anytime before an Alpine horn sounded above their heads, and there was Grandpapa, tooting away and calling them to come up and buy their woolen socks; for they were going to start.

So they scrambled up, and picked out their socks, and, each seizing a pair in one hand and an alpenstock with a long, sharp spike on the end in the other, they ran off down the zigzag path to the glacier, two or three guides helping the others along. At the foot of the rocky path the four drew up.

"O dear, it's time to put on these horrible old stockings," grumbled Adela, shaking hers discontentedly.

"'Good old stockings,' you'd much better say," broke in Jasper.

"They're better than a broken neck," observed Tom, just meaning to ask Polly if he could put hers on for her. But he was too slow in getting at it, and Jasper was already kneeling on the rocks and doing that very thing.

"Now I'm all ready," announced Polly, stamping her feet, arrayed in marvelous red-and-white striped affairs. "Thank you, Jasper. Oh, how funny they feel!"

"Shall I help you?" asked Tom, awkwardly enough, of Adela.

"Oh, I don't want them on, and I don't mean to wear them," said Adela, with a sudden twist. "I'm going to throw them away."

"Then you'll just have to stay back," said Jasper, decidedly, "for no one is to be allowed on that glacier who doesn't put on a pair."

"I won't slip — the idea!" grumbled Adela. Yet she stuck out her foot, and Tom, getting down on his knees, suppressed a whistle as he securely tied them on. Then the boys flew into theirs instanter.

"Mine are blue," said Phronsie, as the others filed slowly down the winding path between the rocks, and she pointed to the pair dangling across her arm. "I am so very glad they are blue, Grandpapa."

"So am I, Pet," he cried, delighted to find that he was apparently as agile as the parson. No one could hope to equal little Dr. Fisher, who was here, there, and everywhere, skipping about among the rocks like a boy let loose from school.

"Well, well, the children are all ready," exclaimed old Mr. King, coming upon the four, impatient to begin their icy walk.

"Didn't you expect it?" cried little Dr. Fisher, skipping up.

"Well, to say the truth, I did," answered old Mr. King, with a laugh. "Now, Phronsie, sit down on that rock, and let the guide tie on your stockings." So Phronsie's little blue stockings were tied on, and after Grandpapa had gallantly seen that everybody else was served, he had his pulled on over his boots and fastened securely, and the line of march was taken up.

"You go ahead, father," begged Jasper, "and we'll all follow."

So old Mr. King, with Phronsie and a guide on her farther side, led the way, and the red stockings and the brown and the black, and some of indescribable hue, moved off upon the *Mer de Glace.*

"It's dreadfully dirty," said Adela, turning up her nose. "I thought a glacier was white when you got up to it."

"Oh, I think it is lovely!" cried Polly; "and that green down in the crevasse — look, Adela!"

"It's a dirty green," persisted Adela, whose artistic sense wouldn't be satisfied. "O dear me!" as her foot slipped and she clutched Mrs. Henderson, who happened to be next.

"Now, how about the woolen stockings?" asked Tom, while Polly and Jasper both sang out, "Take care," and "Go slowly."

Adela didn't answer, but stuck the sharp end of her alpenstock smartly into the ice.

"Something is the matter with my stocking," at last said the parson's wife, stopping and holding out her right foot.

The guide nearest her stopped, too, and kneeling down on the ice, he pulled it into place, for it had slipped half off.

"Now be very careful," warned Grandpapa, "and don't venture too near the edge," as he paused with Phronsie and the guide. The others, coming up, looked down into a round, green pool of water that seemed to stare up at them, as if to say, "I am of unknown depth, so beware of me."

"That gives me the 'creeps,' Polly, as you say," Mrs. Henderson observed. "Dear me, I shall never forget how that green water looks;" and she shivered and edged off farther yet. "Supposing anyone *should* fall in!"

"Well, he'd go down right straight through the globe, seems to me," said Tom, with a last look at the pool as they turned off, "It looks as if it had no end, till one would fetch up on the other side."

"I love to hop over these little crevasses," said Polly, and suiting the action to the word.

"Something is the matter with my stocking again," announced Mrs. Henderson to the guide, presently. "I am sorry to trouble you, but it needs to be fixed."

He didn't understand the words, but there was no mistaking the foot thrust out with the woolen sock, now wet and sodden, half off again. So he kneeled down and pulled it on once more.

Before they reached the other side, the parson's wife had had that stocking pulled on six times, until at last, the guide, finding no more pleasure in a repetition of the performance, took a string from his pocket, and bunching up in his fist a good portion of the stocking heel, he wound the string around it and tied it fast, cut off the string, and returned the rest to his pocket.

"Why do you tie up the heel?" queried Mrs. Henderson. "I should think it much better to secure it in front." But he didn't understand, and the rest were quite a good bit in advance, and hating to give trouble, she went on, the stocking heel sticking out a few inches. But she kept it on her foot, so that might be called a success.

The little Widow Gray was not going over the *Mauvais Pas*, neither was Mrs. Selwyn, as she had traversed it twice before. So, on reaching the other side, they were just about bidding good-bye to the others, when, without a bit of warning, the parson's wife, in turning around, fell flat, and disappeared to the view of some of them behind a boulder of ice.

All was confusion in an instant. The guides rushed — everybody rushed — pell-mell to the rescue; Tom's long legs, as usual, getting him there first. There she was in a heap, in a depression of ice and snow and water.

"I'm all right, except" — and she couldn't help a grimace of pain — "my foot."

The little doctor swept them all to one side, as they seated her on one of the boulders of ice. "Humph! I should think likely," at sight of the tied-up stocking heel. "You stepped on that, and it flung you straight as a die and turned your foot completely over."

"Yes," said Mrs. Henderson. Then she saw the guide who had tied the stocking looking on with a face of great concern. "Oh, don't say anything, it makes him feel badly," she mumbled, wishing her foot wouldn't ache so.

Little Dr. Fisher was rapidly untying the unlucky stocking; and, whipping off the boot, he soon made sure that no ligaments were broken. Then he put on the boot and the woolen sock, being careful to tie it in front over the instep, and whipping out his big handkerchief he proceeded to bandage the ankle in a truly scientific way. "Now, then, Mrs. Henderson, you are all right to take the walk slowly back to the hotel."

Parson Henderson took his wife's hand. "Come, Sarah," he said, gently helping her up.

"Oh, you are going over the *Mauvais Pas,*" she cried in distress at the thought of his missing it.

"Come, Sarah," he said gently, keeping her hand in his.

"I'll go back with her too," said little Dr. Fisher.

"Oh, Adoniram!" exclaimed his wife, but it was under her breath, and no one heard the exclamation.

"I think Dr. Fisher ought to go with the other party; he will be needed there," Mrs. Selwyn was saying, in her quiet way. "And I will bathe Mrs. Henderson's foot just as he says it should be done, so good-bye," and anyone looking down with a field glass from the Montanvert hotel, could have seen at this point, two parties, one proceeding to the *Mauvais Pas* and the *Chapeau,* and the other of three ladies, the parson and a guide, wending their way slowly on the return across the crevasses.

XXVI

"WELL, HERE WE ARE IN PARIS!"

Notwithstanding all the glory of the shops, and the tempting array of the jewelry and trinkets of every description therein displayed, after a few days of sailing on the exquisite lake, and some walks and drives, Polly, down deep in her heart, was quite ready to move on from Geneva. And, although she didn't say anything, old Mr. King guessed as much, and broke out suddenly, "Well, are you ready to start, Polly?"

"Yes, Grandpapa," she answered. "I have the presents for the girls. I'm all ready."

"Why, Polly, you haven't anything for yourself," Mother Fisher exclaimed, as Polly ran into her room and told the news — how Grandpapa said they were to pack up and leave in the morning. "You haven't bought a single thing."

"Oh, I don't want anything," said Polly. "I've so many things at home that Grandpapa has given me. Mamsie, isn't this pin for Alexia just too lovely for anything?"

She curled up on the end of the bed, and drew it out of its little box. "I think she'll like it," with anxious eyes on Mother Fisher's face.

"Like it?" repeated her mother. "How can she help it, Polly?"

"I think so too," said Polly, happily, replacing it on the bed of cotton, and putting on the cover to look over another gift.

Mrs. Fisher regarded her keenly. "Well, now, Polly," she said, decidedly, "I shall go down and get that chain we were looking at. For you do need that, and your father and I are going to give it to you."

"Oh, Mamsie," protested Polly, "I don't need it; really, I don't."

"Well, we shall give it to you," said Mother Fisher. Then she went over to the bed and dropped a kiss on Polly's brown hair.

"Mamsie," exclaimed Polly, springing off the bed, and throwing her arms around her mother's neck, "I shall love that chain, and I shall wear it just all the time because you and Papa-Doctor gave it to me."

When they neared Paris, Adela drew herself up in her corner of the compartment. "I expect you'll stare some when you get to Paris, Polly Pepper."

"I've been staring all the time since we started on our journey, Adela, as hard as I could," said Polly, laughing.

"Well, you'll stare worse than ever now," said Adela, in an important way. "There isn't anything in all this world that isn't in Paris," she brought up, not very elegantly.

"I don't like Paris." Tom let the words out before he thought.

"That's just because you are a boy," sniffed Adela. "Oh, Polly, you ought to see the shops! When Mademoiselle has taken us into some, I declare I could stay all day in one. Such dreams of clothes and bonnets! You never saw such bonnets, Polly Pepper, in all your life!" She lifted her hands, unable to find words enough.

"And the parks and gardens, I suppose, are perfectly lovely," cried Polly, feeling as if she must get away from the bonnets and clothes.

"Yes, and the Bois de Boulogne to drive in, that's elegant. Only Mademoiselle won't take us there very often. I wish I was rich, and I'd have a span of long-tailed, grey horses, and drive up and down there every day."

Polly laughed. "Well, I should like the tram-ways and the stages," said Polly.

"Oh, those don't go into the Bois de Boulogne," cried Adela, in a tone of horror. "Why, Polly Pepper, what are you thinking of?" she exclaimed.

This nettled Tom. "Of something besides clothes and bonnets," he broke out. Then he was sorry he had spoken.

"Well, there's the Louvre," said Polly, after an uncomfortable little pause.

"Yes," said Adela, "that's best of all, and it doesn't cost anything; so Mademoiselle takes us there very often."

"I should think it would be," cried Polly, beaming at her, and answering the first part of Adela's sentence. "Oh, Adela, I do so long to see it."

"And you can't go there too often, Polly," said Jasper.

"It's the only decent thing in Paris," said Tom, "that I like, I mean; that, and to sail up and down on the Seine."

"We'll go there the first day, Polly," said Jasper, "the Louvre, I mean. Well, here we are in Paris!" And then it was all confusion, for the guards were throwing open the doors to the compartments, and streams of people were meeting on the platform, in what seemed to be inextricable confusion amid a Babel of sounds. And it wasn't until Polly was driving up in the big cab with her part of Mr. King's "family," as he called it, through the broad avenues and boulevards, interspersed with occasional squares and gardens, and the beautiful bridges here and there across the Seine, gleaming in the sunshine, that she could realize that they were actually in Paris.

And the next day they did go to the Louvre. And Adela, who was to stay a day or two at the hotel with them before going back into her school, was very important, indeed. And she piloted them about, the parson and Mrs. Henderson joining their group; the others, with the exception of the little Widow Gray, who stayed at home to look over Adela's clothes, and take any last stitches, going off by themselves.

"I do want to see the Venus de Milo," said Polly, quite gone with impatience. "Oh, Adela, these paintings will wait."

"Well, that old statue will wait, too," cried Adela, pulling her off into another gallery. "Now, Polly, Mademoiselle says, in point of art, the pictures in here are quite important."

"Are they?" said poor Polly, listlessly.

"Yes, they are," said Adela, twitching her sleeve, "and Mademoiselle brings us in this room every single time we come to the Louvre."

"It's the early French school, you know," she brought up glibly.

"Well, it's too early for us to take it in," said Tom. "Come, I'm for the Venus de Milo. It's this way;" and Adela was forced to follow, which she did in a discontented fashion.

"Oh!" cried Polly, catching her breath, and standing quite still as she caught sight of the wonderful marble, instinct with life, at the end of the long corridor below stairs. "Why, she's smiling at us," as the afternoon sunshine streamed across the lovely face, to lose itself in the folds of the crimson curtain in the background.

The parson folded his arms and drew in long breaths of delight. "It's worth fifty journeys over the ocean to once see that, Sarah," he said.

"Do come back and look at the pictures," begged Adela, pulling Polly's arm again after a minute or two.

"Oh, don't!" exclaimed Polly, under her breath. "Oh, she's *so* beautiful, Adela!"

"Well, it's much better to see the pictures," said Adela. "And then we can come here again tomorrow."

"Oh, I haven't seen this half enough," began Polly, "and I've wanted to for so long." Then she glanced at Adela's face. "Well, all right," she said, and turned off, to come directly into the path of Grandpapa, with Phronsie clinging to his hand, and the rest of his part of the "family" standing in silent admiration.

"We thought we'd come here first," said old Mr. King. "I don't mean to see anything else today. The Venus de Milo is quite enough for me. Tomorrow, now, we'll drop in again, and look at some of the pictures."

"There is beauty enough in that statue," said a lady, who just passed them, to the gentleman with her, "to satisfy anyone; but living beauty after all is most appealing. Just look at that child's face, Edward."

They were guilty of standing in a niche at a little remove, and studying Phronsie with keen, critical eyes.

"It's a wonderful type of beauty," said Edward; "yellow hair and brown eyes, — and such features."

"I don't care about the features," said the lady, "it's the expression; the child hasn't a thought of herself, and that's wonderful to begin with."

"That's about it," replied Edward, "and I suppose that's largely where the beauty lies, Evelyn."

"Let us walk slowly down the corridor again," said Evelyn, "and then come up; otherwise we shall attract attention to be standing here and gazing at them."

"And I'd like to see that little beauty again," remarked Edward, "I'll confess, Evelyn."

So Evelyn and Edward continued to gaze at intervals at the living beauty, and Mr. King and his party were absorbed in the marble beauty; and Adela was running over in her mind how she meant to have Polly Pepper all to herself at the visit to the Louvre the next afternoon, when she would show her the pictures she specially liked.

But they didn't any of them go to the Louvre that next day, as it happened. It was so beautifully bright and sunshiny, that Grandpapa said it would be wicked to pass the day indoors; so they had all the morning in a walk, and a sail on the Seine, — and that pleased Tom, — and all the afternoon, or nearly all, sitting up in state in carriages, driving up and down the Bois de Boulogne. And *that* pleased Adela.

And when they tired of driving, old Mr. King gave orders for the drivers to rest their horses. And then they all got out of the carriages, and walked about among the beautiful trees, and on the winding, sheltered paths.

"It's perfectly lovely off there," said Polly, "and almost like the country," with a longing glance off into the green, cool shade beyond. So they strolled off there, separating into little groups; Polly and Jasper in front, and wishing for nothing so much as a race.

"I should think we might try it," said Jasper; "there is no one near to see. Come on, Polly, do."

"I suppose we ought not to," said Polly, with a sigh, as Adela overtook them.

"Ought not to what?" she asked eagerly.

"Jasper and I were wanting to run a race," said Polly.

"Why, Polly Pepper! You are in Paris!" exclaimed Adela, quite shocked.

"I know it," said Polly, "and I wish we weren't. O dear! this seems just like the country, and —"

Just then a child screamed. "That's Phronsie!" exclaimed Polly, her cheek turning quite white. And she sped back over the path.

"Oh, no, Polly," Jasper tried to reassure her, as he ran after her. They were having their race, after all, but in a different way from what they had planned.

"Dear me! you are running!" said Adela, who hadn't got it into her head what for, as she didn't connect the scream with any of their party. And she walked just as fast as she could to catch up with them. As that was impossible, she gave a hasty glance around the shrubbery, and seeing no one to notice her, she broke out into a lively run.

"Yes, Phronsie," Grandpapa was saying, as the young people had left them, and the others had wandered off to enjoy the quiet, shady paths, "this place was the old Fôret de Rouvray. It wasn't a very pretty place to come to in those days, what with the robbers and other bad people who infested it. And now let us go and find a seat, child, and I'll show you one or two little pictures I picked up in the shop this morning; and you can send them in your next letter, to Joel and David, if you like."

Old Mr. King took out his pocketbook, and had just opened it, when a man darted out from the thick shrubbery behind him, cast a long, searching glance around, and quick as lightning, threw himself against the stately old gentleman, and seized the pocketbook.

It was then that Phronsie screamed long and loud.

"What ho!" exclaimed Mr. King, starting around to do battle; but the man was just disappearing around the clump of shrubbery.

"Which way?" Tom Selwyn dashed up. It didn't seem as if Phronsie's cry had died on her lips.

Old Mr. King pointed without a word. And Polly and Jasper were close at hand. Polly flew to Phronsie, who was clinging to Grandpapa's hand, and wailing bitterly. "What is it? Oh! what is it?" cried Polly.

"My pocketbook," said Grandpapa; "some fellow has seized it, and frightened this poor child almost to death." He seemed to care a great deal more about that than any loss of the money.

"Which way?" cried Jasper, in his turn, and was off like a shot on getting his answer.

Tom saw the fellow slink with the manner of one who knew the ins and outs of the place well, — now gliding, and ducking low in the sparser growth, now making a bold run around some exposed curve, now dashing into a dense part of the wood.

"I'll have you yet!" said Tom, through set teeth; "I haven't trained at school for nothing!"

A thud of fast-flying feet in his rear didn't divert him an instant from his game, although it might be a rescue party for the thief, in the shape of a partner, — who could tell? And realizing, if he caught the man at all, he must do one of his sprints, he covered the ground by a series of flying leaps, — dashed in where he saw his prey rush; one more leap with all his might, and — "I have you!" cried Tom.

The man under him, thrown to the ground by the suddenness of Tom's leap on him, was wriggling and squirming with all the desperation of a trapped creature, when the individual with the flying footsteps hove in sight. It was Jasper. And they had just persuaded the robber that it would be useless to struggle longer against his fate, when the parson, running as he hadn't run for years, appeared to their view. And after him, at such a gait that would have been his fortune, in a professional way, was the little doctor. His hat was gone, and his toes scarcely seemed to touch the ground. He was last at the scene, simply because the news had only just reached him as he sauntered leisurely up to meet Mr. King in his promenade.

When the thief saw him, he looked to see if anymore were coming, and resigned himself at once and closed his eyes instinctively.

He was a miserable-looking man — tall, thin, and stoop shouldered — they saw, when they got him on his feet. Unkempt and unwashed, his long, black hair hung around a face sallow in the extreme. And he shook so, as Tom and Jasper marched him back, escorted by the bodyguard of the parson and the little doctor, that the two boys put their hands under his arms to help him along.

"Well — well — well!" ejaculated Mr. King, as he saw this array. Polly gathered Phronsie's other hand in hers, while she clung closer than ever to Grandpapa.

"Here's your pocketbook," said Tom, handing the article over; "he hasn't spent much."

"Don't, Tom," said Jasper, "joke about it."

"Can't help it," said Tom. "Well, now, shall we turn him over to the *sergents de ville?*"

"Turn him over?" repeated Mr. King. "I should say so," he added dryly, "and give him the best recommendation for a long term, too. What else is there to do, pray tell?"

"Grandpapa," suddenly cried Phronsie, who hadn't taken her eyes from the man's face, "what are you going to do — where is he going?"

"We are going to hand him over to the police, child," answered old Mr. King, harshly. "And as soon as possible, too."

"Grandpapa, perhaps he's got some little children at home; ask him, Grandpapa, do."

"No, no, Phronsie," said Mr. King, hastily. "Say no more, child; you don't understand. We must call the *sergents de ville.*"

At the words *sergents de ville* the man shivered from head to foot, and wrenched his hands free from the boys' grasp to tear open his poor coat, and show a bare breast, covered with little, apparently, but the skin drawn over the bones. He didn't attempt to say anything.

"Oh, my goodness!" exclaimed old Mr. King, starting backward and putting up his hands to his face to shut out the sight. "Cover it up, man — bless me — no need to ask him a question. Why, the fellow is starving."

His little children — four of them — his wife — all starving — hadn't a bit to eat since, he could scarcely say when, it seemed so very long ago since he had eaten last — it all came out in a torrent of words that choked him, and like the true Frenchman that he was, he gestured in a way that told the story with his face and his fingers, as well as with his tongue.

A *sergent de ville* strolled by and looked curiously at the group, but as Mr. King met his eye coolly, and the party seemed intelligent and well able to take care of themselves, it wasn't necessary to tender his services — if they were talking to a worthless vagabond.

"Hum — hum — very bad case; very bad case, indeed!" Mr. King was exploding at intervals, while the torrent was rushing on in execrable French as far as accent went. No one else of the spellbound group could have spoken if there had been occasion for a word. Then he pulled out the pocketbook again, and taking out several franc notes of a good size, he pressed them between the man's dirty fingers. "Go and get something to eat," was all he said, "and take care of the children."

XVII

"I'VE FOUND HIM!" EXCLAIMED JASPER

And for the next few days Phronsie talked about the poor man, and wished they could see his children, and hoped he had bought them some nice things to eat, and worried over him because he was all skin and bones.

"Ah! the bones were real, even if the children aren't," Grandpapa would say to himself. "Well, I suppose I have been taken in, but at least the fellow hasn't starved to death."

And then off they would go sight-seeing as fast as possible, to take up the mind of Phronsie, who watched for Grandpapa's poor man in every wretched creature she saw. And there were plenty of them.

And then Adela went back to school, happy in the thought of the little pile of sketches she had to show as her summer's work, and with ever so many studies and bits to finish up under Mademoiselle's direction; and little old Mrs. Gray, breathing blessings on Mr. King's head, departed for her English country home.

"Now, then, I have ever so much shopping to do," announced old Mr. King, briskly, "and I shall want you to help me, Phronsie."

"I'll help you, Grandpapa," promised Phronsie, well pleased, and gravely set herself to the task.

So they wandered away by themselves, having the most blissful of times, and coming home to the hotel, they would gaily relate their adventures; and Phronsie would often carry a little parcel or two, which it was her greatest delight to do; and then the trail of big boxes would follow them as they were sent home to the hotel to tell of their experiences in the shops.

"And Grandpapa is going to get me a new doll," announced Phronsie, on one of these days.

"Do you mean a peasant doll to add to the collection?" asked Polly; for old Mr. King had bought a doll in the national costume in every country in which they had traveled, and they had been packed away, together with the other things as fast as purchased, and sent off home across the sea.

"Yes," said Phronsie. "I do, Polly, and it's to be a most beautiful French doll — oh!"

And sure enough, Mr. King, who knew exactly what kind of a doll he meant to purchase, and had kept his eyes open for it, stumbled upon it by a piece of rare good luck in a shop where he least expected to find it.

"Oh, may I carry her home, Grandpapa?" begged Phronsie, hanging over the doll in a transport. "Please don't have her shut up in a box — but do let me carry her in my arms."

"Oh, Phronsie, she's too big," objected Mr. King, "and very heavy."

"Oh, Grandpapa, she's not heavy," cried Phronsie, not meaning to contradict, but so anxious not to have her child sent home shut up in a box, that she forgot herself.

"Well, I don't know but what you may," said Grandpapa, relenting. "I will call a cab after we get through with this next shop," he reflected, "and it won't hurt her to carry the doll that short distance." So they came out of the shop, and deciding to take a short cut, they started across the boulevard, he taking the usual precaution to gather Phronsie's hand in his.

As they were halfway across the street, with its constant stream of pedestrians and vehicles, a sudden gust of wind flapped the doll's pink silk cape up against Phronsie's eyes, and taking her hand away from Grandpapa's a second to pull down the cape, for she couldn't see, she slipped, and before she knew it, had fallen on top of the doll in the middle of the street.

A reckless cabby, driving as only a French cabman can, came dashing down the boulevard directly in her path, while a heavily loaded omnibus going in the opposite direction was trying to get out of his way. Ever so many people screamed; and someone pulled Mr. King back as he started to pick her up. It was all done in an instant, and every person expected to see her killed, when a long, gaunt individual in a shabby coat dashed in among the plunging horses, knocked up the head of the one belonging to the reckless cabby, swung an arm at the other pair to divert their course, and before anyone could quite tell how, he picked up Phronsie and bore her to the curbstone. Someone got Mr. King to the same point, too exhausted with fright to utter a word.

When he came out of his shock, the shabby man was standing by Phronsie, the crowd that saw nothing in the incident to promise further diversion, having melted away, and she was holding his hand, her little, mud-stained face radiant with happiness. "Oh, Grandpapa," she piped out, "it's your poor man!"

"The dickens it is!" exploded Mr. King. "Well, I'm glad to find you. Here, call a cab, will you? I must get this child home; that's the first thing to be done."

The shabby man hailed a cab, but the cabman jeered at him and whirled by. So the old gentleman held up his hand; Phronsie all this time, strange to say, not mentioning her doll, and Mr. King, who wouldn't have cared if a hundred dolls had been left behind, not giving it a thought. Now she looked anxiously on all sides. "Oh, where is she, Grandpapa dear?" she wailed, "my child; where is she?"

"Never mind, Phronsie," cried Mr. King, "I'll get you another one tomorrow. There, get in the cab, child."

"But I want her — I can't go home without my child!" And Phronsie's lip began to quiver. "Oh, there she is, Grandpapa!" and she darted off a few steps, where somebody had set the poor thing on the pavement, propped up against a lamp-post.

"Oh, you can't carry her home," said Mr. King, in dismay at the muddy object splashed from head to foot, with the smart pink cape that had been the cause of the disaster, now torn clear through the middle, by the hoof of a passing horse. He shuddered at the sight of it. "Do leave it, Phronsie, child."

"But she's sick now and hurt; oh, Grandpapa, I can't leave my child," sobbed Phronsie, trying with all her might to keep the tears back. All this time the shabby man stood silently by, looking on.

A bright thought struck the old gentleman. "I'll tell you, Phronsie," he said quickly. "Give the doll to this man for one of his little children; they'll take care of it, and like it."

"Oh, Grandpapa!" screamed Phronsie, skipping up and down and clapping her muddy little hands, then she picked up the doll and lifted it toward him. "Give my child to your little girl, and tell her to take good care of it," she said.

As Phronsie's French had long been one of Grandpapa's special responsibilities in the morning hours, she spoke it nearly as well as Polly herself, so the man grasped the doll as he had seized the money before.

"And now," said Mr. King, "you are not going to run away this time without telling me — oh, bless me!"

This last was brought out by an excited individual rushing up over the curbstone to get out of the way of a passing dray, and the walking-stick which he swung aloft as a protection, coming into collision with Mr. King's hat, knocked it over his eyes.

"A thousand pardons, Monsieur!" exclaimed the Frenchman, bowing and scraping.

"You may well beg a thousand pardons," cried Mr. King, angrily, "to go about in this rude fashion through the street."

"A thousand pardons," repeated the Frenchman, with more *empressement* than before, and tripping airily on his way.

When old Mr. King had settled his hat, he turned back to the man. "Now tell me — why —" The man was nowhere to be seen.

"It surely does look bad," said the old gentleman to himself as he stepped into the cab with Phronsie; "that man's children are a myth. And I wanted to do something for them, for he saved Phronsie's life!"

This being the only idea he could possibly retain all the way home to the hotel, he held her closely within his arm, Phronsie chattering happily all the way, how the little girl she guessed was just receiving the doll, and wondering what name she would give it, and would she wash its face clean at once, and fix the torn and muddy clothes?

"Oh, yes, yes, I hope so," answered Grandpapa, when she paused for an answer. Jasper came running out as the cab drove into the court. "Oh!" he exclaimed, at sight of Phronsie's face, then drove the words on his tongue back again, as he lifted her out.

"Give her to Polly to fix up a bit," said his father. "She's all right, Jasper, my boy, I can't talk of it now. Hurry and take her to Polly."

And for the following days, Mr. King never let Phronsie out of his sight. A new and more splendid doll, if possible, was bought, and all sorts and styles of clothes for it, which Phronsie took the greatest delight in caring for, humming happily to herself at the pleasure the poor man's little girl was taking at the same time with her other child.

"Grandpapa," she said, laying down the doll carefully on the sofa, and going over to the table where Mr. King had just put aside the newspaper, "I do wish we could go and see that poor man and all his children — why didn't he tell us where he lived?"

"The dickens!" exclaimed old Mr. King, unguardedly, "because the fellow is an impostor, Phronsie. He saved your life," and he seized Phronsie and drew her to his knee, "but he lied about those children. O dear me!" And he pulled himself up.

"Then he hasn't any little children?" said Phronsie, opening her eyes very wide, and speaking very slowly.

"Er-oh-I don't know," stammered Grandpapa; "it's impossible to tell, Phronsie."

"But you don't believe he has any," said Phronsie, with grave persistence, fastening her brown eyes on his face.

"No, Phronsie, I don't," replied old Mr. King, in desperation. "If he had, why should he run in this fashion when I was just asking him where he lived?"

"But he didn't hear you, Grandpapa," said Phronsie, "when the man knocked your hat off."

"Oh, well, he knew enough what I wanted," said Mr. King, who, now that he had let out his belief, was going to support it by all the reasons in his power. "No, no, Phronsie, it won't do; the fellow was an impostor, and we must just accept the fact, and make the best of it, my child."

"But he told a lie," said Phronsie, in horror, unable to think of anything else.

"Well." Mr. King had no words to say on that score, so he wisely said nothing.

"That poor man told a lie," repeated Phronsie, as if producing a wholly fresh statement.

"There, child, I wouldn't think anything more of it," said Grandpapa, soothingly, patting her little hand.

"Grandpapa," said Phronsie, "I've given away my child, and she's sick because she fell and hurt her, and there isn't any little girl, and — and — that poor man told a lie!" And she flung herself up against Grandpapa's waistcoat, and sobbed as if her heart would break.

Old Mr. King looked wildly around for Polly. And as good fortune would have it, in she ran. This wasn't very strange, for Polly kept nearly as close to Phronsie in these days, as Grandpapa himself.

"Here, Polly," he called brokenly, "this is something beyond me. You must fix it, child."

"Why, Phronsie!" exclaimed Polly, in dismay, and her tone was a bit reproachful. "Crying? Don't you know that you will make Grandpapa very sick unless you stop?"

Phronsie's little hand stole out from over her mouth where she had been trying to hold the sobs back, and up to give a trembling pat on old Mr. King's cheek.

"Bless you, my child," cried Grandpapa, quite overcome, so that Polly said more reproachfully, "Yes, very sick indeed, Phronsie, unless you stop this minute. You ought to see his face, Phronsie."

Phronsie gathered herself up out of his arms, and through a rain of tears looked up at him.

"Are you sick, Grandpapa?" she managed to ask.

"Yes, dear; or I shall be if you don't stop crying, Phronsie," said Mr. King, pursuing all the advantage so finely gained.

"I'll stop," said Phronsie, her small bosom heaving. "I really will, Grandpapa."

"Now, you are the very goodest child," exclaimed Polly, down on her knees by Grandpapa's side, cuddling Phronsie's toes, "the very most splendid one in all this world, Phronsie Pepper."

"And you'll be all well, Grandpapa?" asked Phronsie, anxiously.

"Yes, child," said old Mr. King, kissing her wet face; "just as well as I can be, since you are all right."

"And, oh, Grandpapa, can't we go to Fontainebleau today?" begged Polly.

"Phronsie, just think — it will be precisely like the country, and we can get out of the carriages, and can run and race in the forest. Can't we, Grandpapa?"

"All you want to," promised Grandpapa, recklessly, and only too thankful to have something proposed for a diversion. "The very thing," he added enthusiastically. "Now, Polly and Phronsie, run and tell all the others to get ready, just as fast as they can, and we'll be off. Goodness me, Jasper, what makes you run into a room in this fashion?"

"I've found him!" exclaimed Jasper, dashing in, and tossing his cap on the table, and his dark hair back from his forehead. "And he's all right — as straight as a die," he panted.

"Now what in the world are you talking of?" demanded his father, in extreme irritation. "Can't you make a plain statement, and enlighten us without all this noise and confusion, pray tell?"

Polly, who had Phronsie's hand in hers, just ready to run off, stood quite still with glowing cheek.

"Oh, I do believe — Grandpapa — it is — it is!" — she screamed suddenly — "your poor man! Isn't it, Jasper — isn't it?" she cried, turning to him.

"Yes, Polly," said Jasper, still panting from his run up the stairs; "and do hurry, father, and see for yourself; and we'll all go to him. I'll tell you all about it on the way."

When Mr. King comprehended that the man was found, and that he was "all right," as Jasper vehemently repeated over and over, he communicated that fact to Phronsie, whose delight knew no bounds, and in less time than it takes to write it, Tom, who was the only one of the party to be collected on such short notice, had joined them, and they were bowling along in a big carriage, Jasper as guide, to the spot where the man was waiting.

"You see it was just this way," Jasper was rapidly telling off. "I was going down by the Madeleine, and I thought I would bring Phronsie some flowers; so I stopped at the market, and I couldn't find a little pot of primroses I wanted, though I went the whole length; and at last, when

I had given up, I saw just one in front of a woman who sat at the very end."

"Do hurry, Jasper, and get to the conclusion," said his father, impatiently.

Polly dearly loved to have the story go on in just this way, as she leaned forward, her eyes on Jasper's face, but she said nothing, only sighed.

"Well," said Jasper, "I'll tell it as quickly as I can, father. And there were a lot of children, father, all round the woman where she sat on a box, and she was tying in a bunch some flowers that were huddled in her lap, and the children were picking out the good ones for her; and just then a man, who was bending over back of them all, breaking off some little branches from a big green one, straightened up suddenly, and, father, as true as you live," cried Jasper, in intense excitement, "it was your poor man!"

"The children?" asked Mr. King, as soon as he could be heard for the excitement.

"Are all his," cried Jasper, "and he took the money you gave him, and set his wife up in the flower business down in front of the Madeleine. Oh! and Phronsie, the doll you gave him was sitting up on another box, and every once in a while the littlest girl would stop picking out the flowers in her mother's lap, and would run over and wipe its face with her apron."

XXVIII

"WELL, I GOT HIM HERE," SAID THE LITTLE EARL

*T*hey were really on their way to see the little old earl, after all! How it came about, Mr. King, even days after it had all been decided, couldn't exactly remember. He recalled several conversations in Paris with Tom's mother, who showed him bits of letters, and one in particular that somehow seemed to be a very potent factor in the plan that, almost before he knew it, came to be made. And when he held out, as hold out he did against the acceptance of the invitation, he found to his utmost surprise that everyone, Mother Fisher and all, was decidedly against him.

"Oh, well," he had declared when that came out, "I might as well give in gracefully first as last." And he sat down at once and wrote a very handsome note to the little old earl, and that clinched the whole business.

And after the week of this visit should be over, for old Mr. King was firmness itself on not accepting a day more, they were to bid good-bye to Mrs. Selwyn and Tom, and jaunt about a bit to show a little of Old England to the Hendersons, and then run down to Liverpool to see them off, and at last turn their faces toward Dresden, their winter home — "and to my work!" said Polly to herself in delight.

So now here they were, actually driving up to the entrance of the park, and stopping at the lodge-gate.

An old woman, in an immaculate cap and a stiff white apron over her best linsey-woolsey gown which she had donned for the occasion, came out of the lodge and curtsied low to the madam, and held open the big gate.

"How have you been, Mrs. Bell?" asked Mrs. Selwyn, with a kind smile, as the carriage paused a bit.

"Very well, my lady," said Mrs. Bell, her round face glowing with pride. "And the earl is well, bless him! and we are glad to welcome you home again, and Master Tom."

"And I'm glad enough to get here, Mrs. Bell," cried Tom. "Now drive on at your fastest, Hobson."

Hobson, who knew very well what Master Tom's fastest gait was, preferred to drive through the park at what he considered the dignified pace. So they rolled on under the stately trees, going miles, it seemed to Polly, who sat on the back seat with Tom.

He turned to her, unable to conceal his impatience. "Anybody would think this pair were worn out old cobs," he fumed. "Polly, you have no idea how they can go, when Hobson lets them out. What are you wasting all this time for, crawling along in this fashion, Hobson, when you know we want to get on?"

Thus publicly addressed, Hobson let the handsome bays "go" as Tom expressed it, and they were bowled along in a way that made Polly turn in delight to Tom.

"There — that's something like!" declared Tom. "Don't you like it, Polly?" looking into her rosy face.

"Like it!" cried Polly, "why, Tom Selwyn, it's beautiful. And these splendid trees —" she looked up and around. "Oh, I never saw any so fine."

"They're not half bad," assented Tom, "these oaks aren't, and we have some more, on the other end of the park, about five miles off, that —"

"Five miles off!" cried Polly, with wide eyes. "Is the park as big as that, Tom?"

He laughed. "That isn't much. But you'll see it all for yourself," he added. Then he rushed off into wondering how his dogs were. "And, oh, you'll ride with the hounds, Polly!"

Just then some rabbits scurried across the wood, followed by several more pattering and leaping through the grass.

"Oh, Tom, see those rabbits!" cried Polly, excitedly.

"Yes, the warrens are over yonder," said Tom, bobbing his head in the right direction.

"What?" asked Polly, in perplexity.

"Rabbit-warrens; oh, I forgot, you haven't lived in England. You seem so much like an English girl, though," said Tom, paying the highest compliment he knew of.

"Well, what are they?" asked Polly, quite overcome by the compliment coming from Tom.

"Oh, they are preserves, you know, where the rabbits live, and they are not allowed to be hunted here."

"Oh, do you ever hunt rabbits?" cried Polly, in horror, leaning out of her side of the big coach to see the scurrying little animals.

"Not often," said Tom, "we mostly ride after the fox. You'll ride with the hounds, Polly," he cried with enthusiasm. "We'll have a hunt while you're here, and we always wind up with a breakfast, you know. Oh, we'll have no end of sport." He hugged his long arms in huge satisfaction.

And away — and away over the winding road and underneath the stately trees, rolled the big coach, to be followed by the other carriages, like a dream it seemed to Polly, and more than ever, when at last they stopped in front of a massive pile of buildings with towers and arches and wings.

And the little old earl was kissing her rosy cheek in the most courtly fashion, and saying while he shook her hand in his long fingers, "And how do you do, my dear?" And Mrs. Selwyn was by his other side. And Tom was screeching out, "How do you do, Granddaddy!" And then, "Oh, Elinor and Mary!" to two quiet, plain-looking girls standing in the background. And "Ah, how d'ye kids!" as the faces of his two small brothers appeared. And Polly forgot all about the fact that she was in an earl's house, and she laughed and chatted; and in two minutes one of Tom's sisters was on either side of her, and the small boys in front, and the little groups were moving in and out of the old hall, as Grandpapa and the rest came in, and the head housekeeper in a black silk gown that seemed quite able to stand alone, and a perfect relay of stiff figures in livery were drawn up underneath the armor hanging on the wall.

And the little old earl worked his way up to her, and he had Grandpapa on his arm. "Well, I got him here," he said with twinkling eyes, and a chuckle.

But the next morning — oh, the next morning! — when Polly tried to compass as much of the thronging attractions as she could, and Jasper was at his wits' end whenever he was appealed to, to decide what he wanted to do first — "cricket," or "punting on the river," that ran through the estate, or "riding through the park, and to the village owned by his grandfather?" "I always go see the tenantry as soon as I get home," said Tom, simply.

"Oh, then, let us go there by all means," said Jasper, quickly.

"I mean — oh, I'm no end awkward," exclaimed Tom, breaking off, his face covered with confusion. "It's not necessary to go at once; we can fetch up there tomorrow."

"Oh, do let us go, Tom," begged Polly, clasping her hands. "I should dearly love most of all to see the tenantry and those dear little cottages." And so that was decided upon.

And Tom had his beloved hunt, several of the gentry being asked. And Polly rode a special horse selected by the little old earl himself.

"It's perfectly safe; he has an excellent disposition," he declared to old Mr. King, "and he'll carry her all right."

"I'm not afraid," said Mr. King, "the child rides well."

"So she must — so she must, I was sure of it," cried the little old earl, with a series of chuckles. And he busied himself especially with seeing her mounted properly when the party gathered on the lawn in front of the old hall. The hounds were baying and straining at the leashes, impatient to be off; the pink hunting-coats gave dashes of color as their owners moved about over the broad green sward, — under the oaks, — and Polly felt her heart beat rapidly with the exhilarating sights and sounds. It was only when they were off, and Tom riding up by her side expatiated on the glory of running down the fox and "being in at the death," that the color died down on her cheek.

"Oh, Tom!" she said, reining in her horse. If he hadn't been the possessor of a good disposition, he certainly would have bolted in his disappointment at being pulled up so abruptly. "It's so cruel to kill the poor fox in that way."

"Eh — what!" exclaimed Tom, not hearing the words, falling back to her side, consternation all over his face. "Why, I never knew Meteor to break in this way before."

"Oh, it isn't his fault," said Polly, hastily, and patting her horse's neck. "I pulled him up. Oh, Tom, it's all so very cruel."

"Eh?" said Tom, in a puzzled way.

"To kill the fox in this way," said Polly, her heart sinking as she thought how dreadful it was for her to object, when visiting, to anything her host might plan. "O dear me!" and she looked so distressed that Tom turned comforter at once.

"We all do it," he was saying, as Jasper rode up.

"Anything the matter?" he asked in great concern. "What's happened?"

"Nothing," said Tom, "only Polly doesn't like the fox-hunt."

"It's so cruel," cried Polly, turning to Jasper, with a little pink spot coming in either cheek. "I ought to have thought of it before, but I didn't; it only seemed so very splendid to be rushing along with the horses and dogs. But to chase that poor fox to death — O dear me!"

"We'll go back," suggested Tom, in distress; "don't be afraid, Polly, I'll make it all right with granddaddy." He concealed as best he might his awful disappointment as the echoes of the horn, the baying of the dogs, and now and then a scrap of chatter or a peal of laughter was borne to them on the wind.

"Polly," said Jasper, in a low voice, "it isn't quite right, is it, to disturb the party now? Just think, Tom will go back with us."

The pink spots died out on Polly's cheek. "No, Jasper," she said, "it isn't right. Tom, you needn't say one word about going back, for I am going on." She gave the rein to Meteor and dashed off.

"We'll have a race through the park some day, Polly," called Tom, as he sped after her, "without any fox."

"Too bad, Polly, you weren't in at the death," said the little old earl, sympathizingly, when at the hunt-breakfast following, the brush dangling to a victorious young lady's belt, had been admired as an extremely fine one. "Never mind; better luck next time, little girl."

But the fête to the tenantry, oh! that was something like, and more to Polly's taste, when this annual affair, postponed while Tom's mother and Tom were away, took place. For days before, the preparations had been making, the stewards up to their eyes in responsibility to carry out the plans of the little old earl, who meant on this occasion to outdo all his former efforts, and show his American friends how an Englishman treats those under his care.

Oh, the big joints of beef, the haunches of venison, the fowls, the meat pies and the gooseberry tarts, the beer and the ale, and the tea for the old women, with nuts and sweeties for the children! Oh, Polly knew about it all, as she went about with the little old earl while he gave his orders, her hand in his, just as if she were no older than Phronsie, and not such a tall, big girl.

And Mrs. Selwyn was busy as a bee, and Mother Fisher was just in her element here, in helping her; for flannel petticoats were to be given out, and stuff frocks, and pieces of homespun, and boots and shoes, as prizes for diligent and faithful service; or an order for coals for the coming winter for some poor cottager, or packages of tea, or some other little comfort. And before any of them quite realized it, the days flew by, and in two more of them the King party would be off.

"It's perfectly useless to mention it," said the little old earl, quite confident in his power to influence old Mr. King to remain when he saw how happily everything was running on. "My dear sir, you were asked for a fortnight."

"And I accepted for a week," retorted Mr. King, "and I go when that time is up. We've had a visit — I can't express it to you, what a fine time — as near to perfection as it is possible for a visit to be; but day after tomorrow we surely must leave."

Tom was so despondent, as well as the old earl, that it was necessary to cheer him up in some way. "Just think what a splendid thing for us to be in the midst of that fête for the peasantry," exclaimed Polly, with sparkling eyes. "It's quite too lovely for our last day."

But Tom wasn't to be raised out of his gloom in this way. "We've had only one game of cricket," he said miserably.

"And one afternoon at tennis, and we've been out punting on the river three times," said Polly.

"What's that? only a bagatelle," sniffed Tom, "compared to what I meant to do."

"Well, let's have the race on horseback this afternoon," proposed Polly, "down through the park, that you said you were going to have, Tom. Wouldn't that be nice?"

"Do," urged Jasper. "It would be so capital, Tom."

"All right," assented Tom, "if you'd really rather have that than anything else; but it seems as if I ought to think up something more for the last afternoon, but the fête; and that doesn't count."

"Oh, nothing could be finer," declared Polly, and Jasper joined. So Tom rushed off to the stables to give the orders. And Polly on Meteor was soon flying up and down with the boys, and Elinor and Mary. And the two small lads trotted after on their Shetland ponies, in and out the winding roads of the park confines, without any haunting fear of a poor red fox to be done to death at the end.

And on the morrow, the sun condescended to come out in all his glory, upon the groups of tenantry scattered over the broad lawns. There were games in abundance for the men and boys; and others for the children. There were chairs for the old women, and long benches for those who desired to sit under the spreading branches of the great oaks to look on. And there were cups of tea, and thin bread and butter passed around by the white-capped maids, superintended by the housekeeper and the butler, quite important in their several functions. This was done to appease the hunger before the grand collation should take place later. And there was music by the fiddlers on the upper terrace, and there was, — dear me, it would take quite too long to tell it all!

And at last, the order was given to fall into line, and march around the long tables resplendent with their cold joints and hot joints; their pasties, and tarts, and cakes, and great flagons of ale. And over all was a wealth of bloom from the big old English gardens in the rear of the old hall. The posies filled Polly with delight, as she and Tom's sisters and Phronsie had gathered them under the direction of the gardeners in the early morning; and then — oh, best of all — Mrs. Selwyn had allowed her to give the finishing touches to them as they became the decoration for the feast.

And the little old earl called the large assemblage to order, and the vicar asked the grace, and the feast was begun!

And then one of the tenants found his feet, and leaning on his staff, he thanked the Earl of Cavendish for all his goodness, and he hoped there would be many blessings in store for 'im and 'is, and sank on his bench again, mopping his face with his big red handkerchief.

And then the little old earl responded in as pretty a speech as could well be imagined, in which he forgot nothing that he ought to say. And there were many "God bless 'ims!" to follow it, and then there were cries of "Master Tom, Master Tom," who appeared to be an immense favorite; and the earl, well pleased, pulled him forward, saying, "Go ahead, youngster, and give it to them."

And Tom, extremely red in the face, tried to duck away, but found himself instead in front of the longest table, with everybody looking at him. And he mumbled out a few words and bobbed his head. And everyone was just as well pleased. And then they gave cheer on cheer for the earl, and as many more for his oldest grandson. And then the little old earl raised his hand and said, "And now, my men, give a rousing good one for my dear American friends!"

And didn't they do it!

And on the following morning, the old hall, with its towers and its wings, had only the memory of the happy week to sustain it.

*J*asper ran up to Polly on the deck. "We ought to go," he said, "the order has been given to leave the steamer."

"Yes, Polly," said Mother Fisher, "we must go, child."

"Give my love to dear Grandma Bascom," said Polly, for about the fiftieth time. "Oh, Mrs. Henderson, and don't forget to take over the new cap just as soon as you can, will you?"

"I won't forget," promised the parson's wife.

"And take mine to my dear Mrs. Beebe," begged Phronsie, twitching gently at Mrs. Henderson's sleeve, "and tell her I got pink ribbon because I know she loves that best."

"I won't forget," said Mrs. Henderson, again.

"Oh, and give the big handkerchief to my dear Mr. Beebe," said Phronsie, "please, Mrs. Henderson, to tie his throat up in, because, you know, he says it gets so cold when he goes out."

"I'll remember every single thing," promised the parson's wife. "Don't you worry, children. Oh, how we hate to leave you, only we are going to see our boys. We really are, Polly!" And her eyes shone.

"Polly! Polly!" called Jasper.

"All off who aren't going!" roared the order out again.

"Polly!" The little doctor seized one arm and Phronsie's hand. "There now, here you are!" and whisked them off, amid "good-bye — good-bye" — and a flutter of handkerchiefs.

"And give my love to dear Grandma Bascom," piped Phronsie, on the wharf by old Mr. King's side, as the big steamer slowly pushed from its moorings.